EAGLE'S CLAW LAKE

ROSS RICHDALE

Doctor Reid Tucker's intention to spend the summer at a remote cabin at Eagle's Claw Lake in northeast Washington State with only his dog, Cinders, never eventuates. On the trip there, pilot Kate Meltz calls in with the amphibian to a commune at the other end of the lake. While waiting on board, Reid pulls a desperate and distressed teenage girl, Lorie Somerville, from the water.

This begins a frightening chain of events as fanatical commune leader, Peter Littlejohn, tries to find Lorie and prevent her from leaving. Though he doesn't find her on the aircraft, he sabotages it so the trio are left stranded at Reid's cabin. It soon becomes obvious that the place is more than just a remote religious commune. The girl is terrified of being caught and begs Reid to look for Jennifer and Sassy, two of her friends who have also escaped.

Though pursued by Littlejohn, Lorie leads Reid and Kate to a cave where the girls are waiting.

But why has Erika Somerville, Lorie's elder sister, returned to Eagle's Claw Lake and found savagely beaten in the commune's cabin cruiser?

National Library of New Zealand Cataloguing-in-Publication Data

Eagle's Claw Lake : contemporary thriller / Ross Richdale.
Previously pub.: 2001 (e-book)
ISBN 978-1-877438-20-2
ISBN 978-1-877438-21-9 (e-book)
I. Title.
NZ823.3—dc 22

Paperback published by:-

Purrbooks
Palmerston North
New Zealand

CHAPTER ONE

Timber Wolf Air did not even have a counter in the terminal at Felts Field Municipal Airport but Reid Tucker eventually found a sign directing prospective customers to an office a hundred meters beyond the building. At least the sign shaped like a stylized timber wolf looked professional.

"Well, I'm at the right airport this time," he muttered to nobody in particular and headed outdoors. It was early morning and still quite chilly with a drizzle hanging over the airport. He grinned at the expectant look of his Black Labrador waiting, without even a leash on, at the corner of the rental car lot and noticed his trolley filled with his luggage had been left untouched. Cinder was a placid creature but when asked to guard something, she did it with vengeance.

Reid rubbed the dog's ears, spoke a few kind words and pushed the trolley along the pavement. With his wild black beard, he seemed to compliment the Black Labrador that followed him through the throngs of people. Most hastily stepped aside to let him through but one irate businessman stopped in front of him.

"Can't you read?" he muttered. "Dogs are not permitted in the airport grounds. I have a good mind to report you to the authorities."

Reid stopped and fixed his eyes on the man. "My Dear Sir," he replied in a cultured voice. "If your safety is affected so adversely by my companion here, by all means go ahead and do it. You will find a security guard just inside the main entrance."

The man flushed when a couple of bystanders chuckled and turned away. "Damn hippie," he muttered and disappeared.

Reid returned the grins of the small group around, patted Cinders on the head, and continued towards his destination. In his eyes, Cinders was worth a hundred of the stupid bureaucrats he'd just spoken to. Oh, he'd had his day of wearing suits and ties but he doubted if he ever would do so again.

The covered walkway stopped without any sign of the *Timber Wolf Air Terminal* so Reid pulled his jacket collar up and strolled on until he came to a second sign and arrow pointing towards a hanger with a small floatplane parked on the apron in front. This looked hopeful.

Adjacent to the hanger was a small office with the stylized wolf painted above the door. Reid told Cinders to stay with the trolley and entered the building. The interior smelt of fresh paint and had the appearance of being recently renovated. He was about to knock on an inner door when it opened and a woman glanced out and smiled. She looked about twenty-eight, was quite tall, slim and had short dark hair. Unusual though, was the baseball cap and mechanic's coverall she wore and a smudge of grease across her cheek.

"You aren't the pilot they sending me?" she asked.

"Sorry," Reid replied. "I was told you could help me. I was redirected here from Spokane International Airport. I had tickets with Resolution Air but it seems they've just disappeared."

The woman grinned. "Well, I'm all that remains of Resolution Air. They went bankrupt and I bought two of their aircraft and ground facilities." She nodded around and smiled again. "So how can I help you Mr...."

"Reid Tucker. Call me Reid."

"Hi Reid. I'm Kate Meltz, managing director and chief pilot of Timber Wolf Air." She held out a hand that had a strong grip.

"I need to get to Eagle's Claw Lake. I've rented a cabin on the north arm for the summer season."

"I know it," Kate replied. "The place is somewhat remote..."

"It's what I want," Reid replied with a shrug.

"Okay," she replied. "You're in luck, Reid. I'm flying the Canadair out to the Elf Commune on the south arm after lunch."

"Elf?" Reid queried.

"Eagle Love Family is the commune's full title," Kate replied, screwed her nose up and added, "Strange lot. They'll be your neighbors but I doubt if you'll see much of them. They're one of these self-sufficient places, a hundred or so men, women and kids. I fly them in supplies once every couple of weeks and bring out stuff they have to sell, mainly cheese from their farm and hand-woven rugs, you know the sort of stuff?" She shrugged. "As I said, you're lucky. I was due to fly in yesterday but my plane has been held up. This will be cheaper for you than a special flight in the Beaver." She smiled again and nodded at the aircraft out the door. "I honor Resolution Air tickets, too."

"Great," Reid replied. "What time?"

"Noon," Kate replied. "That's if my plane arrives. It's been up in Vancouver BC getting an overhaul and was promised back today. Yesterday, actually, but now it's today."

"And you don't mind flying my dog?"

"Reid," laughed Kate. "I fly anything. Half my passengers are hunters with dogs."

4

When Reid returned just before noon he was pleasantly surprised. A bright yellow amphibian aircraft sat in front of Timber Wolf Air's hanger. The Canadair CL-215 had high wings; twin piston engines and was the size of a commuter airliner. The fuselage, though, was squarer in design with the underside shaped like a cabin cruiser. Floats extended down from the wing tips. Two wide doors on the nearest side were open and ground staff was loading piles of equipment from a small tractor and trailer unit. Reid spied his luggage wedged between the gear.

"Well Cinders," he said to his dog. She stood beside him with her tail lashing and wide brown eyes gazing up as if she understood every word. "It looks as if we'll be in our new home tonight, after all."

However, Kate Meltz looked worried as she walked out from the hanger and changed direction towards him. "No pilot's come, I'm afraid," she said. "I couldn't even entice the ferry pilots to stay around a few days. I think the idea of landing on water scared them away."

Reid nodded at the Canadair. "It's bigger than I expected. I suppose it needs two pilots."

"Usually," Kate replied. "I would take the Beaver but the Elf Commune has heavy stuff they want transported that won't fit in the smaller plane. I'm licensed to fly the Canadair solo but would prefer a co-pilot, especially now I have a passenger."

"Oh, I don't mind," Reid replied and broke into a grin. "I would imagine you're quite capable." He was becoming impressed with his chatty companion.

"Okay," the young woman replied. "The weather will be closing in later this evening so we'll head out as soon as everything's loaded."

*

Eagle's Claw Lake did, indeed look like a claw with three long narrow forks of water joined at one end in a mountainous valley filled, except for the lake, by endless fir forest. As Kate dipped the CL-215 and approached the nearest fork, Reid noticed an area of cleared land at the upper end of the fork. Half a dozen buildings, cultivated gardens and several green fields hugged the steep hillsides and smaller triangular flat section intersected by a mountain stream. A road or track followed the river to the apex of the triangle before disappearing into the firs. At the lakeshore, a crossroad followed a small beach area to a wooden jetty that reached out over the water.

"It's like a small town," Reid commented as the view disappeared when the amphibian circled down.

"Military camp, more like it," Kate replied with a touch of cynicism in her voice. "You know the whole area is ringed in a high fence topped in razor wire. " She stopped talking for a moment as she concentrated on leveling the amphibian off ready to drop onto the lake. "They told me it is to keep the bears and other wild animals out but it is more to keep the locals in." She shrugged. "Not that there is anywhere for them to go even if they decided they wanted to leave."

"As bad as that?" Reid observed.

Kate glanced across at him and smiled. "Oh, I guess not. They're friendly enough when I come but never invite me up for a cup of coffee. The head guy gives me the creeps. Anyhow, you can see for yourself in a few moments. Take my advice and don't tell them you're shifting into old Shelton's place."

"Shelton?"

"The old hermit whose place you're renting. He died a couple of years back. As far as I know, the lodge has been empty since then. I would imagine some relation owns it now."

"You could be right," Reid replied. "I rented it through this reality firm and have an option to buy."

Kate caught his eye but made no comment. She reached across to the twin throttles and, with the casualness of an expert, lowered the amphibian onto the lake. The craft surged forward, bounced a couple of times and came to an almost abrupt halt in the water. Kate opened the throttles a little, the nose rose and they surged forward like a boat with white wake fanning out behind them. A moment later the amphibian circled around, engines were cut and it drifted the last few meters to the jetty where a man reached for an unseen handle and tied the nose to a pole. The rear or the craft was pulled in and they were parallel to the jetty with the port wing stretching across the wooden decking. The outer float cleared the surface by a mere half a meter.

"I'll give them this much," Kate grunted. "They built this new jetty to handle the CL-215 perfectly. This section floats on the surface so I can come in close no matter how high or low the lake level is." She glanced at Reid. "Remember, don't mention you're going to be a neighbor."

"Sure," Reid replied.

He followed her to the front hatch and opened it. Two men stood there and, with a minimum of conversation, unloaded their gear into an ancient trailer hitched to a tractor of similar vintage. Reid was introduced and was met by cold eyes but firm handshakes.

"New pilot for Miss Meltz?" one man asked.

"Yes," Reid lied. The man was quite unlike what one would expect. In the remote hinterland, visitors were usually welcomed and regarded as a source of information. These two were as grim as guards at a top-secret military establishment.

He jumped down onto the jetty and offered to help load the trailer.

"Thank you but no," the elder man replied. "We don't require any assistance."

"Okay," Reid shrugged and stepped back. As he did so he noticed the women. They were across the gravel road behind the tall chicken-wire fence Kate had mentioned on the way in. Most looked as young as the men were old and wore identical red tartan skirts, white blouses and had long hair tied back under blue hair scarves. Their faces all looked similar, thin with no make up and large hollow eyes. They stood silently in a line with children ranging from babies to teenagers. Only two of the youngsters gave a quiet smile and one girl wiggled her fingers in a secret wave.

Reid caught Kate's eyes and saw her briefly shake her head. He nodded but still caught the young girl's eyes and smiled. Inwardly, though, he fumed. He'd seen refuges like this from a stint he'd had as a medic in Bosnia, even down to the thin frames and soulless faces, the faces of people with no control over their lives. In disgust, he turned, climbed back in the CL-215 and strolled back to where Cinders sat mournfully in her animal cage.

"No, Girl," he said. "I know you hate the cage but you wouldn't want to get out here."

Somehow, the beautiful lake had become sinister and foreboding, the blue water looked black and the silence, ominous.

He turned and saw Kate's head appear in the door. "Got to you, did it?" she whispered. "I thought it might."

"Yeah," Reid responded.

"Look, I'll be about ten minutes. There's a small backload of stuff on the jetty if you wouldn't mind loading it then you could shut the rear door. The Elf commune always pays me in cash, always exactly the right amount and always in crisp new bills." She chuckled at Reid's raised eyebrows. "No it's genuine money. I checked it the first time. Damned if I know where they get it from, though. I suspect they have a floatplane of their own but I've never seen it. There's no other access. The nearest road would be twenty kilometers away and that is only a forest access road."

"Interesting," Reid replied.

He watched as Kate slipped out of her coverall. Beneath she had a neat maroon jersey and dark skirt that covered an attractive figure. She saw Reid's gaze and flushed.

"More of the protocol," she explained as she reached for a pair of black low heeled shoes and replaced the boots she had been wearing. "They don't like women in trousers or jeans beyond the main gate. It was only after my third visit they even let me inside their compound and that was only when I wore a skirt."

"You look nice," Reid said.

Kate appeared annoyed for a second until she noticed Reid's genuine expression and smiled back. "Thanks," she said in a whisper. "I'm not used to compliments nowadays."

The ten-minute wait became twenty, then thirty. Reid loaded the boxes of cheese, several large cardboard boxes the size of a refrigerator and two crates of fresh vegetables. He shut the back door and sat down beside his dog to wait.

*

It was Cinders who heard the noise first. Her ears shot forward and she gave a low growl.

"What is it, Girl?" Reid asked.

The dog was looking at a closed hatch, not the door Reid had recently shut. This was a smaller opening about a meter square on the starboard side away from the jetty. Reid frowned and listened. A slight tapping sound reached his ears. "You're right, Girl," he said. "Perhaps a log has drifted in against the plane. I'll check it."

He walked across to the hatch and gazed through the tiny porthole built into it. Outside was nothing except water and distant trees across the inlet. He was about to turn back when he jumped in fright. A sharp knock rung out from the metal at the bottom of the structure.

He frowned and swung the hatch up on its overhead hinges.

"Help me, please!" quivered a voice.

Two enormous blue eyes stared up at him from the water. A tanned face, long wet blonde hair and full lips were those of a young woman, hardly more than a girl. She clasped a small handle below the hatch and appeared to be having difficulty treading water.

"Your other hand!" Reid said, grabbed the frozen hand and yanked the surprisingly heavy girl up.

She came out, fully clothed in clinging blouse and skirt, and managed to get a bare foot on the bulkhead and propel herself inside. For a second she lay down gasping and shivering before she turned and gazed at the cargo door and jetty beyond.

"They mustn't find me," she cried. "If I'm found I'll be thrashed or worse. I can't..." A rush of tears replaced her words.

Reid nodded grimly. He searched around for something to help, spied Kate's coveralls and wrapped them, like a towel, around the girl's shaking shoulders. Her lips were shivering from cold and her eyes looked anxious.

"Your name young lady?" Reid asked as he slammed the hatch down and stepped across to shut the other door. Somehow it seemed safer with the view of the jetty shut out.

"Lorie," the girl replied, " Lorie Somerville." she gulped.

"Okay Lorie," Reid replied. "You are safe with me. Nobody will hurt you."

"They will," the girl cried. " They'll forcibly remove me and even a big guy like you can't stop four or five of them."

"And you risked a beating and freezing water to swim out here?" Reid replied.

The girl nodded miserably with her eyes downcast. It was as if her courage had evaporated.

"Okay, so we hide you," Reid replied in a soft voice.

He searched around. The interior was half filled with his gear and the boxes he'd just loaded. With a few heaves he pulled the boxes forward so there was a gap in front of the rear wall. "Get in there, Lorie," he said.

She nodded, sprung into action and within seconds was squatting behind the cargo. Reid shifted it back but grimaced. It was an obvious place to search but what else could he do?

"Cinders," he gasped and opened the dog's cage door.

Cinders bounded out all licks and wagging tail.

"Sit, Girl" Reid ordered. "Guard Lorie, Cinders. Understand!"

The brown eyes stared up and the Black Labrador sat on her back haunches in front of the cargo. The tail stopped wagging and remained straight out behind her. Nobody would touch a thing unless she was called her off. Cinders was a pet but also an excellent guard dog who had been trained with military precision.

They were only just in time. Without even a knock, the jetty door swung open and three men walked in. "We need to search the plane," the old guy who had originally spoken to Reid said. He glared around. "Why is the floor wet?" he hissed.

Reid, though, was not intimidated. "Can I help?" he asked.

"One of our flock is missing," the same man replied.

"So why would he come here?" Reid snapped purposely using the wrong gender.

"Your visit is too much of a coincidence. This girl is a highly neurotic girl. She can not survive on her own."

"So she's gone for a walk along the shore or to the back of your farm? I have not seen her."

The man glowered and stepped towards the boxes. However, a low growl interrupted his intentions.

"I wouldn't," Reid snapped. "Cinders there is protecting my gear."

"Call it off," the man ordered but stopped as Cinders rose and growled again.

"You are on my employer's aircraft," Reid stated in a cold voice. "This is our property, not your land. I respected your customs on the jetty. Here, you can respect mine. I have not seen your missing girl. She is not here. Surely if she had come to look over the plane, your man would have seen her." He glowered at the second man who had, he now realized, been watching the plane since their arrival." As for the wet floor, I opened the door and got some water for Cinders to drink." Reid then decided to bluff and gave a casual shrug. "However, if you wish to move all the boxes, I'll give you a hand." His eyes held the older man's gaze.

For a moment the cold stares held before the man spoke again. "And you never saw a young woman in our uniform on the shoreline or outside the fence?" he asked.

Reid never flinched. "Only the group watching us unload," he said, "They were all behind your gate."

"Perhaps I was wrong then," The man turned to the other two who returned from inspecting the cockpit. "Joseph, go and search the barn; Jacob, the shoreline."

"Right, Peter," both men replied. Reid was sure there was a sadistic gleam in their eyes as they departed.

Peter turned to Reid and now sounded almost friendly. "If you see her, please tell us," he said and held out his hand. "As I said, she is a highly disturbed young woman half way through her treatment. To stop at this stage could be very detrimental to her health."

"Sure," Reid replied as he gripped the hand.

*

He watched as Peter walked away and smiled when Kate appeared a moment later and scrambled aboard. "Trouble?" she asked.

"You are perceptive. Why would there be trouble?"

"Peter Littlejohn and his henchmen are always trouble," she replied. "Also you look tense about something."

Reid grimaced. Usually he had complete control over his emotions but this woman seemed to be able to read him like a book. "I'll tell you when we're in the air. Shall we go?"

Kate frowned but said no more.

A moment later, they were racing forward across the lake's surface with engines screaming at almost maximum revolutions. Water cut out behind until the violent shuddering stopped, the lake sunk away and they were airborne.

"Oh damn!" Kate muttered above the howling engine noise, mere seconds later.

"What's wrong?"

"Look at the clouds," she yelled.

Reid stared out the front windshield and saw the object of Kate's concern. The sky to the north was an inky black and already large drops were hitting the amphibian.

"I don't think I'll be able to get you down and get off again," Kate yelled. "We need to climb up above the mountains and head back to Spokane."

*

The storm hit the Canadair with fury. Rain turned to hail so violent, the wipers could barely cope while the craft bucked and rocked. Reid could only nod and put his trust in his pilot.

Kate held onto the controls and turned the craft ever so slightly into the storm, one wing lifted and she succeeded in turning in a semicircle. The wings shook and both motors screamed as yet another squall hit them.

"What's wrong?" a frightened voice called from the door.

Kate frowned but never moved her eyes off the scene outside. "Who the hell is she?" she screamed.

"Our passenger," Reid replied with a slight grin. "Meet Lorie Somerville. She's hitched a ride back to Spokane"

Kate glanced back for a second and suddenly burst out laughing. "Oh my God, Lorie. You did it!"

"You know each other?" Reid asked.

"Sort of," Lorie shouted as she pulled herself into the third seat in the cockpit and held on with knuckles that were almost as white as here face. "It was Kate who suggested we go up the beach and swim back to the plane. She said you would help us get aboard."

"We?"

"There were two others but they chickened out."

Conversation was interrupted as the sky ahead lit up in blue streak lightning that cut across the aircraft's nose. Mere seconds later, the thunder rumbled, the Canadair CL-215 shook like a leaf and the port motor spluttered. Kate frowned and reached forward to a different control, the engine roared for a second, spluttered and cut out.

"Hell!" she muttered.

The two passengers could only wait as their pilot did everything possible to control the aircraft. The starboard engine continued to function without even a cough but two attempts to restart the port one failed. Another streak of lightning lit the cockpit but the thunder took slightly longer to rattle their ears.

"What can you see below?" Kate screamed to Reid. "My instruments tell me it should be water. I can't make any height and the starboard engine is overheating."

"Water!" screamed Lorie. "I can see white caps."

"Hang on," Kate yelled back. "We're going down."

With infinite care she throttled the good engine back and manipulated the controls so the amphibian dropped. It hit the water with an almighty bump, Lorie screamed and Reid felt something snuggle between his legs. It was Cinders who must have decided his company was necessary at the moment. Kate opened the throttle but the plane pulled sideways and the offside wing dipped. She changed tactics, cut the throttle and the plane dropped sickeningly into the choppy waves.

"We're down," Kate gasped and edged the throttle forward. "What can you see?"

"Trees," Reid yelled. "About twenty meters away to our left."

"Just water on my side," Lorie shouted from immediately behind Kate.

"Good. Thanks!" the pilot replied. "You two are as good as any second pilot."

"I doubt it," Reid answered as he gazed out through the bucking side window. "Look!"

"What is it?" Kate replied.

"There's cabin and jetty in a sort of inlet."

"Your new home, Reid," Kate replied. She grinned for the first time and wiped a strand of hair out of her eyes. "It looks as if you're going to have a couple of guests for the night."

*

CHAPTER TWO

Whoever had chosen the site of the jetty and accompanying building had done it well for, although the lake itself had choppy swells buffeting the amphibian, once they had taxied around the tiny headland the water was calm. Even the rain stopped as fast as it had arrived and a gap showing in the black sky. The sun appeared and a gigantic rainbow glowed across the cloudbank.

"This often happens," Lorie explained to Reid. "We have a downpour and half an hour later the sun is shining." She gulped. "In summer that is. It's always snow during the winter and the lake freezes over."

Kate interrupted. "I'll get in as close to the jetty as I can and will shut down," she shouted but never turned her face away from the outside view. "There are two coils of rope hanging by the front cargo door. One is tied on at this end so it can be used to pull the plane in. The other can be tied to the front and the jetty. With one engine out of action I haven't got my usual maneuverability."

"I'll do it," shouted Lorie.

Reid gazed at the water outside the opened door. Though the small shingle beach was just beyond the CL-215's wing tip, the water was deep.

"You will not. Not after your last freezing swim. I will."

"Let me!" Lorie pleaded and before an argument could develop she placed the loose coil of rope around her shoulder, grabbed the other rope end and jumped. It was deep. She disappeared beneath the surface and came up spluttering with her tartan skirt ballooning up around her. Her eyes caught Reid's; she smiled and kicked backstroke style to shore. She scrambled up the small bank and pulled the rope in until it was taut, walked the few meters to the jetty with the amphibian swinging slightly around so the tail pointed to shore.

"That young lass has got guts, you know" Reid shouted at Kate, realized that without the engine noise, this wasn't necessary so continued in a normal voice. "She was terrified before but gritted her teeth and kept going."

Kate's voice came back from the cockpit. "You either become that way or become completely servile at that commune," she replied. "If the others had Lorie's guts we would have three of them right now, instead of one."

"More likely there would have been three caught," Reid added. "I doubt if I could have hidden more than one."

"True," Kate called back.

*

Lorie used her initiative and tied the rope to one of the jetty supports and scrambled up on the jetty itself. She reached up, grabbed the port wing and walked up the jetty with it. The amphibian swung around so the fuselage came in parallel to the structure and bumped against three old tractor tires tied to the planking. Reid stepped off without even getting his feet wet and smiled at the shivering girl.

"You did well," he said, reached out an arm and gave her a tiny hug.

It was obvious this small gesture made Lorie pleased. She placed wet hair against his chest for a moment and glanced up at into his eyes. "At the commune we were just expected to do the right thing," she whispered. "Nobody ever touches us." She stopped and swallowed. "I mean we are not we allowed to touch anyone without it being sinful?"

"Is that so?" Reid replied.

"My girlfriends and I used to just hug and hold each other at night when we were lonely and it felt so nice to be held but..." Again she stopped but still remained in Reid's arms.

"Come on," Reid said quietly. "Let's get the plane tied up, shall we? You must be freezing again."

"Who cares," Lorie replied. "I'm away from there. I'd swim the length of the lake to get away, if necessary. Thank you, Reid. You just don't know what it is like to be just a thing."

She swung around and kissed him on his bearded cheek, flushed a bright red and almost skipped away to tie the remaining rope onto the steel eyelet under the nose of the aircraft. She lopped the other end around a jetty pole. Reid's helped her tie the plane securely to the jetty.

Reid now examined the cabin that was to be his home. It was more modern than he anticipated with a steep A-frame roof like a Swiss chalet. There was a door to the right, one window on the left and a pentagonal attic window above. Half a dozen steps linked the cabin and the jetty. The whole cabin was wooden with only the window frames painted white. Everything else was stained a natural brown. Faded red curtains were pulled across the downstairs window while, at the rear; fir trees boughs grew over the roof.

Though smelling musty through lack of use, the inside was surprisingly clean. The whole front was an open-plan room with a stone hearth on the right. Sitting on this was an enormous potbelly stove with exposed cylindrical chimney that stretched up through the ceiling. The far end of the L shaped room was a kitchen with the usual facilities. Off this was a tiny bathroom and toilet and steep stairs leading up, Reid guessed to bedrooms. The floor was bare but covered in several large oval shaped mats while sheets covered the furniture.

"It's lovely," Kate remarked.

"They told me there's a generator in a cellar at the back," Reid said. "If you two would like to get things sorted here, I'll go and see if I can get it going then I'll light the stove." He nodded at the pile of dry wood stacked neatly on the hearth.

"Can I?" Lorie asked with her eyes almost shining.

"Of course," Reid replied and caught Kate's eyes. Lorie would be about sixteen, he guessed but seemed to be very young in her mannerisms. But no, he was wrong. In others she seemed old before her time.

"Like the commune she's got to you, hasn't she?" Kate remarked an hour later when the potbelly stove was blazing away and the pipes behind it had heated enough water for Lorie to have the first bath.

"The opposite," Reid replied. "The commune felt foreboding and ominous. Lorie is like a breath of fresh air or a butterfly released from a cocoon."

"A good description," Kate replied. "Do you know she just told me she has never used shampoo before? Luckily, I always carried an emergency bag of clothes in the plane so I shampooed her hair and have given her some shorts and top. Her size isn't too different than mine." She glanced at Reid. "Her hair was quite dirty and she has a nasty rash over her body, too."

"I see," Reid replied. "Perhaps I can help there. I'll get my bag."

He walked across to where his gear had been piled by the kitchen sink and pulled out a very professional bag. Inside was a whole selection of medical supplies from tablets and ointments to a stethoscope.

"That's handy," Kate commented. "Have you a doctor as a friend?"

"Well actually, I was a doctor," Reid replied in a whisper. "Still am, I guess."

"Are you?" Kate replied. "I knew you weren't just a drifter, Reid. And how long have you had your beard and scruffy hairdo?"

"A few months," he replied. "Oh, I used to be so prime and proper, short hair, daily shaves, even a flash house and wife to go with it."

"But now?"

"Gone," Reid replied with a shrug. "I have Cinders." He smiled at the dog stretched out asleep in front of the pot-bellied stove. "She's all I need for a while."

"How do I look!" squealed a happy voice that interrupted the pair before Kate could reply.

Lorie stood in front of them all red from the hot water. She was dressed in shorts and top with her hair wrapped in a towel. As they watched, she pulled the towel aside to reveal damp hair just touching her shoulders rather than waist long as it had been.

"I gave Lorie a haircut," Kate said in a modest voice. "It was so long and knotted."

"You look just like a film star," Reid laughed.

"Do I?" Lorie replied and again seemed to absorb compliments like blotting paper. She flushed, "You're just kidding me, aren't you?"

"No, better than a film star," Reid continued. "They're always too painted up."

"And my clothes fit you quite well," Kate added.

Lorie bit on her bottom lip. "I've never worn shorts before. It was another great sin at Elf. Are you sure it is okay?"

Reid noticed for the first time that the girl's arms were only tanned from her elbow and legs from below the knee. The rest of her skin was as pale as a European gets after a long, cold winter.

"Far better than I look in them," Kate said and changed the topic. "Reid said he's a doctor who may be able to help with that nasty rash you have."

"A doctor?" Lorie frowned.

"Is something wrong with that?" Reid replied quietly.

"No, of course not," the girl replied. "We weren't allowed doctors, that's all."

"And if people got ill?" It was Kate who spoke.

"The elders prayed for them and they got better."

"And if they didn't?" Kate persisted.

"They died," Lorie whispered. "Mom died. She was all I had." Her face contorted and tears bubbled from the corners of her eyes. She turned and ran, sobbing into the bathroom.

"I'll go," Kate said and placed a hand on his arm Reid. "I think this is why she wanted to leave the commune.

Reid nodded. "Poor kid," he said and wondered what other deprivations the youngster had been exposed to at the commune. He'd read about these places but this was his first direct contact with anybody from one. During his time as a doctor he'd seen many abused patients and Lorie showed every symptom of emotional and even physical abuse."

He shook his head and wandered over to the smaller bottled gas stove in the kitchen where a large pot of stew was bubbling away. The smell premeditated the room and he realized how hungry they must all be.

"Your turn," Lorie's voice again interrupted his thoughts. Reid turned and saw the girl, red eyed but smiling, looking intently at him.

"What for?" Reid replied.

"Haircut. If I can have one why can't you?"

Reid grinned. "Oh, I don't know, " he protested.

"I'll do it," Kate cut in. "Just the hair, though. You can sort your beard out yourself."

"You don't mind?" Reid replied.

"My dear Doctor Tucker, when you get to know me a little better, you'll find out I never say anything I don't mean."

*

Nightfall arrived quite late in the evening and Lorie was asleep on a massive old couch with an arm around Cinders. Reid, with haircut and trimmed beard was helping Kate complete the washing up of dishes.

"So what is your story, Reid?" Kate asked in a quiet voice. "You're too nice a person to squander your life out here in the wilderness. What happened to you?" She stopped and placed a hand over her mouth. "I'm sorry, it's really none of my business."

"No, I don't mind," Reid replied. "In fact, like our young friend here, it is nice to have someone who is interested. We all keep our little secrets don't we?"

"We do."

"It was just burn out, I guess," Reid sighed." Let's finish the dishes, I'll make us a cup of coffee and tell you.

"I'd like that," Kate replied as she dried another plate.

*

The court trial was in its fourth day in Minneapolis, Minnesota.

Defense Attorney Jonathan Mossop tugged on his black robe and faced the jury with his final summing up. "Ladies and Gentlemen of the Jury, you now have to weigh up the evidence of this case and decide whether Doctor Reid James Tucker is guilty of the crime of manslaughter by failing to provide adequate supervision of staff, willful negligence for the same reason, lesser charges or, indeed, is innocent. The prosecution's case is based on the accusations of Consulting Surgeon Marcus Kalmus, at the Northern Lights Hospital whom, you know has already been proven guilty of negligence and causing the deaths of Mary Anne McAlfir and Josephine Elizabeth Smaus.

My client was a not accomplice, Ladies and Gentlemen. In fact, if it was not for his astute observations, the unlawful operations performed by Kalmus and the other surgeon who is awaiting trial may never have reached the light of day. Kalmus has accused my client of being an accomplice in a crude attempt to defend his own actions and seek revenge. His statements to this court have not been substantiated by facts." Mossop paused and purposely glanced at the jury.

"Doctor Reid Tucker was appointed managing director and head surgeon of Northern Lights Hospital three years ago and, in that time, built the hospital from one that the locals avoided if possible, to a vibrant hospital with an excellent reputation and surgical department. As character witnesses told us, this was against tremendous odds with the Board of Trustees continuing a long standing feud on whether to provide a general facility for the local citizens or to concentrate on more exotic surgery for, what I would call, wealthy customers. I'd hardly call them patients.

Reid would not let this feud overflow into the wards and was highly regarded by all except a few who found their powers in the hospital community eroded. This included Doctor Marcus Kalmus, a man who wanted to use the hospital's facilities for personal gain. When his unethical operating procedures were discovered, he attempted to shift the blame onto the hospital in general and my client in particular."

The Defense Attorney stopped and eyed every jury member in turn. "This trial should not even be happening, ladies and gentlemen," he said. "Everything is based on the statements of a convicted man who found he had lost his standing the medical profession and has set out to get his revenge on the one person who, in his warped eyes, caused his downfall. It will not work. Reid is not guilty. He did not participate in this crime in which these unfortunate women lost their lives.

Ask yourselves this. Where was his motivation? Why would he tear down the reputation of the establishment he was trying to build up? Why would he rip apart the social structure of the hospital community he was trying to cement together?' The attorney paused for almost a full minute. "The answer, of course, is that he wouldn't.

Remember, too, that unless it is proven beyond doubt that my client had full knowledge of the methods being used by these surgeons and gave his approval or even, as my learned colleague was quick to suggest turned a blind eye at their practices, he must be found not guilty. I charge there is no proof at all, merely an accusation from a man already proven to be dishonest. Remember too, the crimes committed by Doctor Kalmus dated back five years, that is two years before my client was appointed to the position at Northern Lights Hospital." Jonathan rolled his eyes in disgust. "I don't see the previous chief surgeon on trial here."

The Defense Attorney waited again in the hushed courtroom before continuing. "Doctor Reid Tucker should be given accolades for his efforts to built a viable district hospital against tremendous odds, not standing here accused of a crime he was instrumental in stopping. He is innocent of all accusations and that is the only conclusion you can make. Thank you."

He strolled across in front of the jury bench, turned, gave Reid Tucker a brief smile and sat down.

"Thank you, Mr. Mossop," The judge stated and turned to face the jury. "This is a difficult case, Ladies and Gentlemen of the Jury, based mainly on circumstantial evidence and the reliability or otherwise of the conflicting statements of Doctor Kalmus and the defendant," he began. "You must weigh up the evidence presented to you over the last week..." The judge continued his summary for another fifty minutes before ordering the jury to retire and reach a verdict.

Reid Tucker grimaced and glanced at Jonathan Mossop. The case against him was quite damning with the circumstantial evidence built up and made plausible by the outright lies made by his former colleague, a man hell bent on sabotaging every improvement he'd made in the hospital.

He shrugged. It was too late now, anyway. He'd never go back to the place. Sure, he had friends there but it had wrecked his career and his marriage but for what?

"Don't worry, Reid," Jonathan interrupted. "I'm sure it will turn out okay."

Reid's shrugged. "It is too late, Jonathan. Quite frankly, I don't care any longer."

He stood and walked out of the courtroom towards the holding cells. His career of fifteen years was over. Even if let free his reputation was in tatters. All the good he'd done or tried to do would be forgotten. It was as if his efforts over the years had never happened.

Society in heartland America could be very unforgiving.

*

Eight hours later the jury filed back into the courtroom with the jurors' eyes avoiding Reid so there was no way he could read any message. After the usual formalities, the chairperson stood to announce the verdict.

"To the charge of Manslaughter of Mary Anne McAlfir and Josephine Elizabeth Smaus we find Reid James Tucker not guilty, Your Honor," she said in a clear precise voice. "To the charge of Failing to Provide Adequate Supervision we find the defendant not guilty." The woman coughed before continuing. "To the lesser charge of Failing to Account we find the defendant guilty, Your Honor. "

Reid just stood and stared ahead without any outward sign he had even heard the verdict and only his eyes fluttered when the judge started to speak.

"You have been found guilty of the charge of Failing to Account," he stated after the usual preamble. "Throughout the trial I have been impressed by your fortitude, compassion and complete frankness. Also I am impressed by the effort you put into your position as administrative head as well as practicing physician of an inner city hospital reflecting the multitude of problems prevalent in our community. However, you unwisely, shall I say, failed to account for the operations being performed illegally at the Northern Lights Hospital. I don't believe you intentionally broke the law but ignorance of the law cannot be a defense in itself."

The judge's eyes linked onto Reid who never noticed compassion in the gaze. "Reid James Tucker you are hereby convicted of the crime of Failing to Account and discharged. Court is dismissed."

That was it. Reid frowned and glanced at his attorney. "What happens now?" He asked.

Jonathan Mossop smiled. "It means you can go, Reid. Even though you are convicted on that lesser charge, the judge decided not to impose any punishment."

"I see," replied Reid, He knew he should be thankful but wasn't. In some ways it only continued the state of limbo he had been through for almost a year. All he thought was that, Ashleigh; his wife had not even bothered to attend the court that day; nor any other day, actually.

He turned and walked away, a lonely figure with no penalty to pay to society but with a shattered life ruined because he had tried to help others.

*

Reid drove home, walked in the door and glanced at the woman waiting by the living room door.

Ashleigh Tucker was a woman with enormous hazel eyes that always reflected her personality. Reid remembered when they sparkled and laughed as they ran along the Florida beach together. They would chase each other through the surf and cuddle on the sand. He always loved holidays at the beach. But in the last few years, the eyes had turned cold and impersonal. They were like that now.

"They let me go," Reid shrugged.

"I see," Ashleigh answered in a neutral voice. "I'm pleased for you, Reid."

"Are you?" he replied. "If they'd put me away it would have solved your problem, wouldn't it?"

The woman's eyes turned hard. "That's not fair, Reid," she retorted. "I stuck by you through everything. Hell Reid, it affected me, too you know? That horrible hospital."

She glanced down, walked across the room and sat on a kitchen chair. When she looked up her eyes brimmed with tears. "When I walked in the market opposite the hospital, the woman would turn their trolleys and find another aisle. I suffered, too, you know."

Reid found another chair by the table and also sat down. "I realize that, Ashleigh," he said. "I tried..."

Ashleigh reached across and took his hand. Her eyes looked into his and softness Reid hadn't seen for years returned. "I know, Reid," she replied. "You tried. You've always tried. Right throughout your career you tried and the more you tried the more you got trodden on. These last two years have been sheer hell. I can take no more."

"I'm resigning from the position," Reid said.

Ashleigh stared at him. "It's too late Reid," she whispered. "Perhaps if we'd had children." She stood up and walked over to gaze out the window.

Reid shrugged. The present conversation wasn't unexpected. He knew it was only out of mutual loyalty they'd stayed together until the trial. Without it, they would have probably departed when the trouble first began, or even earlier.

"What now?" He continued.

His wife turned. "I'm moving out Reid. I've won a teaching position in Rochester that starts in September. I was going to tell you last week but..."

"I know," Reid replied. "I saw the letter. Perhaps it's the best way."

"It's the only way, Reid," Ashleigh replied. Her eyes found his again. There was a flash of kindness before the old cold stare returned. "The packers are coming tomorrow."

Without another word, Reid turned and walked into the back yard to be immediately greeted by a bark. Cinders rushed up to him with her tail wagging and large brown eyes staring into his.

"Well, Girl," Reid said as he squatted down and rubbed the dog's ears. "I guess there's only us now. I think we're going to be close companions for a while."

*

Reid glanced up to see not only Kate's but Lorie's eyes fixed on his. "It's a pity humans aren't as loyal as pets," he said.

"The cow," the teenager snapped. "She could have stuck by you."

"I guess," Reid replied, "Our marriage had really been that in name only for a number of years."

"Like ours," Lorie snapped. "Peter has two wives and is about to select his third. The man disgusts me but I've been told he likes me. The other women just laugh at me and said I should be honored to be able to bare his child."

Kate looked aghast. "And how old are you, Lorie?" she asked.

"Sixteen, come June," the girl replied. "We are untouched until our sixteenth birthday and after that we are regarded as women."

"What's that?" Reid said, his eyes hard.

"The men can select us for, well ... you know." She flushed and rolled her eyes. "Oh it is all well organized. We are told it is our duty." She frowned. "It's all prescribed in The Oracles. Everything is prescribed in The Oracles."

"What's that?" Kate asked.

"The book that explains the Bible. We have the Bible and The Oracles."

"It's disgusting," Kate retorted. "They should all be arrested."

"... So you're still a virgin? " Reid said in a quiet voice.

"Yes," the girl replied without even a hint of embarrassment. "We have what is called a Womanhood Celebration. It's the only birthday we're allowed to celebrate."

"...And the boys," Kate asked, in spite of herself

"They have to wait until they're eighteen before they're allowed to be a man and can mate. I don't know why they have to wait two extra years."

"The bosses don't like the competition," Reid felt so angry that even Cinders looked up in alarm.

"One of the last things Mom told me was to escape before I turned sixteen," Lorie added in a somber tone. "The others who tried are usually caught and given a public caning. One girl disappeared and they brought back her body weeks later. It seems she got lost in the forest and froze to death." She stared wide-eyed at Reid and on to Kate. "I can never go back. I'd rather die first. Please let me stay with you two."

*

CHAPTER THREE

Reid smiled when Lorie screwed up her nose and rubbed the arm where an injection had just gone in.

"And you say that will stop me getting a whole multitude of diseases?" she asked. "How does it work?"

Reid gave an explanation and was amazed how Lorie understood quite sophisticated details. On many topics, she was very knowledgeable while on others she remained completely ignorant. One of these was medical items. Apparently no medicines or drugs of any sort were used at the commune so, at least, the place appeared to be drug free. She had, though, none of the normal children's immunization programs such as those for smallpox or polio. Luckily, her rash appeared to be no more than an allergy to wild berries they had gathered and ate with abundance.

"I'm giving you some general supplementary tablets to take, Lorie," he said. "They'll build up your iron intake."

"Iron?" she asked. "You mean like nails?"

"The same chemical but we won't have you swallowing nails," Reid laughed.

"I'm dumb aren't I?" Lorie said with a pout. "I know nothing. I've never seen television and don't even understand things first graders know all about."

Reid said nothing but handed a medical book in his hand over to her. He pointed to one paragraph. "Can you read it?" he asked.

Lorie nodded and read the paragraph out orally with amazing expression and only stumbled over a few of the medical terms. "See, I told you I was dumb," she said after the second stumble.

"That passage could not normally be read by an eighteen year old and even I have trouble pronouncing the words you stumbled over."

"Really?" Lorie replied with a smile. "I've always loved reading and we'd often make up and write little skits together." She giggled. "Some were quite naughty and us girls only shared them together in our quarters. No men were allowed there, not even Peter."

"So you are not dumb, Lorie" Kate, who had been listening to the conversation, interrupted.

Lorie smiled. "Can I ask one thing, Kate?" she asked.

"Sure."

"Those shortie pajamas. I noticed you had in your bag. Can I wear them tonight?

"Sure can," Kate laughed. "I was going to wear the heavier ones, anyhow."

Reid grinned and stood up from the bed where he'd been sitting. "I'd better leave you two ladies and retreat to my room," he said.

"Why? " Kate gave Reid a searching look.

Reid flushed. "I'll go and make us all a cup of coffee," he said. "Do you want me to bring it up?

"At the very least," Kate replied.

"Oh, and switch your flash light on," Reid added. He glanced at his watch and saw it was after eleven. "I'm going to check the generator. I may have to turn it off until the morning."

He disappeared downstairs and found Cinders waiting, all eyes and wagging tail. "Hi, Girl," he chuckled. "You've been asleep for hours. Now I suppose you want supper, too?"

Ten minutes later, he went back upstairs to find Kate and Lorie sitting up in bed.

"How do we look?" Lorie giggled as she wrapped bare arms around her knees sticking up under the blankets.

"Beautiful," Reid breathed but he was looking at Kate and was sure she had applied some fresh makeup and there was a distinct whiff of perfume in the air.

*

At dawn, Reid awoke feeling more refreshed than he could remember and thought of the previous day. Funny, this time yesterday he didn't even know Kate or Lorie existed. It was funny how one's life could suddenly change.

"Come on, Girl," he said. "Our morning walk. Okay?"

It was a tradition that every morning he'd take Cinders walking. They'd spend an hour together before the world awoke, doing things a lonely man and his dog enjoyed; walking, chasing sticks or even a swim together. Afterwards they would return home to breakfast, ham and eggs or crunchy variety dog food, none of that namby-pamby stuff.

They were sixteen minutes along the shoreline on a small animal track when the real world returned abruptly to Reid. He heard it first, and then saw a high-powered motorboat appear from the direction of the lake's northern fork.

"Oh hell!" he hissed to Cinders "Come on Girl. We're going back."

Even as they zigzagged through the firs, Reid heard the boat come closer and stop. He stole a glance through the boughs and noticed it was on their side of the tiny peninsular. The cabin was across the opposite side. If the occupants of the boat came ashore here, he'd be cut off from the girls.

"Damn," he whispered and held Cinders by the collar.

She sensed his tension and stood as silent as a statue but with all senses on full alert.

There were at least four men aboard and one was Peter. His silhouette was recognizable anywhere. A jumble of voices crossed the water but no words could be distinguished. However, their intentions became clear when the men brought oars out and began to paddle the motorboat around the point.

My God, if he hadn't taken this walk the men would have been on them before they even realized a boat had arrived.

"Come on, Girl!" Reid whispered and headed home.

After a steep climb and equally steep descent over the peninsular, Reid arrived gasping for breath, scratched and sweaty at the front deck. It had taken only a few minutes and he hoped he was in time.

"Guard the door, Girl," he ordered. "If anyone comes bark, Girl. Bark like hell. Understand!

Cinders ears, eyes, lolling tongue and thumping tail showed she did.

"Good Girl," Reid said. He glanced out but the inlet was still empty and silent. In seconds he was upstairs shaking Lorie and Kate, just as Cinders began to bark.

"Kate," he whispered after he explained what was wrong. "Intruders! Get downstairs and remove anything that could be Lorie's, especially her clothes. I think they're in the washing machine."

"Right, Reid," she replied.

"What about me, Reid?" Lorie stuttered. Her face showed she was terrified. "They'll come up here, I know."

"But you will not be here, Sweetheart," Reid said. "Put on Kate's coverall. You're going to climb a tree."

Lorie's reaction was as fast as Kate's. Without asking why or where, she jumped out of bed and slipped into Kate's clothes.

"Okay," she whispered. "I'm ready."

Reid moved to the small balcony at the rear of the cabin. The tiny deck outside was overgrown with fir tree branches. One had grown so close they could barely squeeze out the door.

"Can you climb it?" he whispered.

Lorie nodded.

"Climb up as far as you can but stick to the main trunk. Don't take any risks. When you are as far up as you can get, move around the side away from the cabin. Make sure your feet aren't showing."

"Right, Reid," the girl whispered, squeezed his hand and, within seconds, was out of sight.

Reid shut the door, returned and pulled up the blankets on Lorie's bed so it looked unused in and headed down stairs. Meanwhile on the other side of the building, Cinders continued barking and growling.

*

"Call your God damn dog off or I'll shoot it," Peter snarled at Kate who had opened the door.

He looked mean and one of his henchmen lifted an ominous handgun up ever so slightly.

"She won't obey me," Kate replied in a cold voice. "It's Reid's dog. "

"Get him and the girls while you are at it," Peter hissed. "It will save an awful lot of unpleasantness."

Kate stood deviant but her mind raced. Girls! Why had he spoken in the plural? "Only Reid is here," she replied. "Wait one moment. I'm sure he is awake after all Cinders' barking."

"I'm here, Kate," a husky voice cut in and Reid stepped out.

"We're coming in," Peter snapped. "I told the girlfriend, here I'd shoot the dog if you don't call him off." He leered at Kate still dressed only in floral pajamas and made no attempt to disguise his gaze.

"Shoot him and the National Guard will be swarming over your commune before the day is out. That's a promise." Reid replied in a slow determined growl that sounded a little like Cinders. His eyes bore into Peter and the fists clenched at his side were so tight, muscles on this neck throbbed. "I am a captain in the local reserve unit and we look after our own. You may be able to intimidate your so-called flock, Mr. Littlejohn, but don't try it with me."

"The airport authorities know my CL-215 is here," Kate added. Her voice was also strong but she felt nervous. "If I don't call in by before seven thirty this morning, a search plane will be over looking for us."

"We want our girls," Peter hissed. "Call your dog off."

"Hush, Girl. Come here!" Reid whispered.

Cinders immediately stopped growling and ran to stand beside Reid. Both eyes moved from Littlejohn's face to stare at the man holding the gun. Teeth bared and hair still stood up on the Black Liberator's back. She was quiet but ready to protect her master.

"There is nobody here," Reid said. He stood aside and Cinders followed. "Search the place if you wish, then get out and leave us in peace."

"We will," Peter replied but made sure he avoided Cinders on the way in. One man went with him and the third stayed on the deck. The fourth, Reid assumed, had stayed by the boat. For a religious group, they were amazingly militant in their methods."

Kate avoided Reid's eyes but her hand went out and squeezed his.

*

Forty minutes slipped by before Peter returned to the veranda where Reid, Kate and Cinders remained.

"It appears I was wrong," Peter stated. "There is no evidence of our girls. I apologize for the inconvenience."

"So that's it," Reid replied. "You leave a nasty taste in my mouth. Anyhow, why is it so necessary for your girls to be returned?"

"This is a hostile wilderness, Mr. Tucker. "

"I agree but your methods are despicable. If you'd come asking our assistance instead of threatening us at six o'clock in the morning, we would have only been too pleased to help find these young women. My advice is to call the state police and report their disappearance. Search crews and aircraft can cover a far greater area than you can in your boat."

"How did you know we had a boat?" Littlejohn asked suspiciously.

Reid never blinked. "You never came by aircraft, it is too far to walk so how else could you have come?" he replied.

"True," the man acknowledged. "I only hope they never left the lake shore. One of our girls died when she was lost in the forest only a few months ago. We don't want it to happen again."

"So how many are missing?" Reid asked. "Back at your commune, you told me there was only one girl."

Peter frowned, glanced at his men and turned to face Reid again. "A few," he muttered. "We believe they had planned to leave weeks ago and would attempt to approach your aircraft. In hindsight, I think your plane was a diversion and they went inland. There is a trail leading back to a forest road but it's at least a day's walk," he said with almost a smile. "Don't worry, I have a jeep checking that route. The chances are they have all been found by now."

"So if they are found and want to leave your commune, will you let them?" Kate asked.

"If you had a fifteen or sixteen year old daughter, would you let them her just leave your home, Miss Meltz?" Peter replied. "It is a vulnerable age."

"No, I guess not," Kate replied innocently. "It's a big world out there."

"Exactly," Peter replied. " I hope this small incident won't spoil our contract for airlifting our supplies."

"It shouldn't," Kate replied. "You're one of my few regular customers."

"Good. I hope your aircraft can be repaired and you can get our produce to market before it spoils."

He turned, nodded to his men and they left. Moments later the boat they heard the faint sound of a motorboat moving away.

"And how did he know the CL-215 was crippled?" Kate said to Reid.

"A thoroughly evil man," Reid replied. "I wouldn't put it past him to have sabotaged the aircraft."

"My thoughts, too," Kate replied. Her frown turned into a smile. "My God, I expected them to return dragging a screaming Lorie with them at any time. Where is she?"

"And I thought they'd find her clothes," Reid replied after explaining where he'd sent Lorie.

"They're in the toilet cistern," Kate laughed. "I'm glad none of them flushed it as I doubt if there was much water left. It's the only place I could think of at such short notice."

"Oh Kate, you are one bright lady," Reid laughed.

"No problem," she replied but appeared to flush slightly.

"Come on, Girl," he said to Cinders and walked out to search the jetty and shoreline. It was not beyond Peter to drop a man off to spy on them. However, even with Cinders' help, nobody was found and he returned to find Lorie and Kate both dressed and waiting expectantly for him.

"Nobody around," he asked

Lorie looked serious. "You know, they were right under the tree I was in. If they had looked up, I'm sure they would have seen me. God, I was terrified but I remembered to keep my feet in out of sight."

"And you're safe now," Reid replied. " We're all going to look after each other until we're safe and back in Spokane," he said. "That's a promise."

*

When Kate walked out to check the amphibian she saw that the CL-215 wasn't floating beside the wharf. It was at a grotesque angle with the nearest wing tipped up at an angle of eighty degrees and the far one below the surface. Even as she watched, the craft shuttered, there was a groan of stretched ropes and the fuselage sank beneath the water.

Kate jumped down the steps, tore along the jetty and was about to leap in the still open rear cargo door when two powerful arms grabbed her.

"Leave it Kate!" Reid said in a quiet voice.

"Let me go! I have to get to the radio," she screamed. She flung an arm out but was held and could only stand; ashen faced and watch the aircraft slide beneath the surface.

"The water is deep," Reid continued in a kind voice but he still held her in a vice grip. "If you'd climbed aboard you'd have been trapped inside."

There was another eerie groan of ropes followed by an enormous twang. The rear mooring rope spun off the top of the small pole it had been looped over and whip-lashed across the fuselage. In the same instant, water reached the cargo door and water poured inside.

"See, you would have been caught," Reid said quietly.

Kate stopped fighting but instead, turned slightly and let Reid hold her trembling body. They watched as the yellow fuselage dropped beneath the surface, a gigantic bubble rolled out the door and the wing over the jetty hit the decking. There was a scream of metal against wood and the wing slid away. Rope held the forward rope but water now covered the entire fuselage and wings.

"The rope is holding the nose up." Reid said.

Kate's throat trembled as she continued to stare at the sunken plane. "How could they?" she finally whispered. "What harm have we ever done them?"

"Because you stood up to Peter," Lorie replied. Their youngest companion had followed them down to the jetty and now stood beside them with a white face and trembling lip. "He is insane, I am sure. He bends people's minds but cannot accept that he is a mere man." She put out a hand to hug Kate. "Anyhow, that's what Mom told me not long before she died."

"I sunk everything into that plane, my entire a fortune," Kate whispered. "Everything! I sold my home and raised two mortgages to buy it and start the company. When Resolution Air collapsed, I was told I was wasting my time and money trying to run a profitable business but I thought I could do it. " She stared up at Reid. "I was a fool, wasn't I?"

"No," Reid replied. "Anyhow, I'm sure the plane can be salvaged and you must have insurance."

Kate nodded. "Our radio has gone, though. Nobody will worry about the plane being overdue. When I last reported in I confirmed we were safe and would probably not return for a couple of days. I thought, I could get the engine sorted out today and would fly out. Serves me right for being so arrogant. I should have asked for a rescue craft yesterday."

"This is an entirely different situation," Reid added. "We couldn't predict the plane was going to be sabotaged."

"And they'll be back," Lorie whispered. "They wrecked the plane to keep you here. When they don't find me, they'll know I'm with you. There's nowhere else I could be."

"But the others!" Kate said

Lorie flung around so quickly her newly cut hair swung out. "What others?" she gasped.

"Peter said they were looking for others who were missing."

"Oh my God, Jennifer and Sassy did it! They told me if I got onto the plane they'd run away and try to get to the cave."

'Where's that?" Reid asked.

"We found a small cave in the middle fork," Lorie explained. "One thing we were allowed to do was to go out in kayaks in the weekend. I guess they knew that we couldn't go too far. One day we set out on an all day expedition and followed the shoreline right around into the middle fork. Half way along was this tiny cave sort of hidden behind rocks. It became our secret place and we said if there was ever any need we could meet there." She stared at Kate with wide eyes. "I'm sure nobody at the commune knows about it and that's where the others would head."

"I see," Reid replied and turned to his companions. "Let's go inside and get everything sorted out," he said quietly. "The last thing we want to do is to panic and do something we may regret afterwards."

"The plane's stopped sinking," Kate gazed out at the stationary aircraft. The top engine mounting, propeller blades, tail and nose were above the water but the wings and fuselage were submerged. "I guess we're lucky the water wasn't too deep near the shore."

*

"It is no good worrying over the things over which we have no control," Reid said to the others as they sat around the kitchen table a few moments later. Cinders had been left on the jetty with instructions to bark if anything appeared. "We cannot fly out nor can we contact anyone.

However, it won't be too long before the lack of radio messages alerts someone back in Spokane something is amiss." He turned his eyes to Kate. "Is there anyone at your base or home who would be likely to contact authorities when you don't radio in?"

"There's nobody at home," Kate replied. "I live in an apartment by myself. At work there are only the two part-time ground staff who are new and Merve. He's the mechanic who came across from Resolution Air with me. He's an older guy who is somewhat laid back." She grimaced. "Don't get me wrong. He's an excellent mechanic but doesn't worry about the administration. He has been doing quite a large job on the Beaver's engine. My guess is, he'll just keep doing that and not worry too much about my non-appearance until at least tomorrow."

"And the airport authorities?"

"The same. There are dozens of smaller aircraft that fly in and out of the airport. I never had a commercial airport as my destination and there are seven or eight lakes and ranch airstrips where I could have landed. Again, tomorrow with be the earliest any one would suspect the CL-215 is down."

"And at that time, will they come here first?"

"Oh yes," Kate continued. "They knew I had landed here. That was confirmed when we arrived."

"One day is a long time to just wait," Lorie added. "If Peter comes back we'll only get ten minutes warning at the most."

"Not if we're on the opposite shore," Reid replied. "My suggestion is we go across to the other side of the northern fork."

"How?" Kate replied. "If we paddle those kayaks stored under the deck, we could be caught in the middle and it must be kilometers to walk around the shoreline."

"A small cabin cruiser goes with the place," Reid replied. "It is quite ancient but has an outboard motor that the reality agent had serviced. The firm holds a trust over the property. They had also upgraded the generator and filled the oil tank.

"So we a can go and look for Jennifer and Sassy!" Lorie interrupted.

"We'll see," Reid replied. "First things first. I have a small tent and a sleeping bag. I had intended to do some overnight hikes but I never guessed I'd have two pretty companions with me."

Kate smiled. "So let's do it. I get nervous just sitting here. "

*

CHAPTER FOUR

Evening devotions at the Elf commune normally lasted an hour but already an hour and a quarter had slipped by with no slow down in the proclamations of Brother Luke. The chapel was full as over a hundred adults and children watched in silence. The women, all in red tartan skirts and white blouses sat on their knees to the right while men in black trousers, white shirts and red ties sat on benches to the left. Only children below five were absent in the crèche under care of two women who had special dispensation to be absent from the devotions to care for the youngest members of the sect.

"...And the great evil has arrived My Brothers, My Sisters," the man screamed with his gray beard jutting out as he stretched his arms wide. "Satan rode in today on the wings of the yellow aircraft." He stopped, glowered out at the congregation and dropped this voice to a husky whisper. "Oh, you couldn't see him but he was there squatting on the fuselage and ready to seize our young flowers and corrupt them..."

Sassy couched in the fifth row and stole a sideways glance at Jennifer. Her companion was tight lipped and looked determined. A soft hand reached out and squeezed hers.

"...At this moment Brother Peter with John and Paul are out searching for our kidnapped flower, Junior Sister Lorie. Her mind was corrupted, My Brethren; corrupted in the form of the Devil incarnate himself. You saw him in the aircraft, the man with the young woman who piloted the aircraft. We now know he was a surgeon, My Blessed Friends, a man who takes a knife and cuts into your body to perform his foul deeds..." The wild eyes stared around the chapel. "We believe, at this very moment ... this very moment," the voice rose in volume to another scream, "our young flower is being violated like a vampire sucking blood from a child..."

In spite of her earlier promise to herself, Sassy was scared. What if it was true? She bit on her lower lip, swished her hair back and mouthed rather than whispered her real name. "My name is Sassy Rosenblatt and my friends are Jennifer Mears and Lorie Somerville. We can think for ourselves. We can be free..."

Sassy's silent words were interrupted when the back door of the chapel opened and a man in a flowing white robe marched forward. Luke stopped mid-sentence but the congregation did not move their eyes from the floor. To glance up in this shrine when a brother was entering was a sin. Only after the man reached the pulpit and Brother Luke stepped back, did the eyes rise to focus on Brother Peter.

"We shall pray for the soul of Junior Sister Lorie," he whispered. "We were too late. Her soul has been clasped by the devil. She is lost!" He stopped and reached for a pair of black shoes. He screamed and held the shoes high. "This is all that remains of our beloved Lorie!" He stopped and waited a minute in the hushed room. "She is no more of our world, Sisters and Brothers. She has gone to make a pact with the Devil..."

Sassy switched eyes and caught Jennifer's who, ever so slightly shook her head.

"Lies!" Jennifer mouthed but the pale face showed doubt.

Twenty minutes later the congregation filed out of the chapel and returned to the dormitories. Tomorrow, at dawn a special service would be held to cast aside this devil and pray for Lorie's soul.

The two girls placed on long night attire they wore every night but underneath they still wore their day clothes. Beneath their beds each had a sack tied with a ribbon that held everything they needed; food sneaked out over two weeks, warm clothes and the few personal items allowed. As well, there was a third sack, Lorie's, the one she never had time to gather before the brave swim across to the amphibian.

Sassy knew that at eleven the living compound fence was electrified, the same time as the lights in the dormitories were turned off and the Elf communion expected to sleep before the five thirty rise and call to devotions. However, they also knew that there were a few brief moments, fifteen at the most, when the 'protectors' stopped manning the gates and did a routine patrol outside the boundary fence. Their powerful flashlights could be seen every night checking for predators, usually nothing but animals that strayed in from the forest.

Even though Sassy thought sleep would never come, she must have dropped off for she jerked up to find Jennifer shaking her.

"Ready?" her friend whispered.

Watches were not allowed but Sassy pulled an ancient alarm clock from under her pillow and checked the fluorescent hands. Twenty to eleven! My God, it was time to go. She nodded, slipped out of bed, yanked off the nightgown and replaced it with a black jersey, usually only worn in times of mourning. Shoes were quickly pulled on and the sacks grabbed from beneath her bed.

"Let's go," she whispered.

*

Getting out of the building was easy enough. Though the doors were locked they climbed out through a toilet window where they had earlier broken the latch and oiled the hinges so it opened without a squeak. Outside, though, it was different. A half moon shone down from the dark sky with a million stars, a chilly breeze hit their faces and only the dark silhouette of the adjacent building gave them an idea of where to go.

Sassy's heart raced and she was sure that the crunch of her footsteps could be heard a kilometer off. She could hear Jennifer's heavy breathing as they made their way across to the other block and followed it around. In front was a grassed area and the main gate with a tiny guardhouse the protectors used in wet or snowy weather. Sounds were accentuated. Water lapping on the shore sounded almost too close and a swishing noise made Sass jump until she realized it was only the fir tree branches. She let go her last security, the edge of the building and walked directly across the grass in total darkness. She counted her steps as they'd done in the practice session. Eighty-three steps would take them to the small warning wire with the main fence a few meters beyond. In daylight it seemed so easy but in this eerie darkness the grounds were totally different. They made it across the grass, though, stepped over the wire and reached the fence.

Light flashed outside and male voices could be heard.

"The guards!" Jennifer hissed. "Lie down."

Sassy did and sank onto the damp grass.

The voices came closer and two flashlights shone like beacons but seemed to be aimed along the top of the fence. Unless directly caught in a flashlight beam, they would be invisible in the darkness. She hoped!

After the men passed, Sassy squeezed Jennifer 's arm and they were off, heading towards the gate.

"What was that?" Jennifer whispered.

Sassy stopped with all senses on full alert. The fence and the fir trees beyond could be seen to their right. In front, it was inky black but from here came the sound of water lapping on the shore. Another noise, though, was the reason for Jennifer's question.

A low sound, half way between a sob and a moan came from near the guardhouse. Sassy's apprehension turned to terror. Though not superstitious, the months of sermons about the devil and dark forces did affect her judgment. Perhaps there was a devil and he was waiting for them!

"It's the pit," Jennifer whispered. "Someone's in the pit! I'm going to check."

"Don't!" hissed Sassy but she was too late. Jennifer had already disappeared into the darkness. God, she was alone!

She swallowed bile and set off across the lawn towards the noise. The pit was a punishment hole in the ground beside the guardhouse with a heavy grate placed over the top.

The two girls dropped to their knees and crawled the last few meters towards it. The moans were now quiet sobs, obviously male and it sounded as if the man was in pain.

"Can we help?" Jennifer whispered when they reached the grating.

The moans immediately stopped and Sassy edged forward to see a white face and round eyes staring up. The man's mouth was open in fright and a dark stain showed down his right chin.

"Who is it?" he whispered in a hoarse croak. "I told you before I don't know where Lorie is. I never helped her escape. All I wanted to do..." He hesitated ... "You aren't the protectors are you? You're girls!"

"Jennifer and Sassy," Jennifer said. "Lorie's friends."

"Go back!" the man hissed. "If they catch you, you'll get a caning."

"You mentioned Lorie," Sassy whispered.

"I only tried to tell her something before she swam out to the plane"

"How do you know about that?" the girl replied.

"We all know. At least the dozen or more of us working along the shore saw her wade in and swim towards the aircraft. Afterwards we were all accused of helping her and I ... " He stopped and gave a gasp. "I tried to run off."

"And?" Jennifer whispered.

They shot me in the shoulder with a crossbow, dragged me here and tossed me in. Tomorrow I have to go before the elders."

"And your wound?"

"It isn't so bad as long as I don't bump it. My whole shoulder is sort of numb."

Sassy looked at Jennifer and realized who it was. "It's Doug!" she said. "Remember, Lorie got into trouble because they were holding hands in the school gym. He reckoned he was just helping her over the wooden horse."

Now they knew who it was, Sassy relaxed a little. Doug was a senior but a classmate because the high school students were all taught together in their small commune school.

"Come on," whispered Sassy. "We can't stay here gossiping. We have to go."

"No," said Jennifer. "Doug helped Lorie so we will help him. Give me a hand to lift the grating."

"Are you crazy!" hissed Sassy.

"You go if you wish but I am not going to leave Doug here. My God, he's in agony."

"Okay but if we're caught we'll be the ones down there, tomorrow."

The grate itself wasn't heavy but getting Doug out proved to be more difficult. He only had the use of one arm but finally managed to work his way up the pit side while the girls pulled his good arm. Gasping in agony he arrived at the top and was almost dragged the last few meters across a pile of clay to the grass. He staggered to his feet and managed a grin.

"Well girls," he said. "We're in this together now. If we're caught we'll all the thrashed and you will be put in the expurgatorial treatment."

Sassy trembled. Rumors of the treatment were well known. Of three women who had endured it, one died within a few weeks and the other two were reduced from happy cheerful people to haunted creatures who refused to talk of their experience.

"Let's go," Jennifer hissed. "The protectors will be around the perimeter soon and the fence will be turned on."

In spite of Sassy's misgivings, the rest of the breakout was straightforward. The gate was not even latched so, within moments they were across the jetty and following the shore along the bay.

"We have a canoe around the point," Sassy explained. "You know, one of those larger Indian ones. It is better than the kayaks as it is open and our gear can fit in."

"Then what?" gasped Doug as he stumbled along.

"We have a secret meeting place in the middle fork, a cave. We have a few supplies stacked there and with our sacks, we should have enough food for a week or more."

"And after that?" Doug pressed.

"We're hoping Lorie will come with Miss Meltz and the other pilot and rescue us."

"Okay," the youth replied but his voice didn't sound very optimistic.

They had just reached a small stream where the canoe was hidden when the compound behind burst into light and a siren howled.

Sassy stared at the others. "They found we're gone, already," she gasped.

In a frantic dash followed by Jennifer and wounded boy she crashed through the firs and found the canoe moored to a tree trunk that hung out over the water. She and Jennifer helped Doug in, passed over the three sacks and slid in themselves. They pushed off shore and paddled out.

"Keep near to shore," Doug advised. "It's pretty dark. If they send a boat out we'll see it before they see us..."

"Right," Sassy replied and pulled on the paddle, swung over to the other side with the double-ended instrument and started the rhythmic pattern that propelled them forward. Jennifer and herself were quite experienced and between them they were soon moving at a fast pace through the water.

Behind, the siren stopped howling but Doug, who was facing the rear said he could see people running in the lit up gate area. "They'll see I've gone," he grunted. "There's no sign of any boat yet. It'll take them a few minutes to get it on the water. Everything is locked up."

"Yeah, to protect us from wild animals," Sassy muttered sarcastically as she dug the paddle into the water and pulled. "I suppose a moose is going to unlock the boat shed and smash up their precious boat."

They again lapsed into silence as the girls concentrated on the paddling. The canoe rode low in the water and it was heavy work. Sassy's arms and shoulders began to ache and she could tell there wasn't as much assistance coming from Jennifer's paddle but she was not going to stop. She gritted her teeth and pulled the paddle again.

"We'll be at the top of the fork in sixteen minutes," she panted. "I remember that pointy rock we just went by."

"Head in behind it," Doug hissed. "They've got the boat out and it's coming this way!"

They were beside the rock within seconds. Sassy with Jennifer's help, clung to sharp protrusions and pulled the canoe in close to the rock. Nearby, the powerful roar of the outboard motor dropped to an idle. A searchlight came on and hovered over the water.

"Pull back!" Jennifer hissed but Sassy waved for her to keep quiet. She knew a slightest movement would be seen.

"They couldn't have got this far," a voice rolled across the water. "Try the stream. They could have gone up around the first bend there."

"Or straight out," another voice added. "They'd expect us to search the shore..." The searchlight swished around and lit up the lake water further out, the outboard motor accelerated and the boat curved away.

For several moments the three waited in silence until the chugging engine noise disappeared and waves from the boats wake lapped around them.

"It's the tremendous paddling effort you both put in that got us this far up the lake," Doug whispered. "I think it is safe to keep going but stay in close to shore. We aren't out of trouble yet."

"Right," Sassy whispered.

She pushed away from the rock and began paddling with Jennifer now helping with her own frantic paddling. The lights disappeared behind and soon they were alone with the lake shimmering in pale moonlight, the contrasting inky black firs and the sky like an enormous inverted basin punctured by the stars. Slop! Slop! The paddles rang out and an owl hooted in the distance. At one stage, green eyes stared at them from shore but Doug assured the girls it was only a small animal of some sort. Again, Sassy's arms and shoulders ached while Jennifer's puffing became more audible.

"Have a rest," Doug whispered. "We must be close to the middle fork by now."

"We're in it," Sassy replied with a touch of pride. "Look out and you can see the outline of the far shore. The main lake was too wide for that."

"Congratulations," Doug replied and reached out to her arm. Sassy jumped as the warm fingers squeezed her skin for a moment and let go but she realized it was a sign of appreciation and nothing sinister. "How are you going to find your cave?" the boy continued.

"We tied a strip of cloth on a branch where we turn up this small inlet. It looked so clear in daylight we thought it was almost too obvious but now, I don't know," Sassy replied. "Everything is so different at night."

"Okay, I'll keep an eye out for it."

"It's on the other side," Jennifer said. "We have to cross the inlet first and then it's at least two hundred meters in."

"I know," Sassy retorted, "but the inlet narrows further on. We need to stay on this side for a while, then we won't be in open water for so long."

Doug chuckled.

"What's wrong?" Sassy snapped.

"I was just thinking what brave girls you are. Out of everyone in our class you two are the best there are."

"You mean it?" Sassy replied, thrilled by the compliment.

"I do," Doug replied. "Most of the others are either informers, are like indoctrinated zombies or are too scared to move. That includes the boys. If anything, they're worse than the girls. That's why the elders get away with what they do."

They paddled on and crossed the inlet as time slipped by. Sassy was about to suggest they turn back when Jennifer gave a tiny squeal of delight. The marker material was in sight.

"I'll get it," Jennifer laughed and reached up as they paddled under the branch.

Moments later they pushed aside undergrowth and entered a small lagoon. The trees almost touched overhead so they operated almost from memory and found a small gravel spit that was their destination.

"We can pull the canoe up here," Sassy explained.

A few moments later they found the cave. Sassy clicked the flashlight on and the area burst into bright light. "It twists back a tiny way and opens out," she said as she shone the beam in the thin rectangular entrance. "I think water drains through it after rain though last time we were here it was dry"

"And everything is where we left it," Jennifer added and pulled away a small almost invisible piece of twine that stretched at waist height across the entrance. "Nobody's been here."

Doug grinned. "I'm impressed," he said.

"Now we wait and hope Lorie remembers we agreed to meet here," Sassy replied. She turned and noticed the boy's face for really the first time. As well as having a wounded shoulder, his cheek was bruised and swollen. He looked cheerful enough but pale and tired. "Come on, Doug," she continued quietly. "We'll have a look at your wound."

*

CHAPTER FIVE

The Wanderlust was old with paint flaking from its wooden hull but it was waterproof and moved surprisingly fast with the new outboard motor. It was stacked with as many supplies as they could carry and Reid had even tied one of the larger kayaks diagonally across the top of the small cabin.

"In case we get stuck or have a breakdown," he said when Lorie asked why it was needed.

After ten minutes of chugging east further up their fork they saw nothing more of life than a flock of disturbed Canada Geese. Cinders loved the boat and stood with her front paws on the side gazing silently at the birds. She was under orders to keep quiet but her tongue hung out the side of her mouth in almost a droll. Lorie couched in the sunshine with an arm around the dog and gazed at the fir forest that hugged the lakeside.

Only Kate looked downcast. She sat on the opposite side of the outboard motor from Reid staring at the water and had not spoken for several minutes.

"What is it, Kate?" Reid finally asked.

"Oh, I don't know," she replied, caught his eyes and shrugged. "It's just the aircraft. It's as if my whole life is sitting on the lake bottom with it. I tried so hard to get the company established." She glanced up. "I was a pilot for Resolution Air, you know. The guy who ran it had everything going for him but blew it."

"How?" Reid said in a quiet voice.

"He got greedy and began to cut corners and carelessness turned into outright dishonesty when he began to fake records," Kate replied. "He'd fly a plane out in the morning, fly all day around northern Washington and only record a small fraction of the flying time." She shrugged. "It caught up with him after the Cessna had a small accident and the Federal Aviation Administration found it was thousands of hours overdue for a major overhaul."

"So what happened?" Reid added.

Kate stared out over the water ahead. "He blamed me for everything and, without a word, skipped the country before he had to face criminal charges." She pouted. "He took Phillipa, the office secretary with him. I found out later they'd been having an affair for almost a year and that was while he was engaged to me." Her eyes finally looked up at Reid.

"Everything happened within a few weeks. He cleared out, the company went under and Dad died. Dad was a widower and my inheritance helped to pay for the airline. The CL-215 was going to be my main source of income. It was really a wreck and I spent over three hundred thousand getting it upgraded and now it's gone."

"Not really," Reid comforted. "It'll be raised."

"I know but it'll need another complete recondition before it is declared airworthy. The insurance covers the basic cost of the plane but not another recondition. I haven't even paid for the last one. I was counting on the earned revenue to pay for everything."

"I see," Reid replied. "So you need a bit of capital investment?"

"Failed airlines are a dime a dozen," Kate shrugged. "Nobody would be interested. The only way out is to be taken over by one of the larger local airlines that want my landing rights rather than the airline itself. I have international rights to fly up to Kelowna and Kamloops in British Columbia and they are a gem to hold. They'll sell the CL-215 for spares and stop serving the lake communities, not that there are many." She grimaced. "I'm sorry, with what poor Lorie had to put up with and also yourself I should be thankful for what I have."

"It's so hard when no matter what you do, someone else stuffs it up," Reid replied. "I found it is often the honest, considerate people who are the ones trodden into the dust. The ruthless bastards are the ones who get on. What's that old saying? While the liberals display doubt, the rednecks are certain they are right."

"Exactly," Kate whispered. She turned and gazed back as the peninsular in front of the cabin disappeared from view. The wake from the outboard motor made a wide V curve across the water and the air seemed so clear it was as if one could reach out and touch the towering mountains behind the trees. "It's so lovely here, I can see why you came," she whispered.

"I thought so," Reid said. "Just Cinders and me."

Kate turned and nodded. "I wouldn't want to be here alone, though. Scenery like this has to be shared."

"I was going to share with Cinders. Dogs are great companions and never judgmental," he added softly.

"But now?"

Reid smiled slightly and glanced at his companion. "My perspective has changed, I guess." He switched his eyes to the shore ahead, moved the boat out around a partly submerged tree trunk and cut back the throttle. "We're well out of sight of the fork entrance. I think we can cross here without too much of a risk."

A quarter of an hour later they were moving slowly up the south shore and almost in sight of the cabin. This shore was flanked by wide shingle beaches that were a disadvantage as the trees were further back and the Wanderlust was in full sunlight rather than shaded by trees. After a brief discussion they pulled ashore and continued along the tree line by foot.

"I can see the cabin," Lorie who was with Cinders a few meters ahead of the others, called. "Oh my God!"

"What is it?" Reid rushed forward and reached for the field glasses he had earlier slung around his neck.

"We were right," Lorie whispered. "A boat is tied to the jetty near the tail of the aircraft and I can see several people walking around."

Reid caught up to Lorie, raised his field glasses and grunted. An agitated looking Peter came into focus. It looked as if he had just returned from the cabin and the man was gesturing at two other men on the jetty. "I wish I had a listening device," he muttered. "I'd love to hear what he is saying."

"It won't take him long to realize we have a boat," Kate added. "He'll be cursing that he never wrecked it too."

She was proved right when another man emerged from the direction of the boathouse and Peter followed him back. He appeared again moments later and looked up. Lorie, who was using the field glasses, flinched. "He's looking directly at us!" she hissed.

"If we keep under the trees and don't let the sunlight reflect off the glasses, we should be safe enough," Reid replied. "The glasses are army surplus and are pretty powerful."

Kate handed the instrument back and nodded. "I know but it's still scary to know he is so close."

"So what do we do?" Kate asked.

"Wait and watch," Reid replied. "Except for making sure our boat is hidden, there is little else we can do at the moment."

*

The day drifted by and the only change across the lake came around an hour later when the boat left and began a slow patrol along the northern shoreline away from them. Unfortunately, two men were left at the cabin.

"Well, that's something," Kate said. "That's the longer way back to the commune."

"And closer to the mountains so there are quite a few streams to check," Reid added. "If they try examining every stream mouth it will keep them occupied all day. I have a feeling that they won't bother. After all they can afford to wait."

"But we can't get out into the lake," Kate added. "There are cliffs around from us and we'd be completely exposed." She shrugged. "Where is there to go anyway?"

"To look for Sassy and Jennifer," Lorie pleaded. "I know where they'll be."

Reid glanced at Kate and shrugged. "Show us on the map, Lorie," he said. He brought out a large-scale map of the lake he'd found in the cabin and lay it on the ground.

The lake did look like an eagle's claw but could also be described as a capital E with the Elf Commune in the southwestern corner. Reid's cabin was on the north coast about half a kilometer across from where they were now and a couple of kilometers from the top end of the E. The middle fork was a skinny wriggling section on the east coast a kilometer north of the commune. It cut across about two kilometers and would only be about three hundred meters across in its widest part while the main lake was over a kilometer wide at its widest point by over ten kilometers around the west coast or outside part of the E.

"The cave is here," Lorie said. She knelt on hands and knees and pointed to a small inlet about three hundred meters up the northern side of the middle section. It's not marked but I'm sure that's the place."

"Almost three kilometers from here around this coast," Reid muttered.

"And past the cliffs," Kate added. "The fork entrance would be less than a kilometer from the commune, too."

"That's the only place they would be," Lorie said with disappointment in her voice. "Anyhow, where else can we go?"

"We didn't say we wouldn't try to find your friends Lorie," Reid replied in an understanding voice. We don't want to be trapped by Peter and the others, that's all. If we're caught it will help nobody, will it?"

"Guess not," the girl replied.

While the two talked, Kate studied the map. "You know the stream that feeds into the lake splits with a smaller section going to the middle fork while the rest feeds into this one."

Reid followed Kate's finger on the map and saw the two forks almost met at the end and, as she had noted, stream split into a Y and fed into both sections. "Interesting, "he said. "Can you remember seeing the area from the air?"

"Vaguely," Kate replied. "The stream is not very large but there is an extension of the valley there so I doubt if there would be rapids. Why?"

"Let's go up our fork to the end and see if we can get through. If we can, we can go down the middle fork using the back door, so to speak."

"And if we can't?" Kate replied. "It'll be a pretty rough shoreline if we have to walk."

"We stay the night on shore somewhere and reconsider our position. With Peter going in the other direction, now is as good a time as ever to head back up our fork."

*

Thimble Creek at the end of the northern fork was wide and free of large boulders. Water tumbled over smooth stones and entered the deep waters of Eagle's Claw Lake. The only problem was it was shallow and hardly more than half a meter deep when Wanderlust crunched to a halt. Reid had stopped the outboard motor earlier and tipped it up and the three had been using the kayak paddles to punt themselves along.

"Now what?" Kate gasped. All around, the firs hugged the shore and there was no sign of the tributary that flowed into the middle fork.

"Take the kayak down, load everything into it and tow it with a rope," Lorie suggested. "With the boat empty we might even be able to float it again."

"A great idea," Reid replied. He had similar ideas himself but didn't want to take away Lorie's pleasure of being able to contribute.

"Look, I'll take the field glasses and slip back to that last bend where I'll be able to see half way up the fork." Kate added. "If anything comes I should be able to see it at least ten minutes before they get here." She took Reid's smile as approval and slipped overboard. "God the water's cold," she shivered and wadded ashore.

"Are you going to help Kate, Girl?" Reid said to Cinders.

The dog looked at Reid, out to Kate, gave a tiny yelp and plunged into the water. She paddled ashore, ran up the small bank and shook herself dry, all over a laughing Kate who rubbed her ears, glanced up, gave a wave and disappeared in the firs with the dog on her heels.

"Okay, Lorie, there's work to do," Reid chuckled.

Lorie proved again to be a great help. Without hesitating, she lowered herself into the water and guided the kayak Reid handed to her down on the water, giggled as it almost floated away and held it by the side of the larger craft. Within moments, the kayak was full, Reid lowered an anchor in case the Wanderlust decided to start floating and also climbed overboard.

Once his weight was off the boat, it lifted and was almost afloat. "I reckon if I take off the outboard we'll do it," he said.

It took three trips to get everything, including the outboard motor, ashore but in the end the boat did float. Reid smiled in satisfaction and wandered back to find Kate.

"Nobody's coming," she said. "We could be alone in the world."

"I wish we were," Reid replied and reported of their progress.

They began to walk slowly back. Kate smiled as Reid slipped his arm around her shoulder while Cinders almost tripped her up trying to walk just that little bit too close.

Lorie ran to meet them. "The other creek is just over that little mound. I can see where they join. It's not far at all. I already carried some of our stuff across ready to load." She screwed her nose up. "The motor was a bit heavy, though."

"You know," Reid said to Kate, "We might just keep this young lass around for a while. She just about pays for her keep and board, don't you think?"

"Probably," Kate replied. "Mind you she sure eats a lot..."

"Kate!" Lorie retorted. "It was you who said I had to..." She caught their eyes and laughed. "Okay, I'm not used to being teased. We weren't allowed to do it, not even in fun."

"Well, you can now, Lorie," Reid replied. "That's the sort of things friends do."

"And we're friends, aren't we?" Lorie replied in a serious manner. "I mean I'm not just a burden, am I?"

"No," Kate replied. "We're friends, Lorie, good friends who will keep on looking after each other."

"Well, let's get the boat across to the other creek, then," Lorie replied and tied the kayak to the rear of Wanderlust.

Forty minutes later, three shivering wet individuals had the boat in the new stream and Reid had bolted the motor back on. This stream was narrower and, therefore, deeper while ahead, the lake stretched away with firs growing right down to the water's edge.

"Well, shall we go?" he said. "With a little bit of luck, we might find Lorie's friends before nightfall."

He pulled the starter cord; there was a splutter, a cloud of blue smoke and the outboard roared to life to drown all their speech. They headed forward with the kayak bobbing along in their wake. Almost transparent water, green trees and a slit of bright blue sky again became their world. Ahead was the unknown but, at the moment, Reid felt more secure and hopeful.

*

"Oh, Doug," Sassy wailed. "What else can we do for you?"

The young man attempted to smile but it was more of a gasp of pain as he attempted to sit up. His shoulder wound was bloated with oozing pus soaking out through the bandage the girls had applied. Perspiration dripped off his forehead and a large lump had begun to appear beneath his armpit.

"We should have prayed for him," Jennifer said in a quiet voice. "Perhaps we're being revenged for running away."

"Oh don't be stupid!" Sassy snapped. "That sort of talk won't help Doug one little bit."

"That's what they do back home," Jennifer argued. "What do you know, anyway?"

"I know Doug was shot with an arrow and for some reason his shoulder has become infected. It was probably that terrible pit he was tossed in. I'll take the bandage off and bathe it in hot water again."

Jennifer nodded. "Okay," she replied. "I'm sorry, Sassy. It's just that I feel so guilty. We've missed three devotion times and Doug has got worse. They seem to be connected, somehow."

"There is no reason why you still can't have devotion here if you want to," Sassy replied in a more tolerant voice. "It doesn't have to be in the chapel."

"Do you want to?" the other girl asked with a slight tremble in her voice.

"No but from what Lorie's mother told us, that doesn't matter. In the world outside the commune we have a choice. I chose not to do it but if you choose otherwise that is fine. It's called democracy, Jennifer. We choose for ourselves and do what we think is right, not what Peter or the other elders force us to do."

Doug reached up and took Jennifer's hand. "That's true, Jennifer so if you want to go and pray for me, I will feel proud."

Jennifer smiled and withdrew her hand. "We shouldn't even touch each other, should we?"

"I think many of the things we've been told are untrue," Doug replied. "There is nothing wrong in touching a friend."

"I'll boil some water," Jennifer said. She went and stoked up the small fire they'd risked lighting in a small dip near the cave and placed an old aluminum kettle on it. "We'll bathe the wound again"

Sassy sighed. When she had earlier wrapped Doug's wound up, Jennifer couldn't even bare to look. It was difficult for them all and this just waiting for Lorie who may never come made everything worse. Somehow their plan had stopped here in the cave. This was going to be their salvation, but it wasn't! Sure, they hadn't been caught but things they hadn't even thought about were affecting them, Doug's illness, nowhere to wash clothes not to mention having no toilet to use.

They helped each other do what they could for Doug after he dropped off into an uneasy sleep. The wound was still weeping and even began to smell bad. Sassy took the old bandage down to the lake and washed it off before bring it up to soak in the boiling water. She added soap powder and watched the suds bubble up.

"This will kill the germs," she said. "We've only got two bandages so will have to use it again."

"Will Doug, die?" Jennifer asked in a whisper.

"I doubt it," Sassy replied but her earlier optimism had disappeared. It was late afternoon and already quite cold. Another night like the last one could be more than Doug could handle and, of course, Lorie was nowhere around. It seemed hopeless but it wouldn't help to confess her thoughts to Jennifer.

"Look, I'm going for a bit of a walk out to the lake," Jennifer said. "Will you be okay for ten minutes or so?"

"Sure," Sassy replied. "I'll start some supper. We've got plenty of vegetables, eggs and milk so I'll make us all something warm and appetizing."

Sassy smiled and decided Jennifer wasn't a liability. Her friend was an excellent cook and she knew that without her company she'd be quite frightened out here in the wilderness.

Five minutes later Jennifer rushed back into the cave with her face terrified. "Quick," she gasped. "There's a launch out in the lake and it is heading right this way. We need to hide... Now!"

*

CHAPTER SIX

"What about the fire?" Sassy gasped.

"Leave it. There is no time," Jennifer hissed. "Come on. Let's hope they don't bother to search thoroughly."

She ran across to Doug who was still asleep, gently shook him and explained what was wrong.

"Right," he replied and with Sassy's help, staggered to his feet.

It was pitch dark around the first corner of the twisting cave but nobody dared turn on a flashlight. Sassy led and ran her hand along the wall until it disappeared and a slight puff of colder air buffeted her face.

"Here," she whispered and felt her way into a small side cave.

This was barely wide enough to squeeze through but they knew it opened out after a few meters. They had explored this side tunnel earlier and found it continued on for an unknown distance. Now, though, they squatted down in complete darkness and waited, afraid that their footsteps would echo back to the main cave.

Sassy reached for both her companions' hands and found them cold and sweaty but reassuring as nothing could be seen except total darkness. Her friend's breathing could be heard and the damp smell of soil whiffed past her nose.

She heard a dog bark, so loud her body jumped and heart began thumping in her rib cage. It was mere meters away but, though scared, sound reasoning impregnated her mind.

Pets were regarded as unnecessary at the commune and they didn't even use farm dogs. Nobody there owned a dog!

*

As soon as he cut the motor, the smell of wood smoke hit Reid's nose. This was the fourth tiny inlet they had searched and Lorie's earlier confidence had become uncertainty for the whole north side of the middle fork was indented with bays, inlets and tiny creeks tumbling down from the forest.

"Smell it?" he said to his companions.

"This is it!" Lorie exclaimed, her voice tinged in excitement. "It must be!"

"Take it quietly," Reid warned. It was late afternoon, the whole fork was in shadow and everything dim. He reached for Cinders and stroked her head. "What can you smell, girl? Is anybody here?"

Cinders glanced up and gave her tail two wags before she stared at the shore with nose ears and eyes on full alert.

"I'll jump ashore and pull the boat in," Reid said.

"Okay," Kate replied. "Be careful."

Reid nodded, grabbed the mooring rope and stepped from the back deck across to a flat rock. His momentum pushed the Wanderlust out but he tugged the rope and walked forward until he could see beyond the rock he had stepped out on. In front, was a tiny shingle area and a dry creek bed. The distinct smell of burning wood was stronger here but there was no fire in sight. He glanced down and saw several footprints in the damp pebbles. Two were smaller but one looked as large as any he would make.

"Lorie," he called back. "You said your friends would wait for you here. Were any men?"

"No," Lorie replied in a worried tone. "Only girls my age, Sassy definitely and possibly Jennifer ... Why?"

"Look here," Reid replied when the other two caught him up. "That one set of footprints is too big for someone Lorie's size."

"Perhaps they were caught," the girl gasped.

"Okay," Reid replied in a grim voice. "It is no good just guessing. Someone has been here so we need to find out what happened. Agreed!" He turned; saw Lorie's frightened eyes and Kate's apprehension.

"Go on," Kate whispered.

Reid nodded and turned to Cinders. "Search, Girl!" He directed. "Find the girls. Follow the footprints."

Cinders set off at a rapid pace with her nose to the ground. Within seconds they found a commune canoe dragged into a little dip and covered in amateur fashion with a few dead fir limbs. Half a dozen steps further along, was the cave and the embers of the fire they had smelt.

"It's our cave, "Lorie said. "I'd know it anywhere."

"But no people," Kate observed. "You could be right, Lorie. Peter or one of the others must have caught them."

But Cinders did not hesitate. She continued on up to the cave mouth and inside. The trio followed and found the signs of recent occupation including dirty dishes and a still warm kettle. Three sacks were sitting against one wall and a girl's black jersey was looped over a rock.

"It looks tidy," Reid observed as he moved the flashlight around. "There's no sign of a struggle."

"Look at Cinders," Lorie whispered. "She's not stopping."

"Go Girl," Reid said. "Bark if you find anything."

Seconds later the bark made everyone jump in fright.

"I'll go," Reid whispered and followed Cinders up the side cave with his flashlight blazing.

*

Seconds later the two parties met. Sassy and Jennifer wide apprehensive eyes turned to relief when Lorie appeared behind Reid and the panting Black Labrador.

"Sassy, Jennifer!" Lorie screamed and rushed forward.

Tears, hugs, explanations and introductions followed before everyone returned to the main cave and only Doug hung back looking tired and worried.

Reid noticed and turned professional. "I'll look at your wound, Lad," he said. "Kate will you get my medical bag from the boat, please."

"Sure, Reid," she replied and left the cave.

"Reid's not a pilot. He's a doctor," Lorie explained.

Jennifer frowned. "A medical doctor?" she asked.

"That's right, Jennifer," Reid replied and sensed her nervousness. "I know you were taught we aren't needed but I assure you I'll do nothing to Doug without his permission."

"No, that's fine, Reid," the girl replied. "If Lorie trusts you, that's good enough for me. It's just so hard to find everything we've been taught is wrong. It's as if my whole life has been a lie."

"No it's not," Lorie interrupted. "Just some things were, not everything. We've spent hours talking about it over the last two days."

"And I don't mind you helping, Reid," Doug added. "In fact, I appreciate anything you can do. The girls were marvelous and I'm sure without their help it would be worse."

"Okay, let's see." Reid began to unwrap the bandage.

With Cinders keeping guard by the Wanderlust, Reid concentrated on helping Doug. Kate held the flashlight and the commune girls watched. Even Jennifer was engrossed as Reid began his examination.

"You did everything right," Reid stated quietly and smiled up at Jennifer. He turned to Doug. "How far away were you from the bow that shot you?" he asked.

"I'm not sure," Doug replied. "I was running and suddenly it felt as if I'd been hit by a fence post. I stumbled and it was only then I heard the sound of the gun go off. After that, I remember very little. Just pain, shouting voices and I felt my shirt become soggy. I must have blacked out, I guess."

"I see… Unfortunately, Doug, a piece of the arrowhead is still embedded in your upper arm. That is why it has turned septic. I'll have to get it out."

"Okay," Doug whispered but failed to hide the quiver in his voice.

"Don't worry," Reid replied. "I can give you a local anesthetic. It won't hurt."

"A needle into the skin!" Jennifer gasped and turned whiter than Doug's pale face.

"It's not a sin, Jennifer," Lorie defended. "This is not the devil at work. He's a kind man helping us. Understand?"

"I believe Lorie," Sassy supported. "We haven't been able to help Doug and you don't want him to die, do you?"

"Of course not," Jennifer whispered.

"Look," Kate interrupted. "What say you and I go out and see how Cinders is getting on, Jennifer. We can't do anything to help, anyway."

"Okay," the girl agreed. Like Sassy and Lorie's before it was cut, she had long hair that hung down over her face and wore the commune uniform. Her features, though, were darker than Lorie's with brunette hair and olive skin. In many ways she looked like a frightened child rather than a mature teenager and never complained when Kate's arm went around her shoulder and guided her away.

Kate looked up. "Do you want to come, too Sassy, Lorie?" she asked but both the other girls shook their heads and switched their attention back to Reid who had produced a needle and tiny bottle of clear liquid from his bag.

"There will be a slight prick and your arm will go numb but you'll have the funny feeling it is all puffed up," Reid explained to Doug. "What happens is that your mind gets no signal from the area and replaces this with its own, that of something all swollen up. We call it pins and needles." He continued with his description and found his audience clinging to every word.

The two girls watched with fascination as Reid made a tiny incision with a scalpel. He ignored the blood that flowed and used tweezers to dig into the wound. Sassy gasped but held the tiny basin out when asked while Doug gritted his teeth, looked out into the darkness and squeezed Lorie's hand.

"It's done," Reid said a moment later and dropped a tiny fragment into the basin. "They had steel tips on their arrows. When it was pulled out this was left behind. Now I'll put in a couple of stitches and get you wrapped up, Doug. It'll be sore for a while once the anesthetic wears off but by morning the swelling should have gone and within a week you'll be fine. I'll give you a tetanus shot, too if you agree"

"Give me whatever is needed thanks, Reid," Doug replied. "Between you and the girls, I have so much to be thankful for, I don't know where to begin."

"It's okay," Reid replied. "Just get better and afterwards we'll all get away from this horrible commune. That's a promise from me."

"And I reckon you're a guy who keeps his promises," Doug replied with a grin.

*

"So how many motor boats does the commune own?" Reid asked an hour later. It was dark, quite cool but they'd all eaten a solid meal and were sitting in the light of an old kerosene lamp Sassy had brought with them.

"Only one that I know of," Sassy replied. "There could be more, though. The boat shed is outside the compound and we were never allowed near it. The kayaks and canoes we use are kept in a different place."

"What are you thinking, Reid?" Kate asked.

"So far, those guys have really had everything their way. They scuttled your aircraft, driven us out of my cabin and effectively cut off our communication with the outside world. Doug's been shot and the girls made outcasts. I think it is about time we did something. To sit here is useless. We'll either be found or run out of food."

"But by tomorrow, someone will realize the a CL-215 is late. I'm sure search aircraft will be over soon after that," Kate replied.

Reid shrugged "Unless Peter contacted Spokane and told them the plane is at the commune with say mechanical repairs and won't be back for a week. It would be perfectly plausible, wouldn't it?"

"I never thought of that," Kate admitted.

"The lake is only about ten kilometers long," Lorie cut in. "Eventually they must find us. "

"So what, Reid?" Doug asked.

"We hit back," Reid snapped. "They've proved to be utterly ruthless. Look at the way you were treated. If they catch us, I doubt if we'll survive. It would be so easy to fake the sunken plane as a crash and have a few drowned bodies floating around. "

"Reid, don't!" Lorie gasped.

In the flickering light all three of the commune girls looked pale and scared. The exhilaration of finding each other and being free had gone. Now, the grim reality of their situation had to be faced.

Kate nodded with her lips creased in a thin line and eyes determined. "And now is the time, Reid," she said softly. "The longer we wait the more the stranglehold will tighten. What do you suggest we do?"

*

It was after midnight when the canoe paddled along the south coast of Eagle's Claw Lake next to a beach and from exactly the opposite direction from where the pair hoped they'd be expected. Everyone, including Doug and Jennifer wanted to help so a compromise was made with everyone taken in Wanderlust out to the main lake, across to the western shore and south for a kilometer to a small bay and beach. Here, Reid and Lorie continued in the girls' canoe that had replaced the kayak. Kate had wanted to accompany Reid but understood his logic of remaining on the boat with Jennifer and Doug. If they hadn't returned by four, Kate would then head back to the cave before daylight arrived.

The commune was in total darkness but, with the help of the moon, the pair could see the western corner of the compound fence. Here they paddled ashore and pulled the canoe up on the sandy shore.

"Don't touch the fence," Lorie warned in a harsh whisper. "It's charged."

"Okay," Reid replied and stared around. To his left the lake was black, ahead the fence could be seen fading away into darkness while, overhead, half the sky was star-studded and held the moon while the rest remained black. "Come on, Girl," he whispered to Cinders. "Remember, quiet. No barking. Understand?"

Cinders did and walked silently along between her master and the blonde girl dressed again in the black jersey and wearing Kate's jeans. They reached the boathouse without a problem but found the wooden doors open and, after an inspection more by feel than eyesight, they realized it was empty.

"Hell," retorted Lorie. "They're probably at your cabin waiting for us."

"Possibly," Reid whispered. "Of course, the boat could be tied to the jetty ready for an early start in the morning. Come on. We'll keep going."

They moved forward in eerie stillness. The sounds were all natural, water lapping on the shore, the wind in the firs ahead and the occasional hoot of an owl. It was chilly but so clear, Reid was sure that if anyone was by the fence they would see their silhouette. Also, Cinders would forewarn them of anyone nearby.

But all remained still.

"The jetty!" Lorie whispered needlessly when the wooden structure loomed like a ghostly skeleton out of the gloom.

"Okay," Reid whispered back. "We need to be very careful. I would not be surprised if some sort of trip wire or warning device is rigged up somewhere." He turned to Cinders. "Search, Girl. Find anything but no barking. Okay?"

Again Cinders obeyed. Her nose went down and she moved ahead a burst, waited for the pair to catch up and continued forward in a zigzag type sweep of the shore. They were at the base of the jetty when Cinders stopped, the hair along her back rose and an almost inaudible growl came from her mouth.

Reid patted her head in acknowledgment, reached back to where Lorie's hand slipped in his, and moved quietly forward. Something had disturbed Cinders but he didn't know what.

Though expecting something, the cough made him jump in fright. It was above them on the decking and only a few meters away.

They froze. Footsteps sounded on the wooden planking, the heavy tread of boots. So there was a guard, after all!

"Take Cinders, go under the deck and wait," Reid whispered in a terse order. "Don't call out if you hear me talk. Understand?"

Lorie stared at Reid with her teeth biting on a bottom lip but nodded and reached for the dog's collar.

Now alone, Reid retreated inland, scrambled on all fours up a small embankment and reached the road. He squinted around. Nothing could be seen inland except the tops of fir trees that shaded anything in front from the moonlight. There was the fence and compound beyond and the slight scrape of metal against metal. The tree boughs sighed and water lapped below. Reid turned and smiled slightly. A boat was tied to the far side of the jetty.

Now could he cover the twenty or so meters to the boat without being noticed? He had the trees behind so would form no silhouette but all it needed was his foot to crunch on a loose piece of gravel and that would be it. If the guard was alone, he would be alert to the slightest sound; a lonely jetty in the middle of the night would make the most confident person apprehensive. The chances are the man would be armed, too. Reid grunted and decided to take a different approach. He slid back down the bank and moved back towards the fence another dozen steps, swallowed and stepped purposely out on the road.

Nothing moved!

He stepped forward and headed towards the jetty. "Aye," he called out. "I was told to come and replace you. Anything happen?"

By now he'd reached the deck and assumed his adversary was only a little way ahead.

"Shit, don't do that," a voice replied. "You scared hell out of me."

The man had been leaning against the side of the boat and now stepped forward out of the gloom.

"There's been a change of plan," Reid said. "Peter wants you inside. I'm to take over."

"Me. What for?" The voice sounded worried.

"Who knows?" Reid replied. He never slackened his stride and was abreast of the man before any suspicion arose.

The man's eyes stared at Reid. "Who the hell..." he began but managed no more words as a heavy wrench swung out and sliced down on his head above the ear. Reid knew has anatomy and was sure only one heavy blow would be required.

It was!

With barely a moan the guard collapsed forward into Reid who grabbed the shoulders and lowered him to the ground.

"Lorie," Reid whispered over the side. "Come on up but be quiet. There may be more than one guard.

She did so well; it was only when a wet tongue licked his hand a couple of moments later that Reid realized the pair were with him.

"Reid!" Lorie whispered, her voice trembling. "There's something thumping on the boat. Cinders heard it as we came up."

*

My God, she was right. A muffled thump, thump came from the middle area of the boat, probably in the area of the cabin.

"Well it worked once. We'll do it again," Reid whispered. "We're going to walk casually aboard. When I talk, just say anything but keep your voice calm and low without it being a whisper. Okay?"

"Sure Reid." Lorie replied and responded to the slight squeeze he gave her shoulder by bending her head into his chest. His young friend was proving to be a very resourceful young lady. "On three," he whispered.

"...And where on the boat did you reckon you left your shoes?" he said. His voice sounded loud but, he hoped, casual.

"The cabin," Lorie replied. "I'm going to be in deep trouble if I lose them."

"You are already in trouble now," Reid continued. "Coming out here in the dead of night. If I report you..."

"Don't please, "Lorie pleaded. "I only..."

They were on deck and stopped. Everything was quiet and even the thumping had stopped. But, no, there was a noise. Cinders growled, her head stretched forward and hair along her back bristled.

Someone was on board. It was time!

Reid handed the wrench, still in his hand, to his companion, reached in his jacket pocket and pulled out a tiny flashlight. He stepped forward, switched the light on the world blazed out as if a skyrocket had lit up. Head in the glaring light were three steps that led to a small door. Reid moved quickly, turned the handle and ran his shoulder into the door. Eighty kilograms of brute force hit the door but it swung in so easily, Reid almost lost balance as he stumbled inside.

The interior was as bright as day in the flashlight beam and it took only microseconds for him to absorb the scene in front. A woman in her twenties was lying on a narrow bunk opposite the door. Puffed blackened eyes stared out beneath a tangled mass of hair. Her arms and legs were tied to the sides of the bunk sides. A second glance showed that as well as the woman's battered face her arms were bruised, her blouse was ripped so underwear was exposed and her jeans were half off, ruffled and dirty. She was gasping for breath like an asthmatic and the petrified eyes that held Reid for a second moved on to the girl behind him.

She stopped the wild breathing and just stared. "Lorie!" she whispered and burst into sudden tears of extreme emotion.

If Reid was astonished, it was nothing compared with Lorie's reaction. "Erika!" she cried, with the words barely forming in her throat. "But how can it be! I was told you were dead." She turned to Reid and gasped. "Erika is my older sister. I haven't seen her since before Mom's death."

*

CHAPTER SEVEN

Kate stared out over the silver water and shivered. The moon had descended and the sky to the east was now red with the approaching dawn. She gazed at her watch for the third time in as many minutes. Four thirty had long come and gone but she refused to head back to the cave.

"You're keen on Reid, aren't you?" Sassy said as she came and stood at the stern of Wanderlust.

"Me?" Kate retorted. "He's a nice guy but I don't really know him any more than you do."

"Oh yeah," Sassy continued in a quiet voice. "So I guess you're clinging the hand rail with white knuckles and staring out at the water because you're worried about Lorie?"

Kate turned and fixed her eyes on the younger woman. "Of course I am," she replied in a quieter voice, then smiled. "Oh hell, Sassy. Is it that obvious?"

"That you have the hots for Reid?"

Kate smiled. "If you put it that way..."

The girl ran a strand of hair through her fingers and replied, "He's a great guy but we can't stay here much longer, you know. In half an hour it'll be so light we'll be in full view of the camp. Everyone there will be up soon and walking across for morning devotions in the chapel."

"Ten minutes," Kate replied. "Then I promise we'll return to the cave. Okay?"

Sassy nodded. "Fair enough," she replied and turned as Jennifer approached.

"Are we going?" Jennifer asked nervously. "Doug has finally fallen asleep on the bunk and..." He voice trailed off as she gazed out across the lake and uttered a sigh of delight. "Shall we start the motor?" she asked.

"Why?" Kate snapped again.

"The canoe's coming," Jennifer replied. "Look!"

Kate swung around and stared out over the water but saw only a dozen ducks fly off the surface. A series of quacks floated through the air.

"They've been disturbed," Jennifer replied. "That is in direct line with the jetty so it must be the canoe. Every morning on the way to chapel, I'd look out and watch the ducks. They made me feel free, somehow. I got to know their movements quite well."

"Oh Jennifer," Sassy scoffed but her tone turned to delight. "My God, you're right!" she gasped.

Far out on the lake a light flickered three times, stopped and was followed by two longer flashes. This was their prearranged signal meaning that Reid was safe and wanted to be picked up.

Kate grinned, gave Jennifer a massive hug and grabbed the starter cord. It took three pulls before the cold motor, chugged, almost stopped and roared into life.

"Get the anchor up, you two," she yelled. She grabbed the steering arm and waited while Sassy and Jennifer ran to the bow and pulled the anchor up.

"Okay!" called Sassy.

Kate opened the throttle and Wanderlust charged forward, bumped for a few seconds until the nose lifted and accelerated toward the position the flashlight signal had come from. Seconds later the canoe appeared like a black cardboard cutout in the red dawn. Doug joined the others on the aft deck with his wounded arm in a sling. He held the rail with his good hand to steady himself and looked as excited as Kate.

"There're three people!" Jennifer exclaimed again before the others could distinguish individual shapes in the canoe. "A woman!"

Sassy accepted Jennifer's comment and dug Kate in the ribs. "She's got eyes like a eagle," she whispered.

"Yeah, and good hearing, too," Jennifer shot back.

"You're right," Kate added. "There're three in the canoe."

She accelerated Wanderlust forward until they were almost to the canoe, cut the throttle and waited as the boat rode the swell from its own wake and watched the wash buffet the canoe.

"Here, help with Erika," Reid shouted up. "She's a little sore so be careful."

Everyone leaped to action. Doug held the mooring rope from the canoe that Lorie had thrown up to him, Jennifer bent over and held the rear of the canoe while Kate took the stranger's hand and almost hoisted her aboard.

The woman caught her eyes and smiled while Kate frowned to herself. Erika looked strangely familiar. Of course, though shorter, older and slightly chubbier, this could be Lorie. She had the same oval face, hair coloring and cheekbones.

"Kate," Lorie said after she hoisted Cinders aboard and jumped onto the deck. "Meet Erika, my big sister. She came all the way here to get me out of the commune but was caught by Peter when he was searching for us..."

"Hello, Kate," Erika interrupted in a soft voice that even sounded a little like Lorie. "I hope I won't be a burden."

"The bastards beat her up," Reid snarled. "Really bad!"

He pulled himself aboard and was about to start tying the canoe behind Wanderlust when Kate reached forward from behind and tucked her arms around him.

"I thought you were caught," she whispered as he turned around. Her lips quivered and tears appeared in her eyes.

Reid ran a tongue along his bottom lip, held Kate close and brushed her hair. "Don't cry, Kate. We're safe; I've wrecked their boat motor and tossed their spare outboard motor in the lake. It'll be a while before they'll be mobile."

Kate nodded, pulled back and took out a handkerchief. She wiped her eyes. "Well, we'd better get going," she replied.

"Kate," Reid whispered.

She looked up. "Yes…"

Reid reached forward and gave her a bruising, passionate kiss. She responded and, for a moment, the others in the boat were forgotten. Finally, Reid held her back by the shoulders and smiled. "Can I go out and come in again?" he asked.

"Why?" Kate replied.

"Well, with that sort of welcome, I just want to do it all again."

"Oh Reid," Kate whispered, flung her arms back around his neck and buried her face in his neck, before turning up and kissing him again.

Meanwhile, it was Jennifer who guided Erika down into the cabin, sat her on the bunk and placed an arm around her shoulders. "We were told you were dead," she said softly. "What happened and why did you risk coming back?"

"It's a long story," Erika sighed. "I came back as I knew Lorie would be sixteen next week and I didn't want her to go through the three years of hell I endured before I managed to escape." She wiped a hand over her face. "I wanted to rescue you, Sassy and the younger girls too, Jennifer, but you ended up rescuing me. Ironic, isn't it?"

"It was Lorie who made it all possible," Jennifer replied. She sat down and filled Erika in on details the older woman hadn't already heard earlier.

*

On deck, Lorie glanced at Reid and Kate embracing, turned and saw Sassy standing by a bashful Doug and realized Jennifer had helped Erika. "Well Girl, if we don't do something, we'll be here until lunch time," she said to Cinders.

She squatted down, gave the Black Labrador a hug and walked across to the idling motor. With Cinders beside her she opened the throttle so suddenly, everyone aboard staggered.

"Sorry everyone!" she called and headed the boat up the lake. The red sky had turned to a pale blue and, in the gap between the eastern mountains, the first rays of sunlight appeared.

"Where to, Reid?" she shouted above the roar of the motor.

"Straight up the center of the lake," he yelled back. "We're heading back to my cabin."

Lorie swallowed and switched her attention back to the boy beside of her. She reached across and deposited a tiny kiss on his cheek. Both flushed in embarrassment but Doug responded with an equally small peck back.

"I was so worried about you," Doug whispered.

"Were you?" Lorie replied. "Why silly old me when you had Sassy and Jennifer to look after you."

"They're great, too," Doug replied, "but..." He stopped and looked into her eyes. "We're going to be just ordinary people, Lorie, free to be ourselves. It will be hard, I guess, we'll make mistakes but they'll be our own mistakes to make."

Lorie nodded, glanced across, saw Sassy grinning at her and Cinders wagging her tail. Even the dog seemed to approve.

*

The trip north was trouble free with Sassy helping Lorie with the controls while Reid went inside the cabin to give Erika a professional examination.

"I believe you have a couple of cracked ribs," he said. Though his probing fingers were gentle, Erika squinted in pain. "I'll bandage them but there is little more I can do. How did it happen?"

Erika heaved. "I was kicked in the ribs after Peter knocked me to the ground.

"You were sexually violated, weren't you?" Reid added quietly.

"Yes," the woman whispered. "Don't tell, Lorie, please. Reid." .

"If you wish but she is a very understanding young lady. Do you want to talk to any of the others?"

"Kate," Erika whispered. "Can you leave us alone for a moment?"

"Of course," Reid replied. "I won't be a moment." He walked out to the deck and found Kate waiting.

"How is she?" she said.

"Physically bruised and battered. She's baring up well but was raped by Peter and probably others, too."

"Oh hell," Kate whispered. "Does Lorie know?"

"She guesses but Erika wants to hide the truth from her. After I found her in the boat I suspected this had happened but we never discussed it in front of Lorie."

"I'll go to her." Kate squeezed Reid's arm and slipped into the tiny cabin.

Lorie slipped over from where she was sitting with Doug and grabbed Reid's arm. "Peter screwed her, didn't he?" she whispered.

Reid grimaced. "She won't allow me to say," he replied.

"To protect my feelings?"

Reid nodded. As a doctor he had to respect patient confidentiality but as a friend he felt if Lorie knew what had happened, it would help both sisters.

"Can I go and talk to her?" Lorie asked.

"I'll see," Reid replied and slipped back inside to find Erika sobbing quietly in Kate's arms. "Lorie wants to see you," he said when she looked up. "Would you like her to come in?"

"When I was sixteen, she was only nine, so beautiful and tall for her age with long blonde hair. I vowed then I'd never expose her to these filthy animals." Erika managed a tiny smile, "I would like her here, thank you Reid."

"I'll get her," he replied, poked his head out the door. Lorie appeared and grabbed her sister in a tearful hug. "You looked after me for years, Erika, " she sobbed. "Let me do the same for you, now, please. I'm not a child any more."

"No you aren't but you'll always be my kid sister," Erika whispered.

Reid tapped Kate on the shoulder, caught her eyes and they both slipped out into the morning light. The others remained quiet but looked sympathetic. To their right, huge cliffs towered above them and Reid realized they were almost half way up the lake. He moved back and sat by Sassy.

"When you get the north fork, go straight across," he said. There's a headland before the cabin. Pull in there and I'll take Cinders ashore and cut across to the cabin. I don't think anyone will be there but it pays to be careful."

" Right, Reid," Sassy responded.

*

Cinders proved her worth yet again when she stopped at the edge of the path near the jetty and growled. Reid glanced down and saw a thin strand of wire stretched across at waist height, between two trees

"So what have we got here?" he mumbled to Kate who had insisted on accompanying him.

With infinite care, the pair managed to trace the wire to the bough of a tree. From there it looped up over three more branches, on through the branches of three more firs and down to the ground where it connected to a junction box, along with other incoming wires. A larger single cable continued along to under the decking at the front of the cabin.

Reid grunted, crawled under and found the cable was connected to a tiny instrument, similar in size to a cell phone.

"What is it?" Kate asked as she squatted in the confined space and brushed a spider's web out of her eyes. "Explosive?"

"No," Reid replied. "It's a radio transmitter. I guess if someone touches a wire it sends a signal telling our enemy that we've arrived home. No doubt the other wires are connected to the cabin doors, across the jetty or other places we'd walk."

"So what do we do?"

"Disconnect its battery, if we can without triggering it."

"And as soon as you touch it, a signal will be transmitted," Kate replied. "Even if you disconnect it the harm would have been done."

"Suggestions?" Reid replied.

"Jam the junction box. This instrument looks quite sophisticated but the junction box is probably just a circuit breaker that makes a contact when the wires shift. If we can wedge it open no current will pass onto this device."

Kate's theory proved correct. The junction box was homemade and it wasn't too difficult to bend back the contact arm. Reid felt in his pocket, produced a ballpoint pen and wedged it into the gap. Afterwards, he used a small jack knife to cut the incoming strands of wire.

"There may be more," he said and sent Cinders searching. However, nothing was found and everything else in the cabin or around the sunken amphibian looked untouched.

"The place has been done over by professionals," Reid muttered after they searched the cabin. Everything has been moved and placed back in its original place. For a religious cult, these guys are amazingly resourceful. The trouble for them was, it is impossible to re-establish dust over unused objects. Everything is far too clean," He grimaced. "I have the strangest feeling incapacitating their boat won't keep them away for long. We shouldn't stay here any longer than is necessary."

"But where else is there to go?" Kate replied. "There's only the cave and that would be useless in the long term. At least we have facilities here."

*

"We can go out the way I came in," Erika suggested when everyone met in the cabin's living room half an hour later.

"Yes, how did you get in here, Erika?" Doug asked. "I thought the only overland route was south from beyond the commune's farm and even that is really only a walking trail."

Erika pointed to the map they'd spread out on the table. "My jeep is stuck about five kilometers north of here on the trial where I was caught. "

" But how did you get so close?" Lorie asked

"I was devious and determined," she replied and began her story...

*

"This road leads nowhere, Ma'am," the forest ranger said and grinned at Erika who sat in the driver's seat of the old jeep. "Where were you heading?"

Erika turned on the charm and smiled. "Isn't this State Highway 20 that leads into 97? I thought I'd take the scenic route across to 97 before heading up to Canada."

"No, Ma'am," the ranger replied and scratched his cheek. "You sure went wrong. The highway is about sixteen kilometers back. Didn't you realize that when you hit the gravel? This is a dead end road. You'll need to turn around."

"Oh hell," Erika sighed. She was on the road she wanted to be on but wasn't going to tell the ranger that.

"Have you a map, Ma'am?" the ranger continued. "I can show you a loop road that'll take you across to 20. It'll save you five kilometers or so."

The ranger was very helpful but Erika was becoming increasingly frustrated. She was already running an hour late and didn't really relish sleeping the night in the jeep on a deserted forest road.

"So it's a kilometer up and to the left?" she said, after pretending to follow the instructions.

"That's it, Ma'am," the ranger grinned. "Be careful though. There are no signs. If you go straight ahead or to the right you'll end up on private forest roads that really just go in circles. Get onto those and you'd be really lost," He glanced up. "I think we're in for a bit of rain too. Would you like me to follow you back to the junction?"

Erika froze. That was the last thing she wanted. However, she smiled again. "No, you've been most helpful," she cooed. "My husband's an old jeep nut. We bought two of them from a lumber mill and I was following him home." She smiled again and looked into the ranger's eyes. "No wonder I couldn't see him in front. Anyhow, he said he'd wait at 97 for me. I guess he'll be there by now. There's no mobile phone coverage here but I guess you know that."

The whole story was a fabrication but Erika hoped, plausible.

"Okay Ma'am," the ranger replied and tipped his hat. "I reckon you only lost half an hour or so." He glanced at the old vehicle. "You can't beat these old army surplus jeeps, can you?"

"That's what Frank says but having half a dozen of them is getting a bit too much." She started the motor, waved and drove away.

Five minutes later she reached the junction but continued straight ahead for two kilometers. She was now in thick forest and the road ended at a chained and padlocked gate. An old faded sign read "No entrance. Private Lumber Road"

Erika stopped, pulled a massive pair of metal cutters from a toolbox behind her seat and, in a very unfeminine manner, cut the padlock chain and yanked the gate open.

An hour later the storm arrived.

*

"That'll be the one we hit when we flew in," Kate said after Erika stopped and took a sip of coffee from her mug.

"If we'd only known you were coming," Lorie whispered. "It was our fault, you know. If Peter wasn't trying to find us he'd never have gone up that trail and found you."

"But you didn't know, Lorie so don't blame yourself for anything," Erika said.

"So what happened?" Doug cut in.

"I knew this cabin was here and had planned to make it my base," Erika continued, "I thought it would be empty after old Shelton the hermit died. He used to visit the commune on occasions to get supplies. Anyhow, I got caught in the storm and bogged down in mud. That night I did sleep in the jeep and by morning the weather was better so I continued on foot. I was just about out and ran slab bang into Peter." She sighed. "I don't know who got the biggest fright, him or me. I ran for it but never stood a chance. The rest you know. I think they were going to use me try to flush all of you out."

"But they didn't have to... " Lorie almost shouted. "Why do they do those terrible things?"

"Because I was there," Erika replied with a shrug. "Simply because I was there."

*

CHAPTER EIGHT

After a meal and freshen up, everyone pitched together to help make the cabin as comfortable as possible. Kate accompanied by Sassy, Jennifer and Cinders went down to inspect the amphibian and also said they'd take the boat back to the boat shed. At the moment, it was tied to the jetty in sight of anybody who might come by.

Though she didn't complain, Erika looked to be in pain and only made a token protest when Reid ordered her to rest. Lorie stayed with her to talk about the gap in their lives and to make her sister comfortable. Doug's wound needed dressing and Reid was pleased to see the inflamed section looked a more healthy red and his swollen gland had decreased in size.

"You really need more painkillers but I haven't got that many," Reid apologized. "I need to keep Erika on them for as long as possible."

"Then use them for her, Reid," Doug replied. "I can cope. Compared with yesterday, it's a hundred percent improvement."

"Yes," Reid admitted. "Keep it clean and you should be okay. Like Erika, I don't think you should do too much walking today. We don't want the wound to begin bleeding again."

"But we'll need to walk out," Doug protested. "I don't trust the elders one bit. Even if they have no boat, they could walk or paddle kayaks here in a few hours."

"If we're lucky, with their alarm disconnected they won't suspect we're here and will spend their time searching for the cave," Reid replied. "We punched holes in every kayak and canoe we found. There was another smaller motorboat, too. I tossed a handful of sand in its gasoline tank and turned on all the valves in the storage tanks. They'll have no gas."

"There's more in the commune," Doug replied. "They have gas and diesel for the tractors and couple of vehicles they use. It wouldn't surprise me if they had another boat there, too. There's a big implement shed that is fill of equipment."

"Well we can't move out today, even if we wanted to. You could probably make it but Erika needs time to recuperate. "

"So what do we do, Reid?" Lorie asked. She had just come down from the loft bedroom where Erika was resting and joined the conversation.

"Rest up and leave at dawn tomorrow. I think we'll be safe enough today but I wouldn't like to risk a second day here. With a little luck, we could be at Erika's Jeep by mid-morning. She said it was sunk in a mud hole but between us we should be able to get it out..."

The group's conversation was interrupted when the door burst open and Kate closely followed by the girls, burst in. "An aircraft's coming!" she gasped. "It's flying in low up the lake."

"Search and rescue?" Reid replied with excitement in his voice.

Kate frowned. "That's the trouble," she replied. "It isn't a plane they'd use. It's one of those old biplanes used for crop dusting, an Ag-Cat, I think."

"Biplane," Lorie said. "You mean it has four wings!"

"Oh hell," Doug gasped and stared at Lorie. "You remember it, too."

"Why, what's wrong?" Reid replied.

"They had one at the commune crop dusting only a few weeks back," Doug replied. "There's a strip at the back of the farm."

"So it could be someone from the commune? " Reid asked.

"That's what we suspected," Kate replied. "We had just put the boat away and shut the boat shed doors when we heard it. I thought it was a boat at first."

"So we stay out of sight," Reid said.

Doug nodded. "It could be a local crop dusting company searching for us."

"But we can't risk it," Kate added. "If it is innocent, the pilot will see our sunken CL-215 and report it,"

"And if not..." Jennifer whispered.

"Don't worry," Kate replied. "It's a land plane. There is nowhere near it can land..."

The sound of the aircraft, like that of an old World War 2 movie of a fighter attack, suddenly howled almost directly above them. There was a tremendous roar and a bright yellow fuselage flashed over only a few meters above the firs.

"Stay away from windows," Reid directed as everyone stared at each other.

The howl retreated, changed tone and became loud again. Reid squatted by the window and gazed out. The biplane was circling high out over the lake. As he watched, it reached the top of a curve and dipped back in from the east. It screamed down so the wheels almost touched the lake surface and flew straight in; so close everyone automatically ducked and Cinders growled through her throat. At the last moment it pulled up over the jetty and cabin with blue fumes streaming from the engine exhausts.

"Well, he's seen my aircraft," Kate grunted. "That's for sure."

"And it's the enemy," Doug added. "A friendly pilot would have circled, waved his wings or something. This fellow roared in trying to scare us."

"It flashed at the back," Jennifer added.

"How do you mean?" Kate asked.

"The sun flashed off something in the cockpit. Glass or something."

"Field glasses," Reid retorted. "What's the bet someone in the plane was studying the cabin using field glasses?"

As quickly as it came, the aircraft disappeared up the northern fork and Reid gazed out over the lake, deep in thought.

"Well, we remained hidden," Sassy said to break the silence.

"No," Jennifer corrected. "They know we're here. All the curtains are pulled back and the upstairs balcony door is open."

Reid grinned at the girl.

"Why, what's wrong?" She responded. Her cheeks burned red.

"You are our thinker and observer aren't you, Jennifer?" he praised. "That was exactly what I was about to say."

"I guess," she responded modestly but her eyes reflected an inner pride. "I'm not as brave as Sassy or Lorie but like to think things out."

"She was always like that," Sassy added. "Often, we'd think of doing stupid things and Jennifer would give us a more sensible idea."

"So what do you suggest now, Jennifer?" Kate added.

"Leave," the girl said without hesitation. "Peter and the elders will be here today, armed to the teeth and probably surround us."

"We can make it to my Jeep," a new voice interrupted and everyone glanced up to see Erika at the bottom of the stairs. "It's steep and windy but the trail either follows the river or is under firs. There is no way we can be cut off. In both directions there are steep foothills leading to the mountains."

"Will you be up to it?" Kate asked.

"Yes," Erika responded. "If Doug can do it, I can."

*

By mid-morning the seven people and their dog were well up Forbes River, as the map named the stream running into Eagle's Claw Lake, and Reid called a halt. It had been one constant climb with the river now flowing through a steep canyon far below them. The lake filled the middle background in front of two snow-covered mountains. It looked serene and empty with no boats, aircraft or other signs of human habitation. The zigzagging trail ahead seemed to continue its relentless climb up the steep hillside.

Doug said little about his shoulder but Reid noticed him grimaced in pain whenever his arm was jarred. Erika, though, was in far worse state and could barely walk. He squatted down beside the exhausted woman who had taken a sock off to expose an enormous blister on her heel.

"I'll get you some ointment and a Band Aid," he said.

She smiled up in appreciation and sighed.

"It was easier going down than up," she commented. "I'm slowing everyone down, aren't I?"

"Not really" Reid added and squeezed her shoulder. "We'll rest and have some lunch. I think the urgency is over now. Does the trail continue climbing for long?"

"We're almost at the first summit," she puffed. "It then drops down to the river and rises again on the other side. The steepest part is over. We can make it."

Reid smiled, finished attending to Erika's blister, walked over to where Kate was leaning against a rock and plunked himself down.

"So what's Jennifer got to say about the weather?" she asked. Like everyone else Kate was wet with perspiration and her blouse just clung to her skin.

Reid grimaced. "I've no idea. I haven't talked to her. Why?"

"Clouds are building behind the mountains," Kate replied. "They're black and thick. It'll be snowing there right now. Unless I'm mistaken we've only got an hour or even less before it reaches us."

"Snow?" Reid asked.

"Probably not at this lower altitude but it'll be wet and cold, straight in from Canada." She glanced up and added, "I'll keep an eye on Erika She's just about all in."

"I know," Reid replied. "Doug is not too good, either. The three girls are fine, though. I'd say they're fitter than I am."

Kate smiled and gazed across the dip they'd stopped in. Sassy and Jennifer were lying down gazing at the sky, Doug had his free arm around Cinders who was munching a dog biscuit while Lorie had just handed her sister a flask of water. She glanced up, saw Kate looking at her, and smiled.

"Us Somervilles are tough," she called. "We'll make it."

*

The refugees were over the ridge and descending the other side towards the first river crossing when the storm stuck. Large drops the size of a fingernail plopped on the dusty trail out of an inky black sky, the sky across the lake lit up in forked lightning and, seconds later, distant thunder crackled.

That was their only warning, for seconds later the downpour arrived, straight down in the volume of a waterfall, saturating everything below.

"Oh, my God!" Lorie gasped as she stared out from the shelter of the firs. "I'm glad we weren't caught in that lot."

"And who wanted to keep going down the open trail?" Jennifer replied above the hiss of water hitting the ground nearby.

"Okay," Lorie replied with a pout. "You don't always have to be right, though."

"It'll pass," Kate added. "These thunderstorms in the mountains are pretty localized. "

She was wrong! Instead of the expected ten minutes, the downpour lasted forty before it slackened and was replaced by a cold breeze that lowered the temperature ten degrees.

Reid glanced around at everyone. Between his clothes and those the girls brought from the commune, they had enough raincoats for everyone but there was a shortage of warmer garments. Spirits, though, were high and even Erika seemed more refreshed now they were on a downhill section.

Their first real hurdle came half an hour later when they arrived at the river to find a raging torrent of muddy water stretching from bank to bank without even rocks in sight,

"Well, we won't even attempt to cross that," Kate said as she glanced upstream.

On their side, the water lapped the trunks of the firs that grew from an almost vertical cliff. Across the opposite bank the scene was similar with the trail disappearing beneath more trees. Downstream, the river widened a little but again water stretched from bank to bank. The choppy surface swirled in whirlpools with broken branches and larger trunks carried along as the water surged by.

"I think we should stay here the night," Reid said. "With the river this high, nobody will be able to ford the first crossing back near the lake so we're as safe here as anywhere. I reckon we should move away from the trail though, just in case."

The others agreed and split into two groups to look for a possible campsite. There was nothing near the river but by retracing their steps for a couple of hundred meters they came to a small dip that curved back from the trail. The trees weren't too close together and a small grass section next to an area of rush-covered swamp appeared.

"That top part under the trees looks promising," Doug remarked to Lorie and Sassy, the pair with him. "It's flat, quite dry and can't be seen from the trail."

"Aye you others," Sassy yelled. "We've got a place. Over here!"

The others arrived and they all worked together to pitch Reid's one little tent and stretch out a plastic tarpaulin Reid had found at the cabin to form another crude shelter. The girls' sacks and Kate and Reid's more professional looking backpacks were unpacked and spread out. Rain had seeped into one of the sacks and some of the spare clothes were damp. Luckily, their supply of blankets were dry, the food was all in plastic bags or containers and in good order. As well, they had Sassy's kerosene lamp and a small gas cooker Reid had originally intended to use on overnight hiking expeditions.

"I thought there would be only Cinders and myself, not seven of us." Reid grinned as he lit the cooker and placed a pot of canned stew on top.

"I'm sorry your solitude was destroyed," Kate replied with a slight grin across her face.

"Don't be," he replied. "At the moment, I think I have far more wonderful people with me than I've met in years." He glanced around. "All of you," he added when he noticed Jennifer's eyes observing him.

She smiled and continued unpacking a pile of plastic plates from one of the bags. "If it wasn't for Lorie and later Sassy, I'd still be back at the commune getting ready for evening devotions right now," she said as if she felt a need to explain herself. "You know, I was too scared to stay but terrified about going. Now, I feel warm inside and, no matter what happens, I'm glad I came."

"Me too," Sassy replied. "If you told me a week ago I'd be sleeping one night in a cave and the next in the forest, I would have said you were crazy."

"And I was going to pull out of society with only Cinders to trust," Reid added. "I couldn't have been more wrong."

"You mean you can't trust Cinders?" Lorie laughed.

"Cheeky!" Doug chuckled and took the opportunity to place an arm around Lorie's shoulder.

She turned, smiled and reached up to squeeze his hand. "I'm so glad we're all here," she whispered.

"Oh hell," Sassy interrupted. "Come on, you lot, give us a hand to put up a clothes line under the firs. If we don't dry our clothes it's going to be a long, miserable day tomorrow."

She tossed a damp towel at Lorie and screamed as Doug intercepted it and flung it back into her face.

Kate glanced at Reid and smiled. "They bounce back quickly, don't they?" she said.

"They do," Reid replied and, like Doug a few moments earlier with Lorie, took the opportunity to reach out and place his hands on Kate's waist.

She said nothing but moved back so her head was under his chin. He held her closer and rubbed his beard into her hair. The smell of her damp hair, skin and clothes filled his senses and Jennifer's earlier comment about being all warm inside jostled his mind.

"And Erika?" Kate whispered.

"I think she is over the worst but only time will repair the psychological wounds."

The subject of their conversation was, at the moment, stirring the stew and chatting to Jennifer while further away Cinders was hindering the others trying to erect the clothesline.

"No!" screamed Sassy. "The rope isn't for you to chew, Cinders. It's to hang our clothes on."

She tossed the rope end to Lorie who grabbed and held it up over her head as Cinders made a massive jump to intercept the object, did a sort of backwards flip and ended up beside the pair with her tongue dripping saliva and tail thumping like a windshield wiper.

"Cinders likes the company, too," Reid chuckled and kissed Kate's hair.

*

Reid was cold and stiff when he awoke and realized where he was. The smell of the firs was so powerful that for a moment he never noticed the faint whiff hair shampoo but seconds later he heard soft breathing and felt a warm body slide under the blanket next to him. He silently cursed Cinders and opened his eyes. It was not like her to allow anyone close.

However, the fingers that touched his hands were soft and the voice determined. "If you tell a sole what is about to happen I'll deny it in the highest court in the land," Kate whispered and ran fingers down his arm.

"Oh hell, Kate," Reid whispered. "What's wrong?"

"Not a thing," she replied and grabbed his hand and held it to her opened jacket.

She kissed him quietly on the lips and clung on tightly while he stroked her hair. Lips met and foreplay was forgotten as they made almost violent love. Lips met again and he ran a finger up her cheeks to find them moist with tears.

"What's wrong, Kate?" he whispered. "Did I hurt you?"

"No, you silly man," she replied. "You ...oh hell, Reid what must you think," Kate replied, kissed his lips, slipped out of the blanket and stood up. He could hear rather than see her getting dressed, felt her wriggle into him, kiss his lips and she was gone.

There was silence for a moment before another voice cut through the still night air. "God, Man, what have you got that I haven't?" It was Doug who had been asleep a couple of tree trunks away.

"You never heard a thing," Reid replied. "Nothing! There's only the trees in the storm. Understand?"

"Sure Reid, " Doug laughed. "Sure beats lying out here in the cold by yourself, doesn't it?"

"And don't you get any fancy ideas," Reid warned.

"Sure, Boss," Doug replied. "See you in the morning."

"Night," Reid replied. He rolled over, lay in the silence and thought of Kate.

*

Dawn arrived with a roar. Reid leaped in fright and stared out beyond the trees. The Ag-Cat screamed over and headed upstream. Moments later silenced reined but everyone was awake with the harsh reality of the morning filled his mind.

It was so cold, everyone's breath puffed out and the girls stood wide-eyed with blankets still around their shoulders.

"Come on," Reid said softly. "We'll have a hot breakfast and head on out. I'm sure the river will be down by now."

Kate walked up to him, looked in his eyes and kissed him softly on the lips.

"Hi." she said quietly and slipped away.

Lorie looked at Sassy who looked at Jennifer.

"Did we miss something?" Lorie asked.

"Perhaps," Jennifer replied and the three girls all burst out laughing and grinned at Erika who was also smiling.

Reid turned and flushed when he realized the girls were scrutinizing him. "Come on," he ordered. "We need to get going. You don't all need to stand around gawking."

"Right, Reid," Lorie replied. "I'll open a can and feed Cinders. She seems to be the only sane one here at the moment."

*

CHAPTER NINE

Reid stared at the raging water. Sure the flattened grass and mud-strewn bank showed that the water level had gone down over the night but the river was still a dirty brown with the surface water swirling in tiny whirlpools.

"It's not deep," Jennifer said. "No higher than our bottoms, I'd say. As long as we help each other, we'll be fine."

"Sure," Lorie replied but with no confidence in her voice. "We might make it but what about Erika and Doug with his sore shoulder?"

"We cross," Reid said a few moments later after all the alternatives were discussed. He glanced at Erika who stood quietly at the rear of the group. "I'll carry you on my back," he said.

"I can walk it, Reid," she replied.

"No, as your doctor, I do not want you getting a chill. It is strong medical advice."

"Listen to him," Kate added.

"And I'll help," Doug added. Though lighter than Reid, he was of similar height and towered above the women.

"And I'll help support you, too," Kate added. "We'll need some poles to help steady ourselves but if we link arms we should be stable enough."

After some scrimmaging around the river edge they found some suitable tree limbs to use. Kate tied two of the girls' sacks together and flung them around her neck like an enormous life jacket. She was also wearing her backpack and looked quite laden.

"You can't take all that across," Reid argued.

"And why not?" she replied. "You're taking Erika"

"Okay, but it you slip let them go or they'll drag you under." He turned to the girls. "Will you three be okay, together?" he asked.

They all nodded.

"I'll leave Cinders with you. We'll take Erika across first. When we get there you all come across together. The one carrying my pack should be in the middle and one of you will need to carry the other sack. Cinders will be able to swim." He glanced at them all. "Or would you rather I came back for you?" he added.

"No, we'll be fine, Reid," Sassy replied "You just get Erika safely across."

She looked at her two friends and nodded. Even Lorie, who usually made the decisions, was contented to follow her advice while Jennifer, in her usual way, was studying the conditions.

"Go downstream fifty meters, Reid," she suggested. "It's wider there but not as swift or deep."

Reid nodded with a smile and turned to the others. "Well, shall we go that way?"

Everyone agreed and, a moment later were in their new position and ready to cross. Reid crouched down; Erika climbed on his back and clasped his shoulders. Doug stood beside the pair and placed his good arm under Erika's posterior. Kate stepped in the other side, linked her own arm into Doug's and seized a pole with her free hand.

After a couple of remarks and a light-hearted comment by Doug, they stepped into the freezing river. Water seized their legs and attempted to drag them away. Brown foam ripped at their knees and splashed higher.

"Slowly," advised Reid.

Kate nodded; felt forward with the pole, found a secure hold and, in unison, the three stepped forward while Erika acted as a sort of navigator from her higher position. Five minutes later, they were half way across; the water was up to the hem of Kate's shorts but the current now seemed less severe.

However, a moment later, Doug staggered and lurched sideways. He recovered but his body jostled the others. Kate staggered, used the pole to steady herself and grasped Doug's arm tighter. The bags around her neck pulled and her fingers slipped. They were, though, still linked with Doug's and the grip held. Erika attempted to help by boosting herself up higher on Reid's back while he stopped mid-stride and steadied himself. Together, the four managed to maintain their position while water sloshed around with tiny waves building up on their upstream side.

"Sorry, my foot hit a loose rock," Doug muttered.

"All okay?" Reid asked.

"I think so," Kate replied.

"Okay," Reid acknowledged. "We're almost there."

They stepped out again, more cautious but also optimistic. The water became shallower and soon they arrived on the opposite bank. Erika slipped off Reid's back, gave him a hug and helped Kate unload the gear she carried.

"My God, you must be frozen," she whispered.

Kate was wet to the buttocks and even the two men had saturated legs and shorts where the water had splashed up. The sacks and backpack, however, were dry and everyone had a satisfied look.

The three girls across the river glanced at each other. Jennifer, who was the tallest hitched Reid's backpack on and grinned at the other two. "Right," she said softly. "Shall we go?"

Lorie and Sassy both nodded while Cinders looked up at them, then across the river at Reid.

"Go Girl!" Sassy cried.

Cinders' tail wagged; she gave a tiny yelp and plunged into the water. She disappeared beneath the current, came out and with a strong dog paddle, headed across. It took her less than a third of the time of her master to complete the crossing but, in that time, was swept sixty or more meters downstream. Once ashore, she ran out, shook herself wildly so water sprayed everywhere and ran straight up to Reid for a well-deserved cuddle and pat.

"Us now," Sassy said nervously and rolled her commune skirt up under her panties.

She stepped in beside Jennifer, linked arms behind her back to Lorie who had the last sack slung around her neck. Sassy swallowed and gripped a long pole with her free hand.

They were off. Sassy found herself on the downstream side of the trio and noticed that Lorie had most of the current splashing up as high as the shorts she was wearing. Jennifer, like herself had rolled up her skirt but so far it remained dry.

"On step at a time," Jennifer said.

The current was stronger than Sassy anticipated and so cold she was sure her toes had begun to freeze. She fixed her eyes firmly ahead to where the foursome and Cinders stood watching and encouraging them. The distant voices, though, couldn't be distinguished above the roar of water but knowing they were there, helped.

When they were a dozen steps from shore the water deepened and Sassy found the stones beneath her feet slippery. Water swirled around their legs like an enemy trying to rip her away.

One more step and another! They were almost half way and not far from where Doug staggered when it happened!

From upstream, there came a screaming howl of a high revving piston engine and the Ag-Cat appeared. Four wings, the fixed undercarriage and yellow tipped propeller seemed to head straight for them. The howling motor silenced Lories scream as, in those few seconds, the aircraft dipped and plunged at them. The wheels missed their heads by several meters but, to Sassy, it was sheer terror. She gripped both Jennifer and the pole as the downdraft, shrieking engine and now the stench of hot exhaust fumes engulfed her.

Her body toppled forward in an over-reaction and she staggered back.

The Ag-Cat disappeared but so did the others. Sassy found herself falling, she dropped and freezing water seized her. She was tossed away, stones scraped across her legs and an elbow bashed into a rock.

Water poured into her mouth and she spluttered but it did not go away. Thoughts flooded her mind. She was beneath the surface and couldn't breathe!

Panic seized her. She lashed out but all around was dirty foamy water. Water ran in her mouth, her eyes, and her nose. It was so cold and her clothes clung into her skin. Her lungs sent out a spasm of pain and her head hit something solid, so hard she saw stars, bright white stars like sparks. Black blotches appeared and replaced the sparks.

The brown became blue. Her head was out of the water. She coughed, spluttered and sucked in air before being dragged beneath the surface again. More stones banged her body and limbs. She fought to grip something but it was too difficult. Again, she panicked and her chest felt as if it would burst.

But her extended hand felt something sharp. A rock! She gripped it and, in doing so, halted her tumbling thrust down the raging torrent. Her arm ached, it pulled at her socket but she held on. Her clothes felt funny and she noticed her skirt, still stuck in her panties, had ballooned out and seemed to hold her up. Water splashed by her mouth but she sensed she had stopped moving. Her arm ached, a spasm of pain shot from it and she almost let go.

But didn't!

Thoughts became rational and she knew that if she put her legs down she would be able to stand up. The water wasn't too deep.

Sassy rolled slightly and reached forward with her other hand to grip the rock. It cut into her hands but the rough surface could be held. Slowly now, while still coughing and attempting to spit away horrible tasting water, she lowered her feet and managed to stand.

Only then did she focus on the shore and realized it was only meters away. A fir tree limb was above her and a long black haired body rubbed beside her. A rough tongue licked her face. It was Cinders!

My God, Cinders was with her!

But there wasn't only the dog. Massive arms seized and held her so tightly it hurt. A drenched bearded face appeared from out of the water, centimeters from her eyes.

"We're here, Sassy," Reid gasped. "You're fine, Lass. I've got you."

Helping hands hauled Sassy to the bank where she collapsed onto the grass and went into a coughing fit. A towel was tucked around her neck and someone held her close. Only then, did she react. Her whole body started to shiver, face turned pale and her lungs heaved as if they were still trying to suck in enough air and her stomach turned queasy.

"You're okay now, Sassy," Kate, the person holding her, said. "Just relax and take slow breaths."

Suddenly, another though rushed into her mind. "Lorie and Jennifer," she sobbed. "Where are they?"

"We're here and both fine," Lorie replied. "Doug plunged in and hauled us ashore while Reid went after you."

"My God, you should have seen him go," Jennifer added. "He plunged in like an Olympic diver and Cinders followed."

"Thank you "Sassy spluttered. "And the plane?"

"It's still out there, somewhere," Kate answered. "I think it's circling around.

"Yeah and I hope the bastard runs into the mountain," Lorie spat.

They all stopped and listened. The roar of the aircraft could be heard downstream but appeared to be going away. Within a minute the roar became a rumble and afterwards, only the gurgling of the river could be heard.

"Come on," Reid said. "We're all wet and cold. I think we should all change into something dry and have a hot drink."

Sassy glanced around and smiled. The men were as saturated as she was and the others were a little better. Even Cinders looked like a half-drowned rat as she stood with her brown eyes wide and her tail lashing.

"No Cinders," she laughed. "We didn't do it all for your entertainment." She turned and became serious. "Thank you, Reid," she said "Thank you everyone. You are real friends and I love you all." She wiped her eyes, hugged everyone in turn and crouched down to grab Cinders in her arms. "And you came to help, too, didn't you, Girl."

"Yes, and she is becoming utterly spoiled," Reid laughed.

*

Half an hour later they were all in dry clothes and on their way up the next hill, this one was less steep and everyone was in good spirits except Erika who became silent and dropped to the rear. Kate noticed and waited for her to catch up.

"Do you want to rest, Erika?" she asked in a concerned voice.

"No, I'm okay. I was just thinking about everything. That's all."

"Is there anyone out there waiting for you?" Kate pressed. "I mean back in Spokane."

"Nobody," Erika whispered. "When I left the commune I found the outside life so difficult I..." She shrugged. "I went wild I guess. The guys I was with were the wrong sort."

"How do you mean?"

"Oh, you know, all very nice until I went to bed with them then they either began trying to boss me around or moved on. I thought Gary, the last guy I was with, was different, but he wasn't." She sighed. "Actually, we had a terrible row when I told him I wanted to get Lorie away from the commune. He just screamed that he didn't want any kid sister around and things went from bad to worse."

"So you're homeless?"

"No," Erika replied. "That was half the trouble with Gary. He was living in my house and didn't like the idea of sharing it with Lorie. It was lucky I never married him, I guess. When I left the commune, Mom told me to visit her lawyer in Spokane but wouldn't elaborate. The lawyer told me she owned a house in Spokane and had put it in Lorie's and my name five years earlier. That was unusual as the commune members are expected to turn everything they own over to the Elf Trust." She glanced at Kate. "The lawyer said it originally belonged to my grandparents."

"It sounds great," Kate replied.

"The trouble is Peter is not going to let us just drive out.

"What do you mean, Erika?" Kate responded.

Erika glanced across at her companion. "Peter Littlejohn is a fanatic, Kate. He is not about to give up trying to stop us. He has too much to lose. The pilot would have also seen my Jeep. My bet is they'll be coming in from the other side to cut us off. Even if we get to the Jeep there's several kilometers of forest roads before we get to that back road where I met the ranger, then another half a dozen kilometers to the highway."

"So we keep an eye out," Kate responded. "I'll go and talk to Reid."

She moved forward ahead of the group to find Reid a couple of hundred meters ahead at a top curve surveying the valley below with the field glasses. Ahead, the trail could be seen come out far below beside the river.

"Oh, hi Kate," he said. "The trail looks wider down there. I guess that is the beginning of the road Erika attempted to drive along. "

"She reckons Peter will have someone there to cut us off and probably a group coming up behind. Several fit men can go at twice our speed. Our two wounded are doing extremely well but I don't like to press them too much. Erika must be in constant pain. Her bruised legs are quite swollen. Doug's wound is better but still mighty tender. The plunge in the river wouldn't have done it any good. And now poor Sassy is putting on a brave front but she had a terrible fright. So what do we do, Reid?"

She glanced back and saw the others had caught up and were gathered in a semicircle around them.

Reid squatted down and took the crumpled map from his back pocket. It was a large-scale topographical map and showed the area in minute detail. He laid the paper on the ground and placed two small stones on the top corners to stop it curling up in the breeze.

"We're here," he said and pointed to the spot on the map. "The difficult part is over. It's downhill then along that old dirt road. Right Erika?" He glanced up.

"Yes," Erika replied and also squatted down. She studied the map for a moment before pointing to a windy logging trail in the top corner. "The Jeep would be here."

"About four kilometers to go," Reid muttered. He scratched his beard, deep in thought. "Why don't we go straight down through the forest?"

"We'll get lost," Kate replied. "Once we get in the trees we won't even be able to see the sun and could end up walking in circles."

"It's downhill," Jennifer interrupted. "As long as we continue down we must come out at the river."

"But there could be cliffs," Lorie suggested.

"No," Reid replied. "They'd be marked on the map. The contour lines aren't too close together either."

"Meaning?" Jennifer asked.

"The steeper the land the closer the lines. This section is no steeper than the big hill we climbed yesterday." Reid grinned. "I've got a compass, too so as long as we take our bearings we should be okay." He turned to Erika. "Do you think you can manage," he said. "There may be difficult parts."

"I'll manage," she replied in a determined tone. "This trail is far too exposed."

*

The journey down through the forest was difficult and nerve racking. As Kate remarked to Reid, everything looked the same, the ground was quite bare but the dead needles everywhere were slippery on the steep slope. There were ridges to climb down and low boughs from the trees to avoid. On the positive side, the temperature was moderate and they were completely hidden from the meandering Ag-Cat that was heard twice during their descent.

It was mid-afternoon when he called a halt. They were on rolling but mainly level ground and, if Reid's calculations were correct, close to the river and half a kilometer from the Jeep.

"I want to scout ahead and see if any commune thugs are here," he said. "We'll walk out as far as the road but keep out of sight. Everyone can rest up while I explore."

"Not by yourself, you don't," Kate snapped.

"I want you to stay with the group," Reid said and stared, unblinking, at her. Their eyes held for a moment before she ran a tongue over her top lip and nodded.

Lorie glanced at Doug who shrugged. Erika obviously wasn't in condition to help and Sassy appeared hesitant.

"I'll come, Reid," Jennifer said. "And why not?" she retorted when the other girls looked at her in surprise. "I'm as fit as anyone."

"Good on you. We'll take the smaller pack with a few essentials." Reid replied before anyone else could comment. He opened his own pack and extracted a handgun. "I hate these things but it may be necessary. Have you used one, Jennifer?"

"No," she whispered nervously.

"I'll show you the basics but we won't go firing any shots off here. Is there anything else?"

"What do we do if you don't return?" Kate said in almost a whisper. Again, her eyes held his.

"Okay," Reid sighed and reached out for her hand. "Let's sit down and discuss every possibility. I think that is fair on everyone. We've got this far by being cautious. I don't think anything will go wrong now but it may."

They all nodded and sat down around the map. Everyone had input and all suggestions were considered. Disagreements were few and mainly came from Kate who didn't want Reid to do anything risky, or cautions from Erika about how to act if any contact was made with anyone from the commune.

"Don't trust them for a second," she said in a quiet voice. "Hesitate once and they'll be all over you." She stared at Jennifer. "We have a conscience. They don't! Remember that, won't you?"

"I will," Jennifer replied with sheer determination replacing the earlier nervousness.

"And we'll leave Cinders with you," Reid proclaimed and held his hand up when Kate opened her mouth to speak. "That's final!"

"Okay, Reid," Kate replied but looked worried.

*

Every caution they took was necessary as Reid and Jennifer slunk through the fir trees beside the logging trail. They were on a gentle slope and took the uphill side above a small cutting. At the bend they stopped, crouched and peered around to an empty road and another bend.

"Right," Reid whispered and they moved forward to repeat the process at the next bend.

This time, though, it was different. The old khaki Jeep sat in the middle of the road with its inside back wheels sunk down to the axle and front hood tilted up about thirty degrees. Jennifer grabbed Reid's arm.

"Sniff," she whispered.

He did. The air was scented with firs that made one think of Christmas. There was a tang of damp earth and, yes, one more smell. Reid frowned and sniffed again. Though nothing was visible there was a distinct smell of marijuana smoke in the air.

"Hypocrites," Jennifer hissed.

"Why?" Reid whispered back.

"At the commune all tobacco, alcohol and drugs are banned. They are an evil habit created by the devil to warp our minds and numb our souls," she muttered as if the passage was embedded in her mind. "The Oracles Chapter 6, clause 49," she added to confirm Reid's suspicions, "But we don't need that anymore do we?"

Reid grinned and squeezed her shoulder.

"They're there," Jennifer hissed. "See!"

Reid couldn't see anything remotely like a person. He squinted and then followed Jennifer's gaze. On the far side of the Jeep was a tiny semicircle of hair. Someone was on that side. The hair moved and a man appeared beside the hood. He took a couple of puffs on the cigarette he was smoking, flicked it away and stared directly at them.

Jennifer gave a silent gasp and held her mouth with her hand while Reid remained frozen to the spot.

"I'm going for a leak," the man said and another voice from inside the Jeep replied. So there were at least two men!

He stood, holding a powerful looking automatic rifle and walked up the trail in their direction, then across to the downward side of the road and disappeared in the firs.

Reid nodded and indicated Jennifer should follow. Again the girl looked determined and gave a faint nod. Reid slipped off the backpack, took out the handgun and crept forward.

A moment later they were back around the bend where they slipped across the road and moved towards the man's position. He was there, urinating against a tree trunk. Jennifer flushed and hesitated. Reid clicked the handgun's safety catch off and crept forward until he reached the man.

"Just let the rifle drop to the ground and place your arms wide," he hissed.

The reaction was instant "What the hell!" came the response. The man swung around and saw the handgun pointing at him. He next saw Reid, then Jennifer and hastily pulled up his zipper.

"Your rifle!" Reid hissed.

"Hello Abraham," Jennifer added in a grim whisper. "Waiting for us, were you?"

Abraham's eyes were that of utter contempt but he lowered the rifle and spread his hands out with the fingers wide.

"How many are there here?" Reid spat.

"Only me," Abraham grunted. His eyes stayed on Jennifer.

"Lies," the girl replied. "Who's in the Jeep?"

Her voice was so cold even Reid glanced at her in astonishment. Abraham shrugged but licked his lips in apprehension.

"Mark," he finally said.

"And where's James?" Jennifer hissed. "You three are always together."

"Gone back to the lumber yard in our wagon," he muttered. Again eyes never strayed from the girl.

Reid nodded. It seemed feasible as no other vehicle was around. Damn, he should have looked for tire marks but it was too late now.

"Kick the rifle this way but do it slowly," Reid said.

Abraham nodded and placed a heavy boot by the rifle and pushed, rather than kicked it forward so it only moved a meter or so.

Reid grunted handed the handgun to Jennifer and said. "Remember Erika's words and squeeze the trigger, don't pull it."

"What do you mean?" Abraham suddenly retorted. A flash of fear crossed his eyes. "Don't give her the gun."

Reid scowled and watched the pair. Something he didn't understand was going on. He moved sideways so he didn't hinder Jennifer's line of sight and prepared to reach forward for the rifle, again without taking an eye off the enemy.

*

CHAPTER TEN

The counter attack was expected but still came so quickly that Reid almost failed to move away in time when a massive boot kicked out. It would have hit his head if he had reached for the rifle. Instead it connected with nothing; Abraham propelled himself forward with a growl akin to a savage grizzly bear and was almost upon Jennifer when she fired.

Again everything was instantaneous. The man was hurled back, screamed as the report vibrated through the forest. Reid grabbed the rifle, gave Jennifer a quick nod and tore out to the road where Mark had just leapt from the Jeep. Reid, though, had the rifle in his hand ready and aimed.

"I wouldn't!" he snarled as the man began to raise a second weapon. "Drop it!"

Without warning, the handgun fired from behind and another scream filled the air.

Jennifer appeared with her face like chalk and the handgun still in her hand. "He rushed me," she said. "If I'd hesitated he'd have got me. I think he's dead."

"Cover this guy," Reid spat. "If he moves, shoot!"

The girl nodded and raised her weapon with both hands, just as Reid had taught her a mere half-hour before. There was no quiver, no remorse but ice-cold determination of a desperate young woman who was not about to lose her freedom.

Abraham wasn't dead but moaning and lying on the ground in a pool of blood. One arm appeared limp while blood squirted out from his stomach. He was trying to hold it with his one good hand.

"The bitch shot me," he gasped.

"Twice," Reid replied without sympathy. "Lie still and I'll come and patch you up soon."

Reid went back to the road where Jennifer waited with her handgun still aimed at second man. "I'll take over," he said. He reached across, gently took the gun from her hands, clicked the safety catch on and put it in his shorts pocket. "Go back and get the others."

"Abraham was the one who beat and raped Erika," Jennifer said in a monotone. "He is well known for his sadistic treatment of the women at the commune and is in charge of discipline." She glanced up. "Mark is almost as bad."

Reid studied the man by the Jeep. He looked bearded, about forty but not as ruthless as Abraham. "Okay, Mark," he said. "Move to the front of the Jeep, undo your trousers real slowly and lower them to your ankles. Then turn and place both hands on the Jeep's bonnet."

"Sure mister," Mark replied and began unbuckling his belt. He looked worried.

Cinders arrived first, followed by Kate who ran up the road, stumbled, caught herself and continued on into Reid's arms. "When I heard the shots I thought it was you," she cried, plastered him with kisses and almost knocked the rifle from his grasp.

Reid kissed her on the forehead, held her close but kept Mark in his vision. "Don't even think of moving," he hissed at the man.

Meanwhile, the others appeared and soon Mark was searched, escorted over the road and made to sit with his back against a tree trunk. "Guard him, Cinders," Reid ordered.

The dog stared up at her master, sat on her haunches and bared her teeth at Mark. A low rumble came from her throat.

"I wouldn't move if I was you," Reid warned and returned to where the others were inspecting a moaning Abraham.

Erika just stood and stared down at the wounded man. "It's a pity, Jennifer's aim wasn't lower," she stated, her voice if anything, colder than the girl's had been. "If it was up to me I'd let you lie here and bleed to death. It's about what you deserve."

She brushed a hand down her hair, turned and walked back to the road. "I'll watch Mark," she said.

"And I'll slip up to the next corner and keep an eye out in case anyone else arrives." Doug added.

"Listen for that Ag-Cat, too," Reid advised and walked through to examine Abraham.

One bullet had gone clean though his upper arm but the second made an ugly stomach wound. "You'll need hospital treatment," Reid said as he bound the man's stomach.

"The disciples don't believe in it." Lorie said quietly and held the man's dark stare. "But, of course you don't smoke pot either do you, Abraham?"

"Bitch!" the man hissed between the gasps as Reid pulled the bandage perhaps a little too tight.

"Shouldn't it be, 'Bless you, My Daughter?" Sassy added sarcastically. "For a man of God you have a lot of the devil in you, Abraham. Perhaps you need to attend one of Peter's re-education courses."

"Piss off," Abraham retorted with his eyes like venom.

"Gladly," Sassy replied, gave Reid a slight grin and disappeared back up to the Jeep.

She found Jennifer sitting on a grassy knob and plunked down beside her. "You did well, Jennifer," she said.

"I was terrified," the taller girl confessed. "I've never fired a gun before. When I hit him he just snarled like and animal then the second time, he lunged at me. If I'd hesitated..." Her face was still white and her hands now shook. "I just spewed in the grass over there" she whispered.

"So what? Sassy replied. "I'm proud of you, Jennifer. We all are. I don't think I could have done it."

"You would have, just the same as you survived when you slipped during the river crossing," Jennifer added. "When it came to the crunch, I'm sure any of us would. I just happened to be the one here at that moment."

"Possibly but I'm still proud to call you my friend."

"Thanks, Sassy. I appreciate that since it was me who was too scared to follow Lorie out to the plane."

"And if we'd all gone, we wouldn't have Doug with us, now, would we?"

"No, I suppose not," Jennifer replied and broke into a smile. "So everything is working out, isn't it?"

"Yes," Sassy replied. "It is."

While the fit members of the group tried to free the Jeep, Erika and Doug kept the two prisoners under surveillance. Abraham just sat looking miserable but Mark seemed to have gained some of his confidence and kept making abusive almost arrogant comments to irk the pair.

"So Baby Boy has to hide behind all the ladies' skirts, does he?" he snickered at Doug.

Doug flushed and it was obvious the jaunting was having an affect. That was until Erika took the matter into her own hands and very deliberately moved a cartridge into the chamber of the rifle she was holding.

"Doug, here has more courage than you cowardly animals any day," she snapped.

"So he can't even defend himself," Mark sneered. "We're going to have fun with you girls when you're all caught. You'll never get the Jeep out so it's only a matter of time." He grinned. "Your little sister has got quite a figure hasn't she?"

His next words, though, were interrupted when the rifle fired and dust beside the man showered into his face. He sprang up but stopped dead still when he saw the rifle aimed directly at him.

"Nobody will touch Lorie, Sassy, Jennifer or myself," Erika hissed. "If you think I'll just stand here and let you thugs capture us, think again Mark. If any of them come close, you'll get the first bullet. I have nothing to lose."

"Oh come now... " Mark taunted but his words turned to a howl as the rifle fired again and he stared, horrified at his hand what was a squirting blood from the bullet hole that had gone right through and embedded itself in the bank behind.

"My father taught me how to aim when I was a child," Erika said in a whisper. " 'Erika, never hold a gun unless you are prepared to use it,' Daddy always said to me."

Mark's face turned ashen as he stared again at his maimed hand. "You bitch," he gritted as his face contorted in pain.

"The next one will be lower," Erika added and turned as the others rushed in to see why the rifle had fired.

"Is everything okay?" Reid immediately sized the situation up and turned to Erika. "Did he attempt an attack?" he asked

"Only threats," she replied. "If he thinks he can abuse the girls, I'll kill the bastard," she added. "Nobody is going to hurt them."

"The bitch just up and shot me," Mark screamed.

Reid turned to Doug who looked quite shaken. "What was it all about, Doug?" he asked.

"Mark threaten to screw Lorie and the others when we are caught again," Doug replied. "I have no doubt that is exactly what he would do if we are captured."

"She's a maniac!" the injured man howled again and turned to his companion who was leaning against the bank a few meters away with a quiet smirk on his face. "Tell them in graphic detail what we'll do with the little bitches when we're back at the commune?"

"And risk another bullet in me. No way, Pal," Abraham replied. "I'd take Erika seriously, if I was you."

Reid glowered at the pair before turning back to Erika. "These semi-automatic rifles have a very fine trigger, don't they?" he said quietly.

"What do you mean?" Doug screamed again and grimaced with pain as blood continued to pour from his wound. "It was deliberate. She purposely shot me in the hand..."

"I'll get my medical kit," Reid added and turned back to Erika. "You don't mind continuing to guard them do you?"

Erika nodded. "I don't mind, Reid," she replied. "I think we have the situation under control."

It was Kate who intercepted Reid in the trees as he pulled the medical kit from his backpack. "Is it wise leaving Erika with the rifle?" she asked.

"In ordinary circumstances I'd say no," he admitted, "Here though, I can think of nobody better."

"If she kills them we'll all be accomplices," she argued.

"Oh, if she was going to kill them she'd have done it by now," Reid replied. "Only those two don't realize that so won't try anything, will they?"

"Not if they're filled with bullet holes," Kate retorted. Her eyes flashed for a second before she relented. "Okay, Reid," she added in a quiet voice. "I guess the tension is getting to me, that's all."

"I know," Reid replied. "I was thinking about the Jeep. All we've managed to do is to get it stuck further in the mud. Perhaps we're going about it the wrong way."

"Okay," Kate said and appeared relieved the topic was changed. "What do we do?"

"Ask Jennifer," Reid replied with a grin. "It is her idea."

So while Reid went to patch Denial's hand, Kate went back to the Jeep. It was still firmly stuck with mud half way up the wheels and splattered debris everywhere that they'd tried to place in front of and behind the vehicle.

"So what do we do?" Kate asked Jennifer. "Reid said you had a good idea."

"Well," the girl replied. "We've tried going forward and reversing but the wheels just spin. The ditch we dug to drain off water is working but there is still be plenty of mud left."

"So?" Sassy interrupted.

"Go down the side bank," Jennifer said. "I had a look and there is just wet grass there, not mud. If the Jeep hits the grass at least one of the four wheels should be able to grip and that is all it needs."

"But it may roll," Kate warned. "The slope is quite steep."

"We have seat belts and a roll bar," Jennifer added. As long as everyone pushing stays above the Jeep, nobody will get hurt and the driver should be okay. Even if it rolls it will only go a few meters and be stopped by those firs." She nodded at the fir trees about twenty paces down the outside slope. "Even if that happens, we'd be no worse off that we are now."

Reid returned and another small argument began. He insisted on driving but Kate pointed out his strength was needed to push, none of the girls could drive so she was the only one left.

"Okay," Reid uttered, "but make sure your seat belt is tight. If the wheels grip just keep going. Okay."

Kate nodded, sat in the driver's seat and started the engine. Reid and the three girls grabbed the inside rear section and, on his signal, pushed as Kate let out the clutch. The tires again spun and mud arched up from all four wheels to splatter the chassis and pushers behind. This time, though, Kate steered towards the slope and kept the wheels moving just above idling speed.

The wheels still spun but the vehicle didn't sink like on the previous two efforts. The Jeep jerked, Reid shouted and attempted to lift the rear corner. The girls followed his lead, grabbed the rear and lifted instead of pushing. There was another shudder and the Jeep slithered sideways before the right front wheel found solid ground to grip. The vehicle plunged ahead but was on full right lock so turned in a semicircle and bolted, like a runaway horse, down the slope. Kate, all eyes and jutting chin, held the steering wheel and just touched the accelerator a fraction. She was in low ratio four-wheel-drive so extra acceleration wasn't needed. The vehicle toppled dangerously, slithered right around so the rear now faced the trees below and the nose pointed back up to the trail.

Kate held on with grim determination and steered into the slide until motion in that direction ceased and the Jeep stopped bouncing like an untrained mustang. She moved her foot off the accelerator and depressed the clutch to disengage the engine. The Jeep stopped and would have rolled back down the slope but Kate realized her mistake and, with teeth firmly embedded beneath her teeth, engaged gear and accelerated. There was a howl from the engine, a cloud of black smoke belched out the exhaust pipe but all four wheels gripped and propelled the Jeep up the bank. It hit a small mound by the road, bounced, tires spun for a second, gripped and propelled everything forward.

Kate maintained control, though, and drove the Jeep sedately along the trail a dozen meters and stopped!

Sassy reached her first, all smiles and laughs. "That was some driving, Kate," she laughed. "Do you know the old girl just about did a flip?"

"Did it?" Kate wiped perspiring hands down her shorts as the other three appeared.

"Keep the engine going, Kate," Reid suggested. "You girls get all our gear and toss it in. It's going to be a tight fit but we have our wheels."

He gathering up the two backpacks and strapped them on the tiny roof rack. The tent and sacks went in the rear and Reid gazed at the muddy girls grinning at him.

"I'll sit in the front with Kate but will need one of you on my knees. The rest can squeeze in the back."

"I will," Sassy, the smallest by a whisker offered and smiled. "That's if Kate doesn't mind."

Kate studied the girl. She was covered in mud with even her hair and face plastered. "Just this time," she replied in a deadpan voice. "Try to keep your grubby hands off the upholstery."

"I'll get the others," Reid chuckled and walked around the bend to where the prisoners were being guarded.

"Erika, Doug," he said quietly. "You're needed up at the Jeep."

"So you never got it out?" Abraham retorted.

"Yeah," Mark added. "You've got nowhere to go." He almost grinned but stopped when Erika's cold eyes rested on him.

"Guard them, Cinders!" Reid ordered.

He ignored the men and followed his friends back. Except for Sassy standing by the Jeep, they were all crammed in waiting.

"Right," Reid said, curled his legs in the passenger's seat and grunted as Sassy crawled in on top.

"Ready?" Kate whispered.

"Almost," Reid replied, stuck his head out the window and gave an ear-splitting whistle.

Cinders appeared around the bend at full speed and didn't even slow as she jumped into the back where Lorie grabbed her while Jennifer slammed the door. Kate had one quick glance around to see everyone was there and engaged gear. There was a shudder, another cloud of exhaust smoke belched from the worn engine and they moved forward, one overloaded Jeep filled with refugees heading down the deserted logging road.

*

Initial chatter turned to silence as Kate concentrated on the driving and the others immersed themselves in their own thoughts. It was now late afternoon and probably only an hour from dusk.

The dirt road was windy and slippery with surface water filling the dips and mud everywhere else. However, the Jeep coped and headed down through a valley of almost black forest before ascending up a saddle. After a twenty-minute climb they reached the summit and Kate pulled off onto a small grass area. There was another valley ahead surrounded by forested hills cut by the zigzagging road.

"You can drive now, Reid," she said. "That was harder than flying the CL-215

"Okay," he replied. "My knees are numb with this massive weight they have to carry."

Sassy grinned, hit his shoulder and clamored out to meet Cinders and the others already on the grass stretching cramped limbs.

"There's trouble ahead," Reid retorted a moment later.

All eyes turned to where he was studying the road in the valley with his field glasses. Way in the distance a vehicle was approaching.

"James!" Erika hissed. "He'll be coming back to pick the others up."

"Yes, sooner than I would have liked," Reid grunted

"So we hold him up," Lorie added. "We've got the rifle and outnumber him"

"I'd rather hide and let him go by," Reid replied.

"But where?" Kate added. "The verges are too steep. If we drive off the road we'd never get up again. There's nowhere in the last couple of kilometers where vehicles could pass, let alone hide. This is the first wide spot."

"So we keep going," Reid said. "It'll be a good twenty minutes before that vehicle gets to us. We may find a spot. If not, we'll be ready for him. We have the advantage that he will not be expecting anyone. Remember, there's no mobile phone coverage here."

Five minutes later they were between fir trees but a firebreak had been left on each side with a broad grass strip. The steep downward slope had leveled and the road was quite exposed.

"There!" Sassy yelled as she bent down so she could see through the top of the windshield.

Reid slowed to a crawl and glanced out his window. Off the road were a cluster of rocks poking up above grass and thistles.

"It'll do fine," Reid replied. "Not perfect but far better than I expected."

He stopped the Jeep, jumped out and walked ahead for a way before returning. "It's feels solid, too but I think if everyone gets out it'll be better."

The Jeep's tires made an obvious trail of flattened grass and the vehicle was only partially hidden when Reid drove behind the outcrop. All they could hope for was that the driver approaching would be concentrating on the road ahead and not see them. It was a risk but better than an open confrontation.

They all lay on the damp grass or crouched behind the Jeep and waited. Reid had the rifle and Kate, his handgun, just in case.

The wait was short. Less than five minutes later, there was the growl of an engine and a large Toyota Landcruiser appeared. It was travelling slowly but there was no sign that it was about to stop.

Reid caught Kate's eyes for a second before he turned and studied the Landcruiser. There appeared to be only the driver aboard. It came closer until it was abreast of them but there was no braking or gear change as it went by the flattened grass. Nothing happened! The Landcruiser continued and a moment later, disappeared behind the firs.

"All aboard!" Reid said with a broad smile on his face. "Next stop, Spokane."

*

CHAPTER ELEVEN

"Home," Erika said and pulled the Jeep she had driven for the last fifty kilometers, up the service lane and turned into the tiny back yard as security lights switched on. Ahead was a tall wooden house with a large veranda and outside steps leading down from an upstairs balcony. When the stiff and exhausted seven walked in they gazed around the modern open plan kitchen. The three girls looked bewildered and Lorie gasped her sister's hands.

"And this was Grandpop's place," she said. "Oh my God. I never dreamed there was a glorious house like this that belonged to our family."

"It's half yours, Lorie," Erika replied. "That's what Mom wanted."

Sassy stared at Jennifer and also seemed to be awe. "Is that the television, Erika," she asked and nodded at a corner screen.

"No that's my computer," Erika replied. "The television is in the living room next door. Do you want to see some? We have proper stations here, not just those religious video tapes like at the commune."

"Can we?" the girls cried, almost simultaneously.

"Why don't you three have first showers? I never turned the hot water off so there will be plenty of it. There are two showers, one upstairs and one along the corridor. There's also a bath if you'd like one."

"I'll get our sacks," Lorie yelled in excitement and ran out to the Jeep while Erika went to find some towels for them to use.

Kate, though, was quieter while the two men looked almost miserable.

"You can all stay," Erika said when she walked back in the room holding an armful of towels.

"No, I'd better go home to my apartment," Kate said quietly. "I'll need to get to the airport tomorrow. There's plenty that needs to be sorted."

"Yeah, and I can't encroach," Reid said. "There's a motel downtown that doesn't mind pets. I stayed there for three nights last week. If you let me borrow the phone I give them a call."

"And I suppose you're going to walk out, too?" Erika replied abruptly and stared at Doug.

Doug sighed. "I guess," he mumbled and glanced at the floor.

Erika placed the towels on the table, walked across and grabbed his hand. "You are going nowhere, Doug," she said. "There are four bedrooms here so you can stay."

"But I have nothing," Doug replied. "No money and not even any clothes. I can't just live off you, especially since you have Lorie and the other two girls. It's fair on nobody."

Reid turned to Doug. "Listen to her, Lad," he said. "It won't be easy but you're wanted here. We can check out the situation with Department of Social Health Services tomorrow. There must be emergency benefits to help the four of you from the commune."

"There is," Erika added. "I was helped by the DSHS when I came out."

"And who are you to talk?" Kate said in a hurt whisper. Her eyes turned to face the tall bearded man.

"What do you mean?" Reid replied.

"You said a moment ago you were going to a motel then tell Doug to stay here. Doesn't that seem odd?"

"I have no place in Spokane," Reid replied quietly. "Remember, the cabin at Eagle's Claw Lake was going to be my home."

"And you're too proud to let us help you, too. You tell Doug one thing yet you act just as stubbornly yourself."

"I..." stumbled Reid. "It's just that, I thought..."

"Oh God, Reid" Kate snapped. "Do I have to spell it out to you?"

"What?"

"I have an apartment about two kilometers away, I live by myself and I'm inviting you to share it." She turned to Doug. "You, too Doug if you want to come."

Doug smiled and glanced at Reid who looked completely embarrassed. "If you don't mind, I think I'll take up Erika's offer," He glanced at the blonde woman. "I'm going to pay my way, okay."

"And you, Reid?" Kate whispered.

"I'll ask Cinders," he replied. "I'm not sure if she'll like being in a tall condominium block."

"Reid!" Kate retorted. "If you don't want to come just say so."

Reid smiled, grabbed her in his arms and kissed her on the cheek. "It's just so funny," he said. "I've felt as if I've known you all for years, not just a few days. Coming back here is so exciting but then. Oh hell..."

"Like the day after Christmas," Erika replied softly. "You know, you really look forward to something, it arrives and passes by. You feel deflated somehow."

"That's it," Reid said. "We were thrust together and I thought that now we're back in Spokane, Kate has her business and her life. I just didn't want to impose."

"Well, you haven't," Kate snapped.

"And neither have you, Doug," Erika added. She turned to Kate and Reid. "Look, it's almost eleven and you both look as exhausted as I feel. I will be offended if both of you don't stay here tonight. Tomorrow, we can have one of our discussions about what we are going to do for Doug and the girls. I'm going to file a complaint with the police, too. I don't see why Peter and those others can continue on after everything they did." She grinned, "One of the spare rooms has a double bed, you know."

"I'll discuss it with Cinders," Reid replied. He tried to keep a straight face but failed when everyone burst out laughing. "Okay," he said when he saw Kate nod. "As long as you let me cook breakfast."

"It's a deal," Erika laughed. "Now let's unpack and I'll light the gas heater. It's a bit nippy, if you didn't notice. Afterwards we'll sort out the bedrooms and I'll see what there is in the cupboards to eat. "

"I'll help," Kate replied.

"And I think we'll need to give your shoulder a good bathe and rewrap it, Doug," Reid said. "We don't want an infection to creep in."

"Sure Doc," the young man replied and grabbed a kitchen chair to sit on.

*

Their lovemaking was frantic, long and fulfilling but finally Reid jerked up to realize he had been asleep and Kate was snoring peacefully in his arms. It was dawn and the view outside the upstairs bedroom window showed a deserted suburban street lined with seventy year-old houses, all in immaculate condition with neat lawns and cared for gardens. A streetlight was still on and glowed orange while the only occupant of the deserted scene was a ginger cat who slunk across the road towards a neighbor's house. Reid kissed Kate on the cheek and slipped out of the blankets.

Five minutes later he walked along the pavement with Cinders at his side. The world was at peace and as he liked it. In an hour he knew, the streets would be filled with automobiles carrying their drivers to work at some unknown destination, telephones would buzz and computers begin to spit out a million and one email messages.

His mind reflected back to the lake and the events that unfolded. Of course, it hadn't changed. Peter was still there and the commune was functioning as it always did. Just four younger members had left and, no doubt would be replaced by new recruits, more lonely women seeking help or young men who couldn't cope with the strains and stresses of normal society.

He patted his dog and walked around a corner to find a small park ahead. The grass was moist with morning dew and three chipmunks ran around looking for morsels of food beneath a trashcan dangling from a pole.

"No Cinders, let them be," Reid said when the dog's ears shot forward at the sight of the tiny animals. "This is their home. We're the intruders here."

He reached a lone park bench, wiped away moisture and sat down. He took out a tennis ball, heaved it across the grass and watched as his dog ran after it, made an almighty jump in the air, missed but, without hesitation, scooped the ball off the ground and came bounding back.

It was only at the very last moment that Reid noticed two girls slip in on each side of the bench beside him.

"Hi Sassy, Jennifer," he said. "I never heard you coming. Did you both sleep well?"

"We followed you but you were so absorbed with Cinders we didn't want to interrupt," Jennifer said in a quiet voice. She looked at Reid and held her bottom lip with top teeth in apprehension.

"But you want to talk?" Reid said.

"How did you know?" Sassy replied, also in a hushed voice that seemed to fit the early morning conditions.

"I guessed," Reid relied with a shrug. "Well, fire away."

"We're scared, Reid," Jennifer said.

"Of what?"

"That you'll walk away and leave us," Sassy said her voice louder and spoken with urgency as if she wanted to get everything out before she lost her nerve. "You have made it with Kate, Lorie has Erika and even Doug has Lorie. They're smitten on each other but we have nobody, we know nothing about life here in the city, we have no home, no family, nobody..."

"Except you, Kate and Cinders." Jennifer turned to show eyes flush with tears. "We don't want you to just go away back to the lake or whatever. Are we being selfish after everything you've already done for us?"

"And you both feel the same?" Reid asked.

Both girls nodded. Jennifer picked up the tennis ball Cinders had just deposited at her feet and threw it across the park. The throw lacked power and sort of dropped after a few seconds, right into Cinders' waiting mouth.

"See, I can't even throw a ball properly," she whispered.

"But you all planned an escape from the commune and rescued a severely beaten young man. You paddled a canoe to a cave and stayed there surrounded by nothing but danger. That took sheer guts, Jennifer," Reid said quietly. He put both arms out and hugged each girl. "You, Jennifer, anticipated every idea I had and more so. You girls have nothing to feel but pride."

"What about love?" Jennifer continued. "We just want to be loved with our faults and all. We were taught we were nothing, sinners constantly being bad. No matter what we did or tried to do it, was wrong." Her tears now rolled unhindered down her face. "You know they even had a tiny building away from the compound where we had to go when we bled, I don't even know the right word..."

"Menstruation," Reid whispered.

"We were ashamed of our own bodies," Sassy continued. "We were evil and on Earth only to serve the men and have children. Nobody was allowed to touch another person but we used to creep into each others bed and just hug each other."

"If we were caught we'd be thrashed," Jennifer sobbed. "Some of the women were as cruel as the men. One delighted in belting us with a cane. I think she got pleasure from seeing us weep.

"But Jennifer never did," Sassy said. "Not once did she cry like she's doing now. It made Sister Madeline so angry she'd just hit out again."

"But I did," Jennifer added. "I'd shut myself in the toilet and howl my head off. Nobody saw, that is all."

"And you're afraid I'll just leave you with Erika and you'll never see me again?"

"That's about it," Sassy replied.

"Let me tell you something," Reid said. "I've found more love in the last few days than I've had in years. I, too, had a hard time and all I wanted to do was disappear from society with my dog. You see, I'd lost my trust of humans, all of them. I had a wife, a profession, respect and it crumbled away but now..."

"You have Kate," Jennifer whispered.

"Yes and you two, Lorie, Doug and Erika. Love is a funny little word that means lots of things; it's not just how I feel about Kate. I love Kate, I am sure and I love Cinders. I love you too, Jennifer and you Sassy. I love you all so much I don't want to leave you and I'm not going to retreat back into my lonely world again."

He glanced at each of the girls in turn and squeezed them in close with his hands. "You can stay with Erika or you can come and stay with Kate and me. One day, I know you'll want to go out and make your own lives but I want to be there for you and be part of your family." Reid stopped for a moment and threw the ball out for his dog. "I was a very lonely man but now I have you all. So you see, I'm being selfish now, aren't I?"

"No," Jennifer whispered. "You're being the father I never had."

Two heads, one brunette and one, auburn tucked into his bushy black beard and remained there. The Black Labrador trotted up and dropped the sloppy tennis ball on the ground, saw nobody was about to throw it out again, so sat down right across the six damp shoes beneath that park bench that was alone, no more.

*

The first day back in the city had twists and turns that left the seven completely bemused. Erika and Doug both filed complaints with the police force that had jurisdiction over the area of Eagle's Claw Lake. That, though, became their first problem. Local police said it was out of their area, state police insisted half the lake was federal land and therefore not their responsibility and the federal authorities stipulated that crimes against a person or property were the responsibility of the Washington State authorities.

Finally, a very pleasant local police sergeant took all their statements and promised to initiate an inquiry.

"I must admit, Miss Somerville," he said. "Your charge of multiple rape against the three men you named will be difficult to prove. Did you have a medical examination?"

"Reid examined and helped me. He is a qualified medical practitioner."

"But there were no swabs obtained that a medical laboratory could test?"

"Sergeant," Erika retorted angrily. "We were a hundred kilometers from the nearest town, I was in fear of my life. If it wasn't for Doctor Reid Tucker and my sister rescuing me, I don't believe I'll be alive today."

"So you were attacked on the forest road after your vehicle was stuck?"

"Yes. A local forestry officer can verify I was on the road leading into Eagle's Claw Lake"

"But you haven't his name?"

Erika shook her head miserably.

"You were forced onto this boat where the alleged offences took place. Later that evening Doctor Tucker and your sister just happened to board the boat that was tied up outside the commune where your sister was living."

"Yes, I told you that," Erika whispered.

The sergeant looked up at her. "I'm actually on your side, Miss Somerville," he said in a kind voice. "There have been murmurs about the Elf Commune but yours is the first actual complaint. I believe if we pursue the abduction, we may stand a greater chance of building a case. With Mr. Doug Rogers' complaint and statements from your sister and the other girls, I believe we can proceed."

"Believe!" Erika replied.

"I shall do what I can, Miss Somerville," the sergeant replied, stood up and extended his hand. The interview was over.

*

"I had the same trouble," Doug said that dinnertime back at Erika's place. "They asked where the arrow fragment Reid dug out of my shoulder was."

"...And like a fool, I never kept it," Reid added.

"Who could expect you to," Kate added. "My God we had other things to worry about. I have other news, too. I don't know whether it is good or bad."

She had been back at the airport all morning and had just returned.

"Go on," Reid said.

"The airport authorities did send out a search plane yesterday afternoon. It flew over the lake and, you know what?"

"The amphibian was gone?" Erika suggested.

"No, it was floating by the jetty as if nothing was wrong. I'll show you." She reached in her brief case and bought out an aerial photograph. It was dated 1600 hours of the previous day and showed the CL-215 floating beside the jetty. It looked perfectly normal.

"And look at this," Reid retorted. Standing on the decking in front of the cabin was a figure waving. "Damn cheek. I'm sure that's Peter."

Kate grimaced and studied the photo. "Could be," she said. "Oh, I have one more bit of news. My new pilot arrived and he's an old friend from Resolution Air. I tried to get Andy Hadfield earlier but he was following up another offer over in Seattle. It fell through due to his age, I think. He's just over fifty and most airlines like younger pilots. Anyhow, he came back, realized I was stranded somewhere and used the Beaver to do all our regular flights. "

"That is good news," Reid replied. "But what are you going to do about the amphibian?"

"Andy is taking another pilot who does odd contract work and Merve, my mechanic, out there tomorrow if the weather's okay. I don't relish going back."

"Well, that's something," Reid said and glanced around the kitchen. "By the way, where are the girls? It's not like them not to be joining in our discussions."

"Far more important stuff," Erika laughed. " I gave them all a credit limit and my credit card. They're buying clothes and Sassy and Jennifer are getting their haircut. Lorie reckons hers was so well done, she didn't need another one."

"And the DSHS?" Kate asked.

"We have an interview tomorrow. I'd like you both to come, if you can." Erika replied. "It's been a busy morning. Oh yes, Sassy and Jennifer were very apologetic and bashful but told me they wanted to live with you two. They said you knew about it, Reid."

"Yes, well. I did say I wouldn't desert them and they could choose." He glanced at Kate. "I was going to speak to you about it but with everything else..."

"They told me," Kate replied. "Everything ... even down to Cinders chasing the tennis ball. I told them they'd have to share a room and help with chores. My apartment is a lot smaller than this house but there are two bedrooms."

"Lorie was disappointed but when I told her Doug was staying here, she cheered up, " Erika added.

"I still feel guilty about that," Doug said.

"Well don't be!" Erika replied. "It's good to have a man around the place." She grinned. "As I said, I loaned the girls money to buy clothes and personal things. You can have the same amount."

"But I can't," Doug protested.

"Buy a razor," Kate laughed. "At the rate you going, you'll soon have a beard as long as Reid's."

"I didn't like to ask," Doug flushed as he ran a hand over his stubble. "I must admit I do feel somewhat itchy." He grinned, accepted the bills Erika handed him from her purse and disappeared outside, only to stick his head back in again a second later. "Cinders wants to come with me. Can she?"

"Sure," Reid laughed. "You'll need her leash, though. The markets don't like dogs."

"Right," Doug yelled and disappeared again.

"Oh, there's one other job," Kate said and smiled at Reid.

"What?"

"The whole four of them want to learn to drive. I said I'd ask you."

"Oh hell," Reid muttered. "One I can handle, but four!"

"You can borrow the Jeep," Erika replied innocently but winked at Kate.

*

The visit to the DSHS produced another surprise. The three girls and Doug were already on the organization's list with Doug drawing an unemployment benefit and the girls receiving an obscure benefit for caregivers of abandoned children. All of these were sent regularly into bank accounts with Doug's, because he was eighteen and classified as an adult, in his own name.

"I know nothing about it," he muttered.

The woman, with Pauline on her name tag, glanced up at the seven gathered around her desk and turned the monitor so they could see it. "Is that your signature, Doug?" she asked and pointed to the on screen document.

"Looks like it, "Doug replied.

"Well, you have a bank account at the Bank of America, main Spokane branch. Your welfare check is paid into there and has been since last year."

"Have you Doug's bank account number?" Reid asked.

"Sure," Pauline replied. She grabbed a business card and copied it down. "The most recent payment went in yesterday," she said.

"Now the girls. Can their welfare be transferred to them personally," Kate asked.

"As they're under age, I'm afraid it must go to an official caregiver."

"I'm Lorie's sister," Erika said and opened her purse. "I have birth certificates."

Pauline examined the documents "You want Lorie's care transferred to yourself," she asked and tapped on her keyboard after Erika nodded "Do you have a bank account number?" she asked.

"Sure," Erika replied and supplied the details.

"Right," Pauline said. "That's sorted but the other two girls situation is more difficult. I assume you're not related."

"No, but we're not going back," Jennifer snapped.

"...And you're both obviously over twelve," Pauline said.

The girls nodded and gave a slight giggle. Again the woman typed on her keyboard and the adjacent printer spat out two official looking documents.

"I can take a statement from you both that says you wish to transfer your caregiver from," she squinted at the screen before glancing up. "... a Sister Madeline Stalinga, to whom?"

"Doctor Reid Tucker," Jennifer said straight away while Sassy had begun to say Kate's name.

"Make it Kate," Reid said. "She has a permanent home."

"Okay," Pauline concluded. "A case worker will need to interview you all and inspect your place of residence but there should be no problem. The transfer will be through within a week."

*

At the bank, Doug found he had a little over five hundred dollars deposited in his name but a monthly automatic withdrawal had been made to the Elf Commune Trust. He cancelled this and withdrew three hundred dollars in cash.

"I never thought I could pay you back so soon," he said and handed two hundred dollars to Erika.

"No, Doug, you get established first." she replied with a wave of her hands and refused to take the bills.

"Now we need a lawyer," Reid said as they walked out to the Jeep and Kate's car. "This is a clear case of false pretenses. Do any of you have one?"

"My lawyer is pretty good," Kate replied.

She grinned as Jennifer and Sassy piled into the back of her car, where Cinders was waiting, while the others walked across to the Jeep.

"I have a feeling that the commune is going to find it's days of doing whatever it wishes has come to an end," Reid retorted. "If we can't get them one way, we'll use another."

*

CHAPTER TWELVE

"Oh, my God!" Lorie screamed as she stared out the window of the Canadair CL-215 as Felts Field Municipal Airport disappeared below them.

Two weeks had slipped by and the aircraft was back in service after a surprisingly brief time. Reid sat in the cockpit with the pilot but Erika and Doug were both absent. Doug had picked up a low paid job at the local market until he decided what to do with his life. He'd completed school and Erika was trying to persuade him to go onto college. Though the girls were already enrolled at a local high school for their second year in September that was months away and summer now stretched out endlessly ahead.

Sassy gripped the edge of her seat and grinned nervously at Jennifer who appeared the most confident of them all.

"After all," Jennifer said. "Kate's flown the aircraft dozens of times. It's not about to crash now."

"Yeah, Yeah," Lorie retorted as she continued to gaze, awe-struck, at the city below them. "You're just too damn practical at times, Jennifer. You're as bad as Cinders"

The dog lay unconcerned on an old blanket in front of the passengers squeezed into canvas seats at the front of a load of supplies. It was their first fight, ever. Kate invited them on 'the milk run', as she called it that visited half a dozen remote settlements, all necessitating lake landings.

*

If the takeoff from the city runway was scary, their first landing twenty-five minutes later on a lake had the girls hanging on like grim death as the CL-215 hit the surface, bounced and hit again. All they could see was white water rushing past and hear the engines roar. Afterwards the aircraft wallowed in the surf and new feelings filled the girls' sensations, seasickness.

"Oh damn!" It was the confident Jennifer who had turned a ghostly white and reached for a paper bag.

The other two would have laughed but were too concerned about holding their own breakfast down as the amphibian turned and taxied along the shoreline towards a small Native American village that looked remarkably like the Elf Commune buildings. On closer inspection, though, the village was nothing like the commune. Buildings were built haphazardly everywhere and there seemed to be people wandering aimlessly around with little to do.

"Why do those men walk funny?" Jennifer asked in an innocent voice as two youths staggered along a dusty road behind the jetty.

"They're drunk," Lorie retorted.

"Oh, the demon drink," Jennifer replied.

Lorie stared at her friend. "I suppose you could say that," she replied. "At least they have a choice, which is more than we had."

"True," Sassy added. "You can choose to do bad things as well as good."

"But why do they do it?" Jennifer asked again. "I wouldn't do anything that made me stagger around. What's the fun in that?"

"Perhaps you should try it one day and find out," Lorie replied. "I'm going to."

"Lorie!" exclaimed Jennifer in horror.

"Well, there are worse things," the other girl replied. "How will we know about anything if we don't try."

"Kate and Reid don't get drunk," Jennifer retorted. "If we end up like them we won't have done too badly. That's why kids get into trouble. They won't take advice and have to just try everything out for themselves."

"Oh Jennifer," Sassy laughed. "Don't take everything so seriously. You can't change people. That was the trouble with the commune. We weren't expected to think, just obey. "

"Sure," Jennifer replied. "There's so much to learn, that's all."

They wandered around for a while, chattered with a few of the locals until they saw Kate waving them back to the aircraft. A few moments later, the engines started and they were off and flying adjacent to snow covered peaks.

Reid came back and told the girls to go up to the cockpit. "Eagle's Claw Lake is coming up," he said. "Kate thought you might like to see it."

"We aren't going to land, I hope," Jennifer whispered.

"No," Reid replied. "Timber Wolf Air has withdrawn from servicing the commune. Kate said it's not worth the risk."

While they talked the other two girls rushed forward and raced for the co-pilot's seat. Sassy won and Lorie had to be content to squat on the seat behind her and gaze out at the lake just coming up.

"There's the road where we escaped," Sassy called out.

"And Reid's cabin," Sassy added. She turned to the pilot. "Can you fly lower, Kate?" she asked.

"Sure," Kate replied. "Our next destination is only a few kilometers west so what say we buzz the commune?"

"Buzz?" Sassy asked with a frown.

"Fly in fast and low, so they get a fright," Kate replied.

"Why not?" Lorie laughed, "But not too low. I'd hate to crash."

*

With the three girls tucked around gazing at the scene below, Kate slowed the CL-215 and followed the curve of the lake southwest over the water and only a little higher than the cliffs on their left. They swept around the headland close to the cave where the girls hid and headed straight towards the Elf Commune.

"Oh my God!" Sassy cried as it unfolded below them.

They could see the jetty, buildings, roads and the farm below. Tiny faces stared up at them and a few arms waved.

"Probably shaking their fists," Lorie retorted as the aircraft roared over.

Jennifer said nothing but had her eyes were glued to the window. It was only when Kate gained altitude and the farmland disappeared behind them that she turned and faced the pilot.

"Can we circle back, Kate?" she requested. "There's something I want to check."

Kate turned and frowned. "I wasn't going to," she replied doubtfully.

"It's important," Jennifer added.

Lorie frowned. "You saw them, too," she said in an equally hushed voice."

"What?" Sassy snapped.

"The uniforms," Jennifer said. "Look at the women's uniforms."

Kate was now flying higher and checked all the gauges. They had plenty of fuel and time, so a return run was quite feasible. "Okay," she relented. "But this is the only time. We have three other places to visit before we head home, you know."

She dropped the port wing, pulled around in a steep turn, leveled and came in over the forest behind the farm. There she turned ninety degrees and headed directly for the lake ahead.

Their time over the commune was hardly more than a minute but all three girls stared down at a line of women filing to the chapel.

"Oh hell," Sassy said. "You're right."

"What!" Kate replied. She never had time to look and, even now, had to keep her eyes ahead as they flew over the lake and began to climb and circle before the northern mountains came too close.

"They are wearing red head scarves," Jennifer said. "Normally, they wear white or black, if someone has died and the commune is in mourning."

"So what does the red signify?"

"The blood of Christ," Lorie said. "It is a sign that some major decision or change of doctrine is about to be announced by the elders. Everyone has to wear red headscarves while the decision is being made. Usually it's for about a week. I can only remember it happening twice before."

"That's right," Sassy added. "The first was when Peter was appointed our new leader to replace old Matthew who died and the second was later when they brought in a series of new sins and regulations."

"And lowered the age of womanhood from eighteen to sixteen," Jennifer added. "Some of the older girls thought they were so smart," She grimaced and added, "until afterwards."

*

Their curiosity was further aroused when they landed at an adjacent lake at another small Native American community. Randolph, one of the village elders, was with three other men and Reid helping to lift a new generator from the amphibian onto the back of an ancient pick-up when he noticed the three girls.

He placed his edge of the crate on the pick-up and wiped a sunburned hand under his wide brimmed hat. A crinkled smile unfolded from his leathery face. "I know you three," he said in a slow voice. "You're the girls who caused all the commotion over at the commune." He gave a chuckle. "They got their comeuppance when you disappeared, didn't they?"

"Why, what happened? " Sassy asked.

"The head honcho came in here and practically accused us of kidnapping you four," Randolf squinted in the sun and glanced around. "Where's the boy?" he asked.

"Doug's got a job in Spokane," Lorie replied.

"That's spot on," Randolph continued. "Anyhow, I told Peter if he treated his young charges decently, they wouldn't need to walk out. We just about came to blows over that." He sniffed in disgust. "He's bad news, that one. It's all in the eyes. He'll never look you in the eyes as if there is always has something to hide."

"So what's happening at the commune now?" Kate asked. "Is anything different?"

Randolph rubbed a hand over his chin. "Funny you should say that, Kate," he drawled. "Something's going on there but I'm not sure what."

"Why are you suspicious?" Reid asked.

"Well, after our big row over the kids, we stayed away from them." He shrugged. "Not that we have a lot to do with them anyhow."

"Go on," Kate persuaded.

"Well, only a week back Peter and Luke, I think the other guy was, rolled in here in their Jeep and offered to sell us all their cattle, three hundred of them. The price was a bargain so we bought them. When they were leaving they said the strangest thing."

"What?" Kate responded.

"They said we could leave them where they were as they weren't going to need the farm land any more. We could graze the cattle there over summer. I found out later they'd only restocked last year and sold the cattle to us at a lower price than they originally paid for them. It's mighty strange, if you ask me."

"It is," Reid replied. "Have you heard or seen anything else?"

The elderly man shrugged. "It seems that after you girls left there was some tightening up. We heard of a protest by the women that went wrong. It was whispered that some were beat up mighty bad. No proof, though. Just rumors we picked up when we went to inspect the cattle we bought." He sighed. "I did see one girl with an almighty black eye and bandaged arm.

"Who was it?" gasped Jennifer.

"I'm sorry, I don't know her name. She'd be a bit older than you, about twenty, I'd say."

The girls stared at each other. It could be anyone. There were sixteen to twenty women at the commune who could fit that description.

Randolph continued chatting but didn't add any more information. They were invited for lunch and conversations with other locals told them much the same. There had been a clamp down at the commune and the farm animals were being sold off. One guy commented that usually the commune had land plowed to plant crops by early summer but a couple of fields had been left half done.

Something different was happening or about to happen at the Elf Commune and the three girls all suspected it was something sinister.

"Everything looks bad," Jennifer said when they were on their way back to Spokane. "The women wearing red, cattle being sold and unplowed fields. They always had crops planted by now. It was one of the main sources of income for the commune."

"And that beat up woman," Lorie added. "Usually, it is only the kids who are given hidings, not adults. "

"I bet it's because we left," Sassy added. "They had to blame someone. They'd say it was the devil on the loose and find a reason to blame someone."

"It sounds like the seventeenth century when women were declared witches," Reid observed.

"It does but what can we do?" Kate replied in a quiet voice,

"I'm not sure," Reid replied, "There must be someone with authority to go in and check on what's happening. If the local police aren't interested, we'll find someone who is. I don't think we should just ignore them. Imagine if they had something terrible planned and we find out after it is too late."

He caught Kate's eyes and saw she looked as concerned as he felt. The three girls, too, all looked apprehensive and looked back at him for guidance. He smiled at them. "Cheer up," he said. "I'm sure there is someone in Spokane who will help and I'll find out who it is."

*

When Erika heard the news, she frowned and asked who had been contacted.

"Nobody, yet," Reid replied. "I was about to go to the police precinct. That sergeant we spoke to seems to be the best."

Erika sighed. "I wasn't meant to say anything but I think I can help. Just give me a moment. I've got a call to make."

She sounded mysterious but would say no more as she found a number in her address book and punched in a number.

"Extension 786, please," she said. Her eyes glanced around at the others while she waited. "Wallpaper music," she retorted and waited again before the extension was answered.

"Good afternoon, Erika Somerville speaking. It's about the Elf Commune. You asked me to contact you if there were any new developments... Yes... No, I'm not personally in danger," Her eyes grinned at Kate. "No she's here and everyone except Doug. He's still working. They've just returned after a flight over the lake..." Erika continued with a brief summary of everything she'd been told. "I can," she said after listening for a moment. "I can certainly vouch for them all." She listened again before she placed a hand over the receiver and glanced around. "Can we go downtown, right now?"

Kate looked at the others and nodded.

"Okay," Erika replied. "Give us forty minutes... Bye." She hung up.

"That was Parnell Rodriguez. He's a FBI agent I have been helping over the last year." She looked directly at Reid. "It's all classified information and I signed a secrecy clause and wasn't permitted to tell anyone anything.

"But now?" Reid replied.

"I think you've all been cleared as not being a security risk."

*

The office was unmarked and on the eighth floor in an unpretentious building two blocks from downtown Spokane. The building did, however, have a sophisticated security system and stern-faced guards rang ahead before they were allowed to enter the elevator.

Their wait in the foyer was brief and they were shown into a sterile office where two men in civilian suits invited them all to take a seat. Erika introduced the taller of the men as Captain Rodriguez who in turn nodded at the second man, a military type with close clipped gray hair and serious eyes.

"This is Inspector Jack DeHaven from the Royal Canadian Mounted Police," he introduced.

Reid frowned as he shook the man's hand. "Canadian?"

"I'm based at Edmonton, Alberta," DeHaven replied in a soft voice but did not elaborate.

A few more pleasantries were exchanged before the girls were grilled with very thorough and searching questions about their life in the Elf Commune, how they escaped, their reasons for leaving and finally what they had seen that day.

"Have any of you heard of Fort McMurray?" the Canadian asked when the interviews were over and everyone was drinking a welcomed cup of coffee.

Kate frowned for a moment. "Isn't that a small town north of Edmonton?" she said.

"You know your geography, Kate," Jack DeHaven replied. "Over three hundred kilometers north and really one of the last outposts of civilization. North of Fort McMurray is wilderness It's a cold desolate area, frozen for much of the year and infested with insects during the brief summer."

"So what is the connection?" Reid asked.

"The Elf Community has an outpost somewhere there," Parnell Rodriguez explained. "Hence Jack's interest in our commune. We believe their intentions are to shift everyone from Eagle's Claw Lake, north. What you just told us this afternoon seems to confirm what we suspected."

"But why?" Lorie asked.

"Once there, it would be a impossible for anyone to escape. They can do whatever they wish. We have other information about this so-called Peter but I'm afraid it is classified at the moment. Suffice to say both our countries are keen to get this gentleman in our clutches. It seems now, that we cannot afford to wait any longer." Rodriguez continued.

"Peter Littlejohn and some of the others have been seen in Fort McMurray," the Canadian added. "However, we have not found where their new commune is. We do know, though, that there is a skeleton group already there, twenty or so, we think."

"A lot of thinking and guesses," Reid said quietly.

"We had a spy but she disappeared," The FBI man glanced at Erika and onto Lorie. "It was Jane Somerville, your mother."

"But Mom's dead!" Erika gasped.

Rodriguez glanced up. "I'm sorry," he said.

"But why are you confiding in us?" Reid asked.

"Circumstances have changed," Rodriguez replied. "We thought we had time to develop a plan but it seems we now have to move quickly." He stood up. "Remember everything said in this room is classified information. Even a casual comment made to a friend could get to the wrong ears. Thank you for coming. We'll be in touch."

*

Even though it was a warm, fine evening, Jennifer and Sassy forwent the chance to go walking with Reid and Cinders around the suburban streets near Kate's apartment. Instead they hung around the kitchen while Kate prepared a meal.

"Okay girls, what's on your mind?" she asked.

"Is it that obvious?" Sassy replied.

"Turning down a walk with Cinders and not watching one of your favorite soap operas on television is unusual," Kate replied with a grin.

"Okay," Jennifer said and sat on a bar stood beside the raised serving bench. "There are a couple of things."

"Fire away," Kate replied.

"You've taken us in here and made us welcome. We love it here, Kate. This apartment is more than we ever dreamed of, you look after us, spent money on us, take us around and let us be ourselves."

"But?" Kate replied with a frown. She placed the saucepan of potatoes on the stove, sprinkled salt across them and also sat down on a stool.

"A bank statement arrived for my account today," Sassy said.

"Your benefit should be coming through," Kate said. "If not I'll..."

"That's it. The money is there, all of it," Jennifer added.

"So?"

"You are taking nothing, Kate. You provide everything yet take nothing in return," Jennifer continued. "We want to pay our way, Kate, and don't want to be charity cases." She screwed her nose up. "I overheard Reid saying almost the same thing to you the other night."

Kate suddenly broke into a smile. "And do you two realize how you have also helped me with your fabulous company? It's not all one way, you know."

"We want to help with expenses," Sassy replied. "We don't want all our benefits. It is for you, not us."

"Okay," Kate responded. "If you wish, we can transfer some of the money back to my account but I definitely won't take it all."

"Thanks," Sassy replied and reached across to hug Kate. "You're are a real pal. So is Reid."

Jennifer, though, hung back. "There's something else, Kate," she said doubtfully.

"Go on," Kate responded.

"All that news today with the FBI guy. It's just that..." She hesitated and bit on her bottom lip.

"They only told us because they want us to do something," Sassy continued in a rush of words. "Jennifer and I reckon they're going to plan a raid or something on the commune and will ask us to go back to show them where everything is."

"We don't want to go back," Jennifer whispered. "Oh I know you'll say we'll be protected but you don't know what they are really like. We're scared something will go wrong and Peter or the others will catch us and... Oh hell." Her face turned white. "I'm scared Kate. Really scared..."

"She thinks we'll be caught and raped," Sassy added.

"You've been raped?" Kate whispered.

"No," Jennifer replied, "But that was only because we hadn't turned sixteen. The code of behavior at the commune is strictly adhered to and nobody in the junior dormitories is touched. Last year at this time, Geraldine, one of the older girls refused to move when she became sixteen but Sister Madeline dragged her away, literally kicking and screaming. She never seemed quite the same after that and wouldn't tell us much about happened. What she did say made us even more terrified of becoming sixteen." She glanced at the calendar hanging on the wall. "It was going to be the twenty-first of June, actually."

Kate gave a tiny smile. "Why that's grand, Jennifer. We'll celebrate," She turned to glance at the other girl. " And when is your birthday, Sassy?"

Sassy frowned. "It's not Jennifer's or my proper birthday. At the commune, everyone becomes a year older on one date. Lorie, Jennifer and myself all would be declared sixteen at seven three am on June twenty one, the Summer Solstice."

"Oh hell but when are your real birthdays?"

"We have no idea," Sassy whispered. "Other birthday dates were not recognized."

"I see," Kate replied softly. "We'll have to do something about that, won't we?"

"But how" Sassy replied.

"All births are registered. We only need to look up the records and find your actual dates of birth." Kate replied in a resolute tone. "Once we've found out we'll have our own celebration whenever it is your real birthday. Now come on, help me get supper served. I don't know about you but I'm famished."

Jennifer glanced at Sassy who smiled back and walked across to the stove. Supper was bubbling away and steam drifted up to the extraction vent.

*

CHAPTER THIRTEEN

The Timber Wolf Air Beaver was a single engine floatplane that was used by several local companies so if seen over Eagle's Claw Lake nothing would be out of the ordinary. At least, that is what Kate and her friends hoped. Other precautions were taken just in case, with Kate flying the aircraft in from the north and over Reid's cabin before looping around the central arm of the lake. She landed close to the cave where Sassy and Jennifer had originally taken refuge but taxied to the southern shore to let the passengers off.

Lorie glanced nervously at Kate before she followed her sister, Parnell Rodriguez and another FBI agent, Ralph Yates onto the small beach. "Perhaps I should have stayed back home with Sassy and Jennifer," she said. "It's easy to be brave back in your apartment but now we're here, all the memories return."

"You'll be fine," Kate replied. She smiled at Reid who sat in the co-pilot's seat and waited while the other men unloaded equipment from the rear of the Beaver.

Parnell pushed the tail of the aircraft around and the four watched as the engine roared and the Beaver moved out into the inlet. It turned east into the wind and accelerated forward. Wake surged out from the floats and it lifted into the air but remained below the foothills as it disappeared around the rugged shoreline.

"Right," Parnell said. "There's about a kilometer's walk along the shore then we head inland a couple of hundred meters to the cave. Once there, we'll be away from any prying eyes."

Lorie glanced at Erika and bit on a lip. She had volunteered to help as she knew where the sleeping dormitories were and the names of all the children, whereas Erika's knowledge of everything was somewhat dated.

Parnell and Ralph had remained tight-lipped about the reason for the visit so all Lorie knew that it was important to remove the children from the commune and, as well, persuade as many adults as possible to accompany them. There were forty-two children under sixteen who slept in the children's dormitory and another dozen women and five men that the girls and Doug had listed as probably being interested in leaving.

Apparently, the area beneath the commune was a honeycomb of caves, many unexplored but others had been made into the tunnels that linked the commune buildings. Agents had been surveying these catacombs for weeks now and had discovered a northwestern entrance, the one they were walking to now. They had also found a way into the tunnel linking the dormitories with the chapel. It was through here that they hoped to rescue the children.

"There's no hurry," Parnell reassuring voice said after the sound of the aircraft disappeared. "It is more important to remain hidden. Keep yourselves on alert and if you see a boat just freeze and warn everyone. Movement is highly visible from anyone out on the lake but someone standing still is more likely to blend into the background." He grinned. "That's why I asked you to wear dark clothes."

*

For forty minutes they followed the shore without seeing another sole. The shadow from western mountains already covered the lake and thick firs to their left offered room for a quick retreat, if necessary. However, the hillside was so steep it was almost impossible to walk through the trees.

Lorie trudged beside of Erika and the pair spoke in soft voices as they moved along. "This is where we paddled the canoe," Loire pointed out. "I'm sure when we go around that next headland we'll be able to see the commune."

"You're right but we'll move inland before there," Parnell replied. "We follow this creek bed up through a valley. It's more of a canyon really. The cave entrance is at the end. In the spring thaw water tumbles down but, at the moment, there is a mere trickle."

His words proved correct for, once beyond the shore, they followed the narrow twisting canyon up through rocks and were surrounded by almost vertical fir covered walls. It was hot work and Lorie found herself covered in perspiration and tiny mites hovering around. She felt pleased that she managed the steep sections as well as Erika and the men. In fact, she could propel herself up between rocks quite easily while Parnell had to grunt and heave his heavier frame through the narrow sections.

The climb took another half an hour until the canyon petered out into a broad valley of firs.

"Right," panted Parnell. "Let's stop and have a rest. I don't know about you lot, but I'm exhausted. The cave entrance is only a hundred meters further on." He glanced at his watch. "We have about an hour of daylight and then several hours wait before we enter the dormitory around midnight."

"So how about telling us the whole story, now," Erika said after they'd all removed backpacks and canisters of water were handed around. "After all, there's nobody here to tell, is there?"

Parnell glanced at Ralph who gave a little shrug. The younger FBI agent leaned back against the bank and glanced at Erika and Lorie. "Does the summer solstice on June twenty-one mean anything to you, Lorie?" he asked.

Lorie nodded. "That's when we were to be declared sixteen," she replied in a hushed tone. "Everyone is declared a year older on that day. We have special ceremonies to mark the event."

"That's what we learned," Ralph continued, "However, everything has been brought forward a month, probably because of your escape."

Lorie nodded. "Okay but why the urgency? The three of us who were to be declared women all escaped. The next two girls younger than us are only turning fourteen."

"There's more, though," Parnell added. "Those red scarves you saw when you flew over last week confirm what we had suspected..."

"And that was?" Erika interrupted.

"Peter is about to declare Armageddon this Sunday and prepare the commune for The Last Judgment. As I said, it's been brought forward."

"Oh I see," Erika whispered and turned pale.

"Well, I don't," Lorie retorted. "What is it?"

"The end, Lorie," Erika explained. "Everyone at the commune has been told the world will end tomorrow night and they must leave before then."

"How?" Lorie persisted. "On some gigantic spaceship or something."

"Your soul, Lorie." She took her sister's hands. "Surely you were told about it."

"Yeah, sure," the teenager replied. "We were always told of the battle between God and the devil and only the believers would survive."

"But the opposite will happen unless we step in," Ralph added quietly.

Lorie frowned. "How?" she asked.

"Everyone will be expected to commit suicide tomorrow evening," Erika whispered. "Even the children and babies will be given poison to swallow then the whole compound will be set ablaze."

"Oh hell!" Lorie gasped.

"It's even worse." Parnell's eyebrows creased into a frown. "Our dear disciples, Peter, Abraham and the others are going to quietly slip away. An amphibian is due to land shortly and will be waiting to evacuate them and a few of the loyal women, their so-called wives, out. They plan to fly to their new commune up in Canada. It won't be mass suicide but really mass murder."

*

The cave interior was well marked with tiny phosphorescent arrows at every intersection to show the way. After an initial descent down a steep cliff where a wire rope had been secured to the wall, the rest of the cave was level but twisted and turned with side passages going off everywhere. Without the arrows, Lorie was sure they would have all been hopelessly lost. She shone the flashlight Parnell had given her, upwards but the beam did not show any ceiling. In contrast she could almost touch the two walls with outstretched hands. It was single file territory and she was second to last but had the comfort of having Ralph behind.

Their hushed voices echoed around and a fine dust was stirred up by their footsteps as they plodded forward. The section they were in at the moment had damp walls and droplets of water ran down to trickle through cracks in the floor. It was cool but not cold. In fact, if it wasn't for the worry about what was to happen, the journey would have been a pleasant hike.

When they came to a sharp corner after almost an hour's walking, Lorie gave a gasp. Concrete blocks replaced the left wall in front.

"Right," Parnell called back in a hushed voice. "We're on the outside of the tunnel that connects the dormitories to the chapel. We follow it south and end near the children's dormitory." He gave a tiny chuckle and removed his backpack. "They were considerate enough to put in large air vents into this cave. We've unscrewed the one closest to the children's dormitory."

"We wait here until midnight," Ralph added. "Keep very quiet. Our voices could be carried through the vents into the tunnel." He nodded at a small alcove across from the concrete blocks. "This is where we left some gear."

Parnell nodded at three large containers Lorie hadn't noticed in the corner. "There's a radio and other equipment there to defend us," he said. "There's also food, water, clothing and a medical kit. When you arrive back, take it all with you and continue on to the third intersection and wait. It will be safer there as any noises the children make won't be heard."

*

"Sister Madeline Stalinga?" Ralph Yates hissed as he grabbed the woman around the mouth and whispered in her ear. "This tiny needle you feel pressed against your neck will put you asleep for twelve hours if you move one centimeter. Just nod if you understand." The woman's terrified eyes looked up at him and nodded. "We know all about the raspberry drink you were going to give the children as a treat in the morning, Stalinga." His eyes bore into the woman.

"But how?" Her white face turned gray.

"Special Services, FBI, Madam," Yates spat. "You either cooperate or we leave you here. Of course you'll be asleep..."

"You can't!" gasped the woman.

"So you care about the souls of forty two children but don't worry about you own, Sister," Ralph continued sarcastically. "Isn't that sacrilege?"

"It's a fake," the woman whispered. Her eyes darted sideways in an unsuccessful attempt to see the needle. "The children..."

"Oh, we know. You answer the questions I ask and if you hesitate for one second, in goes the needle. Got it?"

"Yes," Stalinga squeaked.

"How many other adults are in this block?"

"None!" the woman replied.

"Liar!" Yates replied and pushed the needle, ever so slightly into the flabby neck.

"Four. There's four!" the woman almost screamed. "Guards are outside the doors at each end of the block and two women are in the nursery to care for the babies."

"Good," Ralph replied and relaxed the pressure on the needle. He followed with questions at such a speed the terrified woman never had a chance to hesitate so probably told he truth.

Finally the FBI man grunted and pushed the needle in. "We can't have you telling anyone we're here now, can we?" he grunted as the woman attempted to scream but failed and slumped unconscious onto the floor.

Lorie looked at the agent in terror before Ralph explained. "This knockout drug only lasts an hour. There'll be plenty of time for her to escape even if they blow the building, tomorrow." He smiled slightly at her. "Do you know what to do?"

"Yes," Lorie whispered. "Wait exactly ten minutes, turn the lights on and start getting the children up."

"That's right," Ralph replied. "Don't worry, those outside are expecting it. The adults here were due to wake the children and give them all the raspberry-flavored poison. I believe the dosage also includes an anesthetic to knock the children out."

"How do you know all this?" Erika gasped, as she stood pale but determined beside Lorie.

"I'll tell you later," the man replied. "I have to dispose of the guards outside the doors and the women in the nursery. See you soon."

He squeezed Lorie's arm and was gone.

*

"Come on," Erika whispered and Lorie followed her to the tiny pantry at the end of the dormitory.

They were in the girls' dormitory and everywhere were the slumbers and snorts of sleeping children. However, nobody appeared to be awake. Lorie suspected that some were but did not want to bring attention to themselves. They reached the ablutions room adjacent to the dormitory where, in spite of herself, she gasped. On the bench was a massive punch bowl filled with red liquid. Tumblers were neatly arranged in orderly rows around it. The smell of raspberry filled the air but it was also accompanied by another pungent smell.

"Almond," Erika whispered. "The poison smells like almonds."

With her face white with fury, Erika grabbed the bowl but it was too heavy to lift so she tipped it over the edge of the bench. The fluid swished out onto the wooden floor in a gush like a small tidal wave and splashed onto her jeans. She ignored her wet attire, lifted the now empty container to the sink and flushed it out with the faucet turned on at full speed.

"The noise!" gasped Lorie as she stared at the water splashing onto the floor and red liquid running away in two long lines beneath the outside door. Her sister's fury surprised her.

"In five minutes the lights go on, anyhow," Erika retorted and again ignored her wet clothes. "I'll go across to the boys' room. You stay here. Remember, be calm."

"Look who's talking," Lorie retorted. "I know what to do. We've been through it a dozen times."

The tension was getting to them both.

A moment later both men appeared and said all the adults in the block had been given knockout drugs.

"Are you okay?" Parnell asked when he noticed Lori's grim expression.

"Yes," she replied and glanced at Lorie.

"Sorry about the outburst before. Seeing that terrible stuff made me so angry, I sort of snapped, that's all," Erika whispered.

"That's okay," Lorie replied.

Parnell cut in. "I've known hardened police officers to react the same way. I would have been more concerned if it hadn't affected you, but now is the time to hide your worries from the children. Can you do it?"

"Yes," Erika replied quietly. "We'll be fine, won't we Lorie?"

Lorie swallowed bile and nodded. She felt anything except fine but was determined to do everything asked of her.

*

"Hi Guys," Lorie said in an enforced light tone as the lights come on. "Do you remember me?"

"Lorie!" called a dozen voices. "But why..." The bubble of voices filled the room and several of the older girls leaped out of bed.

"You're in jeans and jersey," one youngster cried out in an amazed voice. "Oh Lorie, I knew you'd come back,"

"Hi Rebecca," Lisa replied and relaxed a little when the ten-year-old smiled. "Now, listen everyone, I will explain later but you must all get dressed in your warmest clothes. I want the older girls to a go and get the babies from the nursery. The sisters there will be asleep so won't stop you."

"But," argued one of the older girls, "If the disciples come..."

"Do it!" Lorie hissed with her calmness forgotten, "or would you rather be dead, Julie?"

"No, of course not but..."

"Come on, Julie," a tall dark haired girl in the next bed said. "You know we can trust Lorie. Why would she risk coming back here if it wasn't to help?"

Lorie glanced in appreciation at the girl who supported her. "Thanks, Yvonne," she said. "Can you organize the babies? Just see they're wrapped in something warm. Okay?

"Sure," Yvonne replied and turned to those around. "Well, you heard Lorie. Snap to it!"

*

Fifteen minutes later, again exactly on time, the lights went off but forty-two children and babies were assembled in a long line in the darkened corridor. Except for two infants crying, all was hushed and everyone's eyes stared at the two men holding the only lights, two small flashlights switched to show only a dull red beam.

"We are going down the tunnel that leads to the chapel," Parnell said in a quiet voice. "I want no talking and, unless you're holding a baby, I want you to reach your hands out to the people in front and behind you. If you're near someone holding a baby, grab her clothes or arm. Okay! "

"It is perfectly all right to touch the person near you," Erika added. "It does not matter if you are a girl or boy. We're all friends here and friends are allowed to touch each other."

An embarrassed giggle went through the darkness but hands were grabbed and, everyone waited.

"Are you okay?" Parnell whispered to Lorie. "Ralph has gone ahead to check the tunnel and I'll be the rear guard. You lead the children down to the cave and Erika can go behind them, "

"I'm okay," Lorie replied. "But what about the adults in the other building? You said they were going to be given a chance to come."

"Another squad is coming in for them," the man replied. "Our main concern is these kids. When you get to the cave, keep going to that third intersection and wait there. Erika has a radio so we can keep in touch. Remember before lose sight of an arrow look for the next one."

"Right," Lorie replied and swallowed nervously as the man slipped away.

She knew Erika was at the rear but felt somehow alone. "Okay, Yvonne," she gulped. "Follow me."

She moved forward down the ramp and into the tunnel with the others following in single file. Once inside, there were small red pilot lights that gave an eerie glow but made it easier to see. The tunnel curved slightly to the left so when they reached their destination, both entrances were out of sight. Lorie stopped and turned to Yvonne.

"We came in through this air vent in the wall," she whispered. "Give me a hand to pull it out."

"Right," the younger girl replied.

Together, they grabbed the two sides of the rectangular grating and pulled it out to reveal an opening about half the size of a small window. Lorie grinned at the children, wriggled into the opening and let herself down. Her feet found a protruding rock and from there she knew it was only a short drop to the ground. She held the metal edge of the vent for a second, lowered herself down until toes touched the ground and let go.

"Yvonne," she called up. "Get the smaller children and I'll give them a hand. It's dark down here but quite safe."

The other girl's face appeared, looking apprehensive but excited. "Okay," she whispered. "It'll be Trevor first."

The legs of a little boy about six appeared, Lorie reached up, grabbed his waist and gave a grunt as he just let go and flopped into her arms. She stood him on the floor and noticed his grinning face.

"Where's our raspberry drink, Lorie?" he asked. "We were told we were all going to have a raspberry drink when we woke up and were very good."

"Oh, Trevor," Lorie replied and tried to keep the tremor out of her voice. "When we get out of here I'll buy you the biggest soda you have ever seen and it'll be any flavor you like. Okay?"

"Sure Lorie," the little boy replied. "We missed you, you know; Sassy and Jennifer, too. It isn't the same without you all."

"And I missed you, too," Lorie whispered and ruffled the boy's hair. "Now, can you move a little so we can get the next person down?"

She glanced up as two feet and a red tartan skirt appeared. It was one of the girls. Tiny hands appeared and another small body, lighter than Trevor flopped into Lorie's arms.

"Hi Noeline," she said and plopped the little girl next to Trevor and reached for the third child.

The line of children seemed to take forever but after about half were in the cave, Erika's head appeared and the babies were handed down, and past onto bigger children to hold before the rest of the children followed. Finally, Erika appeared with the grating held above her head...

"I had a radio message from Ralph," she called down. "There's some delay with the other squad. He said to pull the grate back and go to our original meeting place. Parnell and himself will meet us there."

She rested her feet on the outcrop of rock and used both hands to pull the vent into place before, with Lorie's help, she stepped down into the cave. Eyes followed her and several children could be heard sniffing back tears. Crying was discouraged at the commune but, in many ways, the self-control by these youngsters was more heartbreaking than if the tears rolled.

Erika flicked on her flashlight, still set on the red beam and smiled around at the children crowded in the confined space. "Right," she said. "Now we want another big line. Join hands again and follow Lorie. Okay?"

"Yes, Erika," three dozen voices whispered and Lorie felt two hands grab hers. Both Yvonne and Trevor both wanted to hold onto her.

She glanced down. "Okay Trevor, you can be behind me, then Yvonne." She smiled at the girl who let go and grabbed the little boy's hand so she was third in line. "Away we go."

CHAPTER FOURTEEN

After making a quick reconnaissance of the dormitory and a brief check outside, Parnell found nothing out of the ordinary. The unconscious adults were made reasonably comfortable and he was about to follow Erika and the others through to the tunnel when his radio buzzed.

"Rodriguez."

"Home Base, here," came the reply, "Arrival of takeover force has been delayed due to low cloud. Estimated time of arrival is now 0500 hours. An aircraft flying south from Canada has been tracked from Edmonton, Alberta and ETA at Eagle's Claw Lake is 0530 hours. This may also be affected by the low cloud base with visibility at dawn expected to be down to sixteen meters."

Parnell reported that the children were in the caves but no adult dormitories had been entered.

"Leave them," said the remote voice. "Keep the children in the caves until advised. Do not attempt to walk them out down the canyon. Helicopters will arrive when the weather improves."

Parnell frowned. A surprise attack was becoming less likely as he knew the commune assembled in the chapel at dawn less than half an hour after the force was due.

"The commune members may have moved to the chapel by that time," he replied. "Also the adults in the children's dormitory will be awake by then. It is paramount that you get here earlier or there may be a bloodbath."

"We'll try, Parnell," the voice replied in a more reconciliatory manner. "But there are no guarantees. If all else fails care of the children is your major concern. The adults are on their own. Use plan B if the enemy enter the caves."

"Okay," Parnell replied and rung off. "Damn!" he muttered, for he knew there were many adults who were not volunteering to take their own lives but what could he do? It would be foolish to expose their presence and risk having the children found.

He slipped into the children's dormitory, locked the doors but left the keys inside the locks and checked the five adults again. It was strangely quiet and the air was cold and still. Something seemed wrong! Maybe it was his imagination but something tickled his mind. Why would they wake the children in the middle of the night to administer the poison? Surely it would be logical to administer in the morning.

"Oh hell," he snapped to himself. That was it. The building would be blown up before the final meeting in the chapel. If the children were already dead any adults who had second thoughts would be so overcome with remorse they wouldn't hesitate to take their own lives.

"The bastards!" he swore and glanced at his watch. That was why Stalinga was so terrified. Even being put out for a short while would be too late if the building was going to be blown early.

But what about the adults here? He couldn't just leave them. He made a sudden decision and ran through to the nursery, lifted the first women over his shoulder and carried her out the furthermost exit. At the rear all was dark and a white fog hung around the ground but he knew there was a small shed across the lawn. He stumbled forward and slung the woman behind the building. Over the next ten minutes he moved all the others and glanced at his watch… twenty to two. Knowing how the commune minds worked, they probably had the building due to blow on the hour. He had to hurry.

Moments later he was in the tunnel and found there was a massive steel door just inside the entrance. He shut and latched it, while noticing the latch only operated from the interior, and headed forward. Ralph was not waiting at the vent as arranged nor were there any signals visible to show he'd followed Erika and the children into the caves.

Parnell took his radio, pressed a remote button and hissed into it. "Ralph, where are you?"

Ralph's voice came straight back. "Along the tunnel where it intercepts the other one. Something's strange is happening. Can you get here?"

"Right. Be with you in a couple of moments."

"Keep damn quiet and show no lights," warned Ralph. "See you soon."

*

"What is it?" Parnell asked when he found his companion lying on the floor and peering around a ninety-degree bend.

"The men have all filed past," Ralph whispered. "They were dressed in dark suits as if they're going to a wedding."

"Or funeral," Parnell spat. "I have a feeling everything has been moved forward several hours and isn't at dawn as we suspected."

"It fits in," Ralph replied and peeped around the corner again. "The women are coming," he hissed.

The two men watched as the women approached, all dressed in their usual red tartan skirts and white blouses. The scarves on their heads were red. Fifty or more filed past in two lines and disappeared towards the chapel.

"Well, that's it," Parnell whispered. "Our orders are to look after the kids."

"Wait," hissed Yates. "There are more coming."

The noise came first; scuffling feet, clanging, low weeping and intermittent moans as another line of women appeared. This was different, though. About sixteen women, mainly young by their appearance were stumbling along in pairs with their hands bound to a long chain along between them. Several were crying and, even as the men watched, an older woman, obviously a guard lashed out at one mere girl with a switch.

"Move!" she snapped as the girl attempted to defend herself.

*

Parnell caught Ralph's eyes and nodded grimly. "We're going in," he hissed. "On three."

Both men were professionals and no other discussion was necessary. Three seconds later, they stepped quietly out in front of the line abreast of them with heavy caliber service automatics held ready to fire.

"FBI!" snarled Rodriguez. "Everyone will stop and sit down. Now!"

The line stopped and the front guard opened her mouth as if to scream but nothing came out. Yates clipped her on the side of the head with his weapon and she collapsed, bleeding to the floor.

"Sit, I said!" Parnell hissed and pointed his weapon at the second guard. "These weapons have silencers and we will not hesitate to use them."

The woman's face drained of all color but she dropped her switch and sat down. Meanwhile the women tied together also stumbled down onto their knees. Expression ranged from relief to uncertainty.

"I'll keep an eye out up the corridor," Ralph whispered and slipped away.

"Now, if you wish to survive you will undo these young ladies," Parnell directed. "Nobody will speak. If anybody attempts to call out it will be the last sound you'll ever make." He almost grinned when he realized it was all a bluff. If the women were about to commit suicide they had nothing to lose. Luckily, though, the flustered women never thought of it that way.

The four remaining guards nodded and began to untie the prisoners.

"We objected to what they intended to do but were being forced to take part, anyway," one of the women prisoners whispered.

"And your name, Ma'am," Parnell asked.

"Geraldine," she replied. "Did Lorie get help?"

Parnell nodded. "And I assume it is the Armageddon pact you're talking about."

"You know?" hissed a guard but swiveled back when the FBI glowered at her and raised his weapon a tiny fraction.

"Everything," he grunted. "Including the hoax."

"Hoax, what hoax?" Geraldine asked.

Parnell stared at her. "I'll tell you later. Right now we need to move quickly."

"My baby!" howled one of the other prisoners as she rubbed her swollen wrists after the ropes came off. "They're going to kill all the children!" She reached out for Parnell and burst into tears.

"It's okay," he replied tenderly.

He glanced up as Ralph returned and indicated all was quiet.

"Right," Parnell ordered. "Bound and gag the guards."

The former prisoners reacted immediately. Guards were seized and, none too gently tussled up and almost choked as their own scarves were knotted around their mouths.

"Bring them and we'll leave then out of sight around a corner," Parnell ordered and nodded up the side tunnel. "We're going back up here."

The women guards were propelled forward as the newly freed prisoners followed Parnell back up the tunnel. Several women stepped back and affectionately guided the some of the more distressed victims along and talked reassuringly to them. They had almost reached the vent when, above them there was clap of thunder and the whole tunnel shook for several moments, a few thuds banged on the ceiling and silence returned.

"The dorm!" Geraldine screamed. "They've blown the children's dorm and the kids are inside." Her face and that of her companions was that of utter terror until the FBI agent's slight smile sent a message through to her. "The children aren't there, are they?" she whispered.

"No," Parnell replied. "They're safe and waiting with Erika and Lorie. We got them out in time."

"Oh my God, thank you," another slim blonde woman who was barely twenty sobbed. "We tried to stop the slaughter but..." Her voice trailed off.

"I know," Parnell answered in a kind voice. "But come on. We still aren't out of danger."

*

"Sassy, are you awake?" Jennifer's voice called softly across the dark bedroom.

"I wasn't but what is it, Jennifer?" came the sleepy reply.

"I thought I heard footsteps in the kitchen."

"Oh, Jennifer," Sassy replied as she sat up in bed and turned the bedside lamp on. She squinted in the bright light and stared across at her friend in the other bed. "It's okay. We're in Kate's apartment, half way up a condominium block with an alarm and two locks on the door. Just because she called last night and said Reid and her were grounded somewhere up near the Canadian border because of low cloud, doesn't mean that every pervert in the city is about to head this way." She was about to say more when a very faint creak came from outside their door. Her face drained of color and she stared at Jennifer. "I heard it?" she whispered.

Jennifer sucked on a bottom lip and stared, wide eyed at the door.

Sassy slipped out of bed, tip-toed towards the door, hesitated, smiled reassuringly and continued forward while Jennifer pulled her blankets up to her chin.

*

Sassy, though, never reached the door!

It was flung back and the main bedroom light flashed on. "So the wayward little devils thought they could just up and leave, did they?" The male voice boomed. "We have a little unfinished business, don't we girls?"

Sassy shrank back but not before Abraham, the disciple Jennifer had shot near Erika's Jeep, reached out and grabbed her arm. In a second the hold was around her waist and she was flung down across the bed.

"Let me go!" she screamed.

"Oh, I will," the man whispered. "It's the other little trollop I want." He flung Sassy aside like a rag doll and leaped at Jennifer, grabbed her by the arm and around the neck in one move. With one yank she was pulled out of bed and crashed to the floor.

"Nobody gets the better of me, Jennifer, my sweetie," he chuckled, "Your night attire is not regulation one for girls to wear," he chuckled as she kicked, screamed and tried to beat him off. The man pulled her close into him, so close his unshaven face tickled her chin and kissed her cheek. "But you're a woman now, aren't you Jennifer? You know I was going to choose you as my fourth wife. Now isn't that a privilege?"

"Leave me alone, you creep!" Jennifer shouted. The words became distorted and almost a screech as the man held her throat and forced her head back.

The man was briefly interrupted when Sassy launched herself at the man. But it was to no avail. Abraham just rose Sassy careered across the room and crashed against the dresser.

"You bastard!" she hissed as she staggered to her feet and wiped a hand down her face. It came away sticky with blood.

Jennifer had no time to get away. She was seized and her continuing screams were stifled when the fingers on her throat became so tight she could barely breathe. She understood, though, the seriousness of the situation. The man was openly fondling her beasts now and the free hand reached up the inside of her leg. Her mind froze in fear and utter revulsion but she was unable to move away.

"Yes, young madam, you'll do fine," the man sniggered and Jennifer barely heard his voice muttering to Sassy. "Jennifer is about to become a woman, Sassy." He chuckled. "Depending on how she cooperates decides whether you should become one, too. Don't bother to try to use the phone. It's disconnected."

He chuckled again but in doing so, his hold on Jennifer relaxed ever so slightly. She kicked out, connected with the man's groin and broke free. She hardly realized the hysterical screams were her own as she headed for the kitchen and outside door.

Abraham caught her half way across the kitchen and grabbed her pajama top, ripped it open and threw her petrified to the floor. "Bitch," the man snarled squeezed her exposed breast until the pain was almost unbearable and held her until consciousness almost disappeared before letting her breathe again as he unbuckled his belt.

"No!" Jennifer shrieked when she saw the male organ pushing out the material of the man's trousers but the only response was a sharp slap across the face.

"I like a good fight," he whispered. "You will now cooperate."

A new sound reached her ears. The firm grip holding her slackened and as Jennifer leaped away in she saw a black shape tear across the room from the balcony and land, full force on the would-be rapist. Abraham was a powerful male but his strength was useless against a growling, snapping, slobbering Black Labrador that seized his arm with such a bite, the skin was ruptured and blood poured out onto the carpet.

Abraham lashed out with his free arm but Cinders turned, let go the one damaged arm and seized the opposing wrist. The man staggered, collapsed to the floor with kicks and screams every bit as terrified as Jennifer's own ones were mere seconds before.

"Call it off!" he screamed with his one bloody arm now trying to protect himself. "For God's sake call it off!"

*

Sassy stood by the door with a chalk white face and just stared at the one sided fight.

"Stop, Cinders!" she ordered in a quiet voice. "Jennifer is safe now."

The dog immediately stopped and sat back centimeters from Abraham cringing on the floor. Her eyes looked up at Sassy, across to Jennifer sobbing by a chair and back to the man.

"Guard!" hissed Sassy. She turned to Abraham. "Don't move! If you do, Cinders will rip you throat out as if you're a spring chicken." It was a lie, of course, for she had no idea what the dog might do. She turned to her friend. "My cell phone is under my pillow, Jennifer. Dial 911 and asked for the police."

Jennifer wiped her eyes, nodded and walked around the inanimate man. She reached the bedroom, found the tiny yellow instrument and pressed in three digits.

"Can you help us, please," she said and burst into hysterical tears.

*

The police patrol car was outside the condominium within fifteen minutes and two officers arrived.

"Our dog saved us," was all Sassy could say as the officers walked in to find Abraham lying on the floor where Cinders had first attacked him.

"And yourself, Ma'am?" one officer asked.

"He was after my friend," Sassy replied. "I was just flung out of the way."

The second officer, a woman, turned to Jennifer who still stood weeping by the inner door with her hand holding the torn pajama top together.

"So this man attacked you but was stopped by your dog?" she asked in a quiet voice.

"He was about to..." Jennifer replied and burst into tears again.

"But he never managed to violate you," the officer added in a kind voice.

"No," Jennifer sobbed. "He would have if Cinders wasn't here."

"It was premeditated," Sassy added. "We know him."

"I see," said the first officer. "Can you call your dog aside, Ma'am?"

"Here, Cinders! Good Girl," Sassy called. Again, the Black Labrador instantly obeyed. She stood, walked across and sat beside the girl, seemingly without a care in the world. Even her tail began to wag as Sassy rubbed her head.

"That dog is an uncontrollable monster," Abraham shouted. "It was an unprovoked attack and I demand the vile creature is put down before some innocent child is killed. I was merely visiting my charges to see how they were coping..."

"So one has a blooded face and the other is so terrified she can hardly talk, not to mention a pajama front with the buttons ripped off," the woman officer interrupted in an icy retort. "I am arresting you on the charge of willful assault and issue the usual warning. You have the right..."

Within a moment Abraham was handcuffed and out the door while Sassy walked across to tuck an arm around Jennifer. "Come on," she said. "What say we go and sit down? I'm sure the officers will want a statement from both of us. I'll turn the coffee on."

Jennifer nodded and squatted down. She wrapped her arms around Cinders and just clung on while the tears rolled down her cheeks.

*

Inside the cave, Lorie stared at Erika when they heard a muffled roar above them and several pieces of rock clattered to the ground.

"What is it?" she gasped.

"An explosion," Erika whispered. She glanced around at the frightened children. "Probably the dormitory."

"What now?" Lorie whispered.

"We wait," Erika replied but her face looked worried. "It is no good going back. If we get separated it will just make things worse."

"Okay but I don't like it. What if Parnell and Ralph are lying wounded somewhere. If we don't help..."

"They're professionals," Erika replied. She glanced back up the cave and reached for Lorie's arm. A tiny red flashlight beam was moving towards them and, at the same time, her radio cackled into life.

"Erika," she hissed into the instrument.

Moments later the FBI men appeared with the commune members they had rescued. Geraldine, at the forefront, rushed forward and swept one of the babies into her arms. Other mothers found children and Parnell noticed some of the women gathered seven or eight children of a similar age around them. Nobody was omitted and every child had an adult to relate to.

"Many of the children are orphans," Erika explained to the FBI men a few moments later. "The women you rescued are mainly the younger ones who spent time as caregivers and teachers for the children."

Lorie interrupted. "Not all the younger ones are here, though," she added in a grim voice... "I'd say a little over half. I guess these are the ones who questioned the way the commune was run."

"Okay, thanks," Parnell replied. "We can't go back for any others and have been ordered to make our way to the cave mouth. There we'll wait until dawn. Helicopters are coming to pull us out."

"Like the last days in Saigon," Ralph added in a whisper and grinned at Parnell when the woman stared blankly at him. "That was before your time, I guess," he added. "My Dad told me all about it."

*

CHAPTER FIFTEEN

"The only problem is the weather," Ralph reported to Parnell. It was still an hour before dawn and he'd just returned from making a surveillance of the route out. "There is a thick ground fog and misty rain over the lake."

"That's similar to the radio report I received?" Parnell replied. "We should be safe enough in here as long as we aren't followed."

"I'll removed all the arrows our men put in," Ralph replied and held out a handful of the phosphorescent arrows. "I've already taken the ones behind us and replaced them with the new ones in case we need to retreat..."

"How are they different?" Erika asked.

"The original arrows can be followed by anyone, even children. The ones we're replacing them with only show if lit by an ultraviolet light. An ordinary flashlight won't show a thing." His lips curled up almost into a grin. "The floor is rock hard so won't show footprints except in the damp sections. There we'll try to brush them out as best we can."

"Okay," Erika replied. "The children are organized into small groups with an adult in charge so they should be no trouble."

"Fine," Parnell replied and turned to Ralph. "If you and Erika lead, I'll come up the rear."

He turned as Lorie and Geraldine came up

"We're all packed and ready," Lorie said. "All the children have eaten, been to the toilet and the gear is distributed around. Most of them are in good spirits."

The group that now numbered close to sixty, moved forward in a long line with younger children holding adults' hands and twenty or more flashlights bouncing off the walls. With the two FBI men covering the front and rear and with the labyrinth of twisting tunnels they moved through, the chance of anyone seeing the lights was remote. It was more important for the children to have the security of seeing where to go. Ralph again disappeared ahead but gave Erika a tiny radio receiver so they could keep in touch.

"I'm at the entrance," he radioed back fifty minutes later. "There's a misty rain but the fog seems to be lifting. Take your time. I doubt if we'll be leaving for a while." His voice hesitated. "That climb up using the wire rope could be difficult for the children," he added. "I'll see if I can get something sorted out."

"Right," Erika replied.

She placed the instrument in her pocket and gazed back along the line. Behind her, Lorie smiled and still looked a bundle of energy. The children, though, were weary and some of the women close to exhaustion. Though none complained, it was obvious several were finding the walk difficult after their initial treatment and wounds...

"I think a break for breakfast would be a good idea," Erika said when they arrived at another intersection of tunnels with a wide area the size of a classroom. She called a halt and everyone fanned out and found a place to sit and relieve stiff limbs.

"We are well provided for, aren't we?" Lorie commented as she slipped off her backpack and began to unpack.

"We are," Erika replied.

There were twenty backpacks in all and everyone held three food cartons containing sandwiches, fruit and energy bars wrapped in tinfoil. Plastic canisters of water and several flasks of hot coffee were also available. Other gear included spare clothing of various sizes, first aid kits, toiletry items and other assortments

Once everybody was settled, several mothers took the chance to breast feed tiny infants while others listened to the children and examined their feet. Blisters were plastered with lotion, Band-Aids applied and wet socks replaced with warm dry ones from the reserves. Tired faces glanced around but morale was high and the conversation, light.

*

Dawn approached outside and the fog lifted like a blanket so the lake was clear but the surrounding hills and mountains remained invisible. Ralph received a radio report from Erika and estimated the party was about twenty minutes behind him but this did not include the time it would take to climb the steep section. He tested the wire rope, found it secure and supplemented it with a nylon rope. His idea was that a small seat could be made for smaller children and they could be hauled up while supported by an adult. It wasn't perfect but all he could do with available equipment.

He slipped into an oilskin jacket and made his way up to a ridge behind the cave entrance and surveyed the area. Above was the blanket of white fog, below the lake looking still and dark but of more interest was the commune itself stretched out in the pale morning light. Flames and bellowing smoke poured skywards from one building and people, rows and rows of them were assembled on the waterfront, either on the jetty or along the beach outside the fence.

"Strange," Ralph muttered to himself and brought a powerful pair of field glasses to his eyes.

Several things were unexpected. For one, it was not the children's dormitory ablaze nor, indeed, the chapel, but a large rectangular building behind it. Ralph pulled a map from his pocket and examined the contents. The burning block was labeled, *Administration offices*. The queues of people included both sexes but the women now wore white scarves over their hair and the men had changed into working clothes.

As he continued to watch, a tractor and trailer laden with suitcases chug out the gate and those on the jetty moved aside to give it room. It was driven to the end of the jetty and the faint chug of the motor stopped. Ralph turned and saw a second tractor, also loaded with gear come out the main gate.

The FBI man made a quick count of the people on gathered around. There were eighty or ninety, with probably two-thirds women. Taking into account the children and adults they had rescued, that was close to everyone in the commune.

So the suicide pact had not gone ahead! Whether this was as a result of the children being rescued or the whole pact a hoax from the beginning, Ralph had no way of telling. He did know, of course, the poisoned raspberry drink was in the children's dormitory ready to be administered and the women they'd rescued had been badly treated. Probably what happened was that the women they'd drugged had awoken and warned the leaders the children had gone and, of course the women they had with them, were missing. It was merely a guess but Ralph surmised there were hastily rearranged plans and everyone was now being prepared for evacuation.

He cursed and reached for the radio. "Can you get the helicopters in?" he asked after reporting everything. "The fog has lifted twenty meters or more and visibility below is 20/20."

"We're still fog bound at base," the voice came back. "Will send the task force out. ETR is twenty five minutes."

"Hurry," Ralph retorted. "Something's happening down there and I think it will be soon."

*

No sooner had he stopped talking when a loud rumble sounded up the lake and a massive four=engine flying boat touched down on the main arm of Eagle's Claw Lake. It stopped after an amazingly short run and turned to taxi towards the jetty.

"Oh shit!" the FBI man swore and barked into the radio.

"Describe it," the controller requested.

"Four piston engines with a radar dome and observation windows in the nose. There's a high tail and... oh my God!"

"What?"

"It's Russian. At least it was. There is Cyrillic writing along the fuselage."

"Any registration numbers?"

"The old Soviet CCCP has been painted out but I can make out the digits 8794. It's Russian all right."

While he was speaking, the flying boat slowed and swung around. A powerboat appeared from the far side of the jetty and headed out to circle around near the cockpit of the aircraft. A head appeared out an opened window, hands were waved and two of the plane's engines switched off. Slowly, under the power of the inboard engines the massive machine maneuvered in parallel to the jetty. The remaining engines stopped and crew appeared in two open hatches to throw out ropes. Within minutes, the flying boat was secure and towering above the jetty. A gangplank stretched to shore and three people walked off to be met by several men in business suits.

Ralph focused his fiels glasses on the group. The new arrivals looked very ordinary Europeans, two men and a woman while one of the commune men was Peter Littlejohn.

"What's happening?" the radio crackled.

"The aircraft at the jetty and, by the look of it, everyone is getting ready to board. How long until the task force arrives?"

"Still twenty minutes. Heavy fog at this end is hindering progress."

"Well, you'll be too late."

There was a brief silence before the voice came back. "Civilian radar found no trace of your intruder. It must have come in low from Canada. We're onto the military tracking stations and will confirm their flight path when it is known."

"That won't do any good now," Ralph snapped.

"The air force is sending up interceptors."

"To shoot down a plane load of women?" Ralph retorted. "I think the Canadians need to be contacted."

"Will do. Report in if the craft leaves... Wait, I have info on the registration. The aircraft was sold to a Canadian private owner a year back. The name is..."

The person was unknown to Ralph but the Canadian ownership confirmed what he suspected. The commune members were going to be evacuated to the new commune somewhere unknown in northern Alberta.

He watched as the lines of commune members filed forward and entered the bowls of the flying boat, gear was lifted in through the second hatchway and a third tractor piled high with gear drove out the main gate. At their rate of progress, everyone and everything would be aboard within a few minutes.

*

After spending the night at a small settlement to the east, Kate found the morning weather conditions clear enough for her to fly out just after dawn. The Beaver landed at Spokane's municipal airport twenty minutes later but her original intention to switch to the CL-215 and fly onto Eagle's Claw Lake was thwarted when the local control tower advised that the lake was still fog bound. There was little else she could do, therefore, except go home and wait.

When the aircraft swung in beside the Timber Wolf Air hanger, the first thing she saw were two girls and a dog standing at the edge of the tarmac. "It's Sassy and Jennifer," she said to Reid. "What are they doing here so early in the morning?"

Reid stared out at the frantically pair. "I guess they were anxious because we didn't get home last night," he replied.

Their apprehension turned to concern when the Beaver's engine spun to a stop and they noticed the girls' appearance.

"Oh my God, Sassy, you look terrible! What happened?" Kate exclaimed as she climbed down from the cockpit.

Sassy had cleaned herself up but had a blackened eye and pieces of Band-Aid plastered across the bottom of her chin. Jennifer, in comparison, would have looked quite ordinary, if it wasn't for the tears in her eyes.

"Jennifer came out worse," Sassy explained in a quiet voice. "Abraham broke into the apartment and attacked her."

"He did what!" Reid snarled.

"Cinders saved me," Jennifer sniffed and wiped her eyes. "Oh Reid, Kate. It was terrible. We thought it was so safe at the apartment but he broke in and attacked us both..."

The words tumbled out and between them; the girls related the full story.

"The police were so good," Sassy added. "They took us to the hospital for a check up and then back home. When they left, we tried to clean the blood up but there is still a stain on the carpet. We didn't want to stay alone so took a cab here to wait. Is that okay?"

"Of course," Kate replied. "How terrible. We thought you'd be safe there," She tucked her arms around both girls and also managed to rub Cinders' head. "Come on, we'll go home and see what's happened but don't you worry about any stains. It is far more important that you're both okay."

*

Except for the wet carpet where the girls had tried to remove bloodstains and the unkempt appearance of the girls' bedroom, Kate's apartment looked surprisingly ordinary.

"Do you know how he got in?" Reid asked after he had searched around.

"The police said he must have picked the door lock. We had it locked but never pushed the top bolt across as we thought you might get back late and would need to get in," Jennifer said. "It was stupid of us, wasn't' it?"

"You weren't to know," Reid replied. "Anyway, he sounded so determined, I doubt if that would have stopped him."

"I was so scared," Jennifer added and attempted to smile. "Why was he so awful, Reid?"

"Revenge because of what happened up at Erika's Jeep, I guess," he replied.

"It was more than that," Sassy added. "He had one thought in mind and that was to get Jennifer. He wasn't even interested in me. I was just flung aside. He muttered something about Jennifer being picked as another of his wives."

"And you told the police all this," Kate added.

"Yes," Sassy replied. "They said they'd like to speak to you when you arrived home, Kate but I think it is because this is your apartment."

"Okay," Kate replied. "I'll give them a call. She picked up the phone, pouted in disgusted when she noticed the cut wire and borrowed Sassy's mobile phone. After a few moments she rung off and stared at the others with a strange expression on her face.

"Well!" Reid asked.

"It seems our Abraham is really a Sean McHardy, a wanted terrorist who has been on the run since he escaped from jail in California several years ago. He is known to be particularly violent and has a history of attacking women and girls. The good news is, he'll be sent back to California to continue his prison sentence."

"Oh hell!" Jennifer whispered.

"And I bet Peter and those others are no better," Sassy retorted. "God, I hope Lorie and Erika are okay."

"So do I," Kate whispered. "We all do."

*

"Damn!" Ralph swore.

The last women were aboard the Russian flying boat and the men seemed to have decided to leave one trailer load of supplies on the jetty. Peter glanced at the sky, gave one last look at the commune and burning administration block before he muttered something and followed the few men left on the jetty aboard. There was a cloud of black smoke when the engines burst into life, a crewmember in his distinctive flying jacket rushed along, undid the mooring lines and was hauled aboard just as the craft moved forward.

It taxied away from shore, turned its nose up the lake and moved slowly forward. The engines howled and, like a bloated whale, the flying boat accelerated, waves cut out behind and the nose lifted. Spray shot everywhere and finally the hull lifted like a hydrofoil.

Ralph stared, fascinated. It looked as if the ungainly beast would never be able to lift itself from the water. The howling motors became a crescendo of mayhem and the hull rose higher in the water until it sort of bounced, wings wobbled and the craft disappeared behind the hills beyond the middle arm of the lake. It was not for long, though, for seconds later it appeared above a nearby gap in the hills, turned north and disappeared in the fog bank until the rumble of its motors was replaced by a high shriek from the opposite direction.

The FBI man turned and saw three F15 Eagle fighter jets, throttled in, wingtip-to-wingtip from the valley beyond the commune.

"You're a bit late, little buddies," he retorted and turned to go back into the cave.

*

Erika and Lorie scrambled out the cave mouth, shivered in the cool breeze and glanced around at the view. In the last hour the fog had largely disappeared and the sun peeped through to dry the foliage.

"Look down at the commune," Ralph said.

"Oh my God!" Loire exclaimed as she took everything in.

The administration building was a blackened ruin but the fire was almost out with no other buildings affected. Everywhere were police and military personnel who had fanned out from seven helicopters lined up on a field at the rear of the dormitories.

"The place is empty," Ralph added. "Not one person has been found."

"What about bodies?" Erika asked.

"None," the FBI man added. "Even those women we tussled up are gone. There are signs of a hasty departure everywhere and one other strange thing."

"What's that?' Lorie added.

"The raspberry drink you tipped out in the toilet of the children's dormitory has been replaced."

"What?" Erika snapped. "How?"

"The punch bowl and the tumblers are back, all neatly arranged and the bowl is full of raspberry drink."

"And?" Erika added with a scowl across her forehead,

"Its ordinary raspberry extract mixed with water and the floor beneath has been washed and reeks of disinfectant."

"Oh hell," Lorie gasped.

"All signs of the women's bad treatment have gone, too. There's no blood, rope, ripped clothes or signs of anyone being mistreated. The women's dormitory is immaculate, almost too neat..."

"So they're running scared?" Erika grumbled.

"Oh yes," Ralph added. "All signs of any explosives has gone, too but this is where, in their haste they failed."

"How was that?" Lorie asked.

"They could remove the evidence but tiny residuals of plastic explosive are everywhere. Apparently, every building was wired with a huge concentration beneath the chapel." He grimaced. "I'd say their intention was mass suicide all right and the resulting fires would have been so intense, it would be impossible for experts to count the number of corpses."

"So nobody would realize some of the commune members escaped." Erika gasped.

"Exactly," Ralph replied. "Our worry is that they'll try to do it all again at their new destination. Their flying boat is at present flying between the mountains of British Columbia but is being traced by satellite. As soon as it lands we'll know where it is. The Canadians are on full alert."

"But we're no better off," Lorie whispered.

"Yes we are," Ralph said and smiled at the teenager. "We have all the children here plus the women we rescued. As well, there are another hundred or more who would be dead by now if we hadn't acted. You have plenty to be pleased about, Lorie and you can be proud of your contribution."

Lorie nodded. "I guess you're right," she said and tucked an arm around her big sister. "So what now?"

"The helicopters are going to take everyone back to the commune's farm. A tent village will be erected, as we don't want anyone back in the commune itself until everything is examined. There may be booby traps, poisoned water supply and food or all manner of nasty tricks. It could take days to check everything."

"I'm going the other way," Lorie chuckled and pointed down the other estuary.

In the middle arm of Eagle's Claw Lake, a yellow twin-engine amphibian was gliding in over the water. The words Timber Wolf Air could be seen written along the fuselage and the stylized wolf on the tail almost grinned at them.

"How did they get here?" Ralph gasped. "I wasn't told they were coming."

"Flew in low beneath the fog, I'd say," Lorie laughed. "Your sophisticated equipment isn't that flash after all."

*

CHAPTER SIXTEEN

"Well, Kids," Erika said to all the children sitting at the bottom of the wire rope. "We have a choice. Either we can all go back through the cave to the dormitory or climb up this steep part and get a helicopter ride back."

"What about Peter?" a boy of about ten called out. "He's going to be mighty angry with us."

"He's gone," Geraldine replied in a quiet voice. "Everyone except those of us here now have gone."

"To heaven?" asked a tiny girl.

"No Deanne," Erika said in a quiet voice. "They didn't want to stay here any more so flew away in a big aircraft."

"Like the one you went away in, Lorie?" another little girl asked.

"Much the same, "Lorie said and smiled at the youngster.

"Except for the office that caught on fire, the whole commune is there and we can go home," Erika continued. "Won't that be nice?"

The silence was unmistakable as the children glanced at each other until another child spoke up. "You said all the disciples and sisters have gone?"

"That's correct."

"And we won't get punished?"

"No. You've done nothing wrong," Erika replied. "In fact you've all been very brave."

"Then that's okay," Deanne replied. "We missed morning devotions, you know. God is going to be so angry with us."

Erika glanced at Geraldine. "I don't think so," she said. "He understands."

"But what about the helicopter?" someone called out and the conversation reverted back to Erika's first question. "I want to ride in the helicopter."

"Yes," chorused half the group so the decision about what to do became unanimous.

The climb was achieved with comparative ease. The children proved to be remarkably agile and the only problem came from a couple of the women who swung too close into the wall. However, Ralph and Parnell helped so, within half an hour, everyone was out on the ridge above the canyon just as a massive Sikorsky S-61N helicopter landed. Someone slid open the door on the side and half the children were helped aboard.

When it was full the ungainly craft rose and was immediately replaced by a second one. Everyone squeezed aboard but Lorie was hesitant. "I wanted to go to Kate's amphibian," she said to Ralph who was the last aboard.

"You'll see them," he chuckled. "We've been in radio contact and told them the commune is empty. They're going to taxi around to the jetty."

"Good," Lorie replied and, like almost everyone else aboard, held on nervously as the engine howled and the helicopter rose straight up, swung its tail around and headed back towards the lake.

*

By the time the CL-215 was tied up at the jetty, Lorie and Erika were standing waiting for those aboard to disembark. First there was Cinders who bounded off with tail thumping and jumped up at Lorie who cuddled the dog in her arms. Her smile turned to a frown when she noticed Sassy for the first time.

"Oh hell, Sassy." she gasped. "What happened to you?"

"Nothing really," the girl replied. "You should see what happened to the guy who did it."

Jennifer interrupted. "Cinders attacked Abraham and just about chewed his arm off."

"What?" It was Erika who spoke.

By now Kate and Reid had joined the group and the full story came out. News was exchanged before they all stopped and stared around.

"So you stopped a tragedy?" Kate said in a solemn voice. "Parnell and Ralph filled me in over the radio."

"And by the sound of it, Cinders did too," Lorie replied. She glanced around. "By the way, where's Doug."

" He's working today but did ask about you," Kate replied.

"Oh well," Lorie replied in a disappointed voice. "I thought he might have come, that's all."

Kate glanced knowingly at Reid. In actual fact, Doug hadn't shown any interest in accompanying them although she knew he could have easily had his work hours changed. Life away from the commune was affecting them all in different ways and Doug was beginning to drift away. It was natural enough, she guessed.

She studied the three girls. In many ways, they were sophisticated beyond their years but in others, were as innocent as twelve-year-olds. That was why Jennifer was so devastated about being attacked, even the chatty Sassy was subdued and now it looked as if Lorie was going to be hurt over Doug. Everyone was affected by the recent events and, from what the FBI had told her; there were still many problems to solve.

She caught Lorie's eyes and the girl smiled.

"It doesn't matter, Kate," she said. "I've still got Erika, you and Reid, haven't I?"

"As well as Sassy and myself," Jennifer added in a quiet voice. "I think we'll go through dozens of guys but we'll be friends forever, won't we?"

Lorie glanced at her taller friend, stepped across and tucked an arm around her shoulders "Oh Jennifer," she whispered. "Here you are, violently attacked and I'm worried about Doug. You must think I'm just a hard hearted bitch."

"No," Jennifer replied. "I think you are the bravest friend one could ever have. If you hadn't swum out... but we know about that and now ... God, we're a screwed up lot aren't we?"

"So who's perfect?" Sassy retorted.

"Kate," Reid whispered with a grin across his face and received quite a sharp jab in the ribs from the lady in question.

"That sort of comment will get you everywhere, old fellow," she laughed, gave him a sudden kiss on the lips and tucked her head into his neck. "But come on, let's go and see what has happened to the commune."

*

The commune buildings were cordoned off with only the road through the center giving them access beyond the rear fence. Here, several large tents had been erected; a mobile kitchen flown in and the children were sitting behind long trestles eating. To many of them, it was a day to remember with no morning devotions and school cancelled for the day. Older children appeared apprehensive and many of the women rescued, openly worried about the fate of their partners and friends who had disappeared in the flying boat.

Kate and Reid were about to accept an invitation to have a plate of food when Parnell walked across to them.

"Can we have a quiet word?" he asked.

"Sure," Reid replied and glanced at Kate who shrugged. The pair followed the FBI agent out of the large tent and along to a smaller one. They were introduced to Lieutenant Ian Norton from the local police.

"We have made an interesting discovery," the lieutenant began. "It really concerns Erika Somerville and her sister, Lorie but we thought we'd ask your opinions on whether they are in fit emotional condition to receive the news."

Kate frowned. "What is wrong, Lieutenant?" she asked.

The lieutenant sighed. "Nothing urgent but... Look, it's probably better if we show you."

Kate and Reid followed the lieutenant and two escorting policemen back through the commune to the smoldering ruins of the administration block.

"They blew it up in the hope of destroying all their records," Parnell retorted. "In that way they succeeded but the fire remained above the surface."

"Meaning?" Reid asked.

"There is a cellar," Lieutenant Norton continued. "The place looks like one of those dungeons beneath a European castle."

He led them through a newly cleared track where the blackened ruins of the building had been pushed aside. The remains still smoldered and the stench of burnt wood and chemicals filled the air. The fire had been saturated by high-powered foam and a dozen or more personnel were still dousing outbreaks of flames with water.

In what would have been the center of the building, several police dressed in safety gear were sweeping debris away from an opening. It was a concrete, entranceway, cracked and blackened by the fire but still intact. Inside, a string of electric lights showed winding concrete steps disappearing below.

"Just be careful," the lieutenant warned. "There may we loose material around and everything at this end is covered in soot from the smoke and is still hot."

Kate grimaced and followed the police officers down the spiral staircase that ended in a long corridor. Except for being constructed of modern concrete blocks, the scene in front could easily have been a castle dungeon. There were even windowless cells with iron barred doors, bolts and chains everywhere. At the end was a larger room with a low wooden table in the center and the usual office furnishings around the walls, including six steel filing cabinets. Two police officers were sorting them into boxes that sat on the table.

The lieutenant gave them a cursory nod and strutted through to another set of steps that descended to another lower level. Kate and Reid found themselves in a cave that wound around until Kate had no idea what direction they were heading.

"Almost there," Norton grunted and turned right into another concrete block corridor that ended at an open steel door.

The police officers stood aside and let Kate and Reid through. Lieutenant Norton followed and turned to face the pair. They were in a living area that, except for the lack of windows, could have been a downtown apartment. Carpet covered the floor, opposite was a small kitchen bench and a wooden table with two chairs poked beneath it full the center. There was no television but an old fashioned radio from the nineteen fifties sat in the corner with two armchairs facing it. Along the opposite wall were four shelves jammed with books, paperbacks, novels, hard-covered books of various vintages and a selection of larger colorful travel books.

"Jane Somerville's quarters," Lieutenant Norton explained before anyone could ask. "Our belief is that Erika and Lorie's mother was held here for several months, perhaps even years."

"But she's gone, now?" Kate gasped. She walked through an archway, past a tiny bathroom onto a bedroom comprising of a double bed and closet. Inside several of the commune's female uniforms hung all clean and pressed. A chest of drawers contained women's clothing and toiletries.

"So why didn't she take her clothes with her?" Kate asked.

"Probably the decision to shift her was made at the last moment and she was just forced out," Norton replied.

"And how do you know these rooms were used by Jane Somerville?" Reid added.

Ian smiled and walked across to the books, found an inconspicuous hardback from the top shelf and handed it to Reid.

"Look inside," he grunted.

Reid sat in one of the kitchen chairs and, with Kate looking over his shoulder, opened the book. An envelope was tucked inside the dust cover.

Ian grimaced. "There are two letters inside," he said. The outer one was dated only last week and was directed at anybody who found it. I'd say Jane intended to take it with her and smuggle it to another commune member. The second note is sealed in a smaller envelope. Read the first letter and it'll explain the second.

Kate nodded, opened the envelope, placed the smaller envelope on the table and extracted two sheets of writing paper. It smelt fresh and appeared to have been recently written.

Can you help? began the neat, square shaped printing. "*This is written on the chance that you are also concerned about how the Elf Commune is being run and want to see changes. Can you please give the accompanying letter to Lorie or Erika Somerville, my two daughters? Lorie, as far as I know, is still member of the commune. Failing that, can you hand it to one of our American Indian friends who visit periodically and ask them to post it to the solicitor whose name is on the envelope? I'm afraid I don't know his address but the firm is a well-known one in Spokane and any telephone book should give an address. Don't use the commune mail as all outward letters are censored.*" The sentence was underlined.

"*Thank you if you can help. Regards, Jane Somerville.*

P.S. No, I am not dead. It is a favorite ruse of these so-called elders to feign the deaths of commune members who are a problem to them. No doubt they wouldn't have hesitated to kill me for I hold information they need. J.S.

*

"I know Erika thought her mother might be still alive," Kate said and glanced up at the lieutenant with a grim expression across her brow. "But I doubt if she realized she was here in the commune right beneath everyone's feet."

"What does the main letter say?" Reid asked.

"That's why we sort your advice," Ian Norton said. "You see, we haven't opened it yet. Even in this bizarre situation, the privacy act is quite adamant that personal property cannot be opened unless it is related to the direct court search order. A sealed envelope is deemed the property of the person it is addressed to."

"So this letter would belong to Erika or Lorie first and, failing them, the lawyer," Reid said.

"That's about it," Ian replied. "Would the emotion of seeing this prison and having this letter given to them be too much? If you think it is, we'll forward the letter to the solicitor"

"Erika and Lorie would both cope," Kate whispered. "However, I wouldn't bring them down here. The thought of that poor woman being confined here for months gives me the shudders and I don't even know her. Imagine how Erika and Lorie would react?" She reread the letter before folding and placing it back in the larger envelope. "Would you like me to give them these letters?"

"Those were my thoughts," the lieutenant replied. "I'm pleased you've confirmed my first opinion of the two young women. I just wanted to be sure. My only advice is to wait for a quiet time, perhaps this evening or even after you've taken them home. I'm sure a few hours won't make a lot of difference."

"Will you need to be with us, Lieutenant," Reid asked.

"Not really. Of course the FBI and ourselves are interested in the contents but it is really up to them." He shrugged. "It may be something entirely personal that has no baring on this case."

"But you don't think so?" Kate replied.

"No!" came the blunt reply.

*

It was late afternoon before the FBI declared the children's dormitory safe and available for use. The women who had been rescued all received medical attention, with Reid helping two police nurses examine them. They were all suffering from bruising and were very thin, almost to the point of being undernourished but had no other serious medical problems. All of them wanted to stay at the commune to help the children. So far, except for a few problems caused by the burnt out building, the commune was in excellent condition. The power supply operated and water supply was free of contaminants. Even the food appeared to be untouched but was not used until further tests were made.

At six in the evening, after Kate declared she needed to return to Spokane as the plane was required for a morning run, she was surprised to find, not only Reid but the three girls and Erika all wanted to return to Spokane with her.

"The commune depresses me," Sassy said. "With the disciples and the bossy sisters gone it might become quite good but I'd never want to live here full time again." She screwed her nose up. "I hate the clothes we had to wear."

"What about you, Jennifer?" Kate asked as she sat in the pilot's seat and noticed the teenager beside her.

Jennifer went quiet for a moment before she spoke. "Your apartment was so secure then Abraham broke in," she said quietly. "I thought I'd be scared too return but I'm not." She gazed out the windshield. "It's people who are important, not places. With all of you, I feel..." She turned to face Kate, "Oh I don't know ... part of a family I never had, I guess."

Kate nodded and was quiet for several moments as she concentrated on flying the amphibian out. The CL-215 lifted off the lakes and headed southeast before she realized Jennifer had sat down in the seat behind her. Reid, as was becoming a habit, occupied the co-pilot's seat while Lorie, Sassy and Erika were in the main cabin with Cinders.

"I think we make a pretty good family, you know," she said.

"So I won't have to return to the commune?" Jennifer whispered.

"Of course not," Kate replied. "Not unless you want to. From what I heard, Geraldine and the other woman are going to stay and try to make a go of everything and I'm sure the FBI and police will provide protection until Peter and his cronies are found. But you made your break and everything is organized; your welfare payments, custody, enrollment at school and everything else will just continue as it was."

"Thanks," the girl replied and smiled. "I'll go and tell the others."

She stood and slipped away through the small door connected to the main cabin.

"Deep waters," Reid commented.

"Yes," Kate replied. "She was probably the hardest one to really get to know but is one great kid."

"They all are," Reid replied and gazed, deep in thought, out at the mountain peaks. "The Russian aircraft must have landed somewhere by now." He sighed. "It'll be good to get home. I'm feeling quite exhausted yet I only have to relax while you do all the hard work."

*

CHAPTER SEVENTEEN

The woman awoke from a deep sleep and realized straight away that something was wrong. For one, the light was on in the living area and her body clock told her it was the early hours of the morning. She glanced at her small bedside clock and saw the tiny phosphorescent hands point to three thirty-five. Why would any of the commune members visit at this time?

She sat up, turned on her bedside light and stared at the door.

"Okay, who is it?" she called.

Two women appeared, both known to her and both grim and determined.

"You're going on a trip, Jane Somerville," the first said and turned to her companion. "Grab her arm, Sister Carmel."

"Like hell you will!" Jane cried, threw the top blanket at the women and dived off the end of the bed. Though confined to her prison for months, she had made a point of keeping fit on an exercise machine she'd been allowed to have and was a match for the women.

She was out through the archway in a second before she thought about where to go. The door was shut and there was only the cave outside, anyway. She turned and glowered as Carmel and her cohort encircled her.

"So you'd rather stay here to starve to death," the leader hissed. "Come now, Jane. Use a bit of common sense."

"You are not injecting me!" Jane retorted.

"Oh, but we are," Carmel hissed and grabbed her.

The fight was brief but violent with Jane kicking hitting, scratching and punching. If there was one opponent, she could very well have succeeded but with two, the odds were impossible. Moments later she found herself in a wrestling hold on the floor while Carmel smiled grimly and brought a hypodermic needle into sight.

"In the arm, Mother Francis?" she asked the panting woman still trying to control the squirming Jane.

"Of course and hurry. We've got problems upstairs, you know." Francis grumbled.

Jane stared at the pair. They were two of the commune's most fanatic and sadistic females, worse than Peter, Abraham or Luke. With the men there was always a chance of a reasonable conversation but this pair... She decided to change tactics, stopped struggling and let herself go limp.

"That's better," Francis hissed and tugged up Jane's nightgown sleeve.

However, just as Carmel moved the needle up to the victim's forearm, she lashed out. There was a sharp prick in her arm but she had the pleasure of seeing the needle snap and clear liquid drip onto the floor.

"We should just leave you to the rats. If Peter wasn't so..." Her voice became a mutter and Jane shook her head. Everything was spinning. Oh hell, the drug must have entered her blood stream. The contorted face of the women grinned at her and the wrestle hold was relaxed. Now was her chance!

Jane tried to lash out but her limbs did not react, the room became like liquid with the archway pulsing. She tried to mutter but even her tongue felt numb and the world went white.

*

She woke with a terrible headache, vomit in her throat, no idea where she was nor how much time had gone by. She swallowed and opened her eyes. It was dark, the air smelt dank but she was alone. A thin line appeared in the blackness, a rectangle of feeble light. It was the outline of a door!

Jane swallowed the terrible bitter taste in her throat and shook her head. It cleared a little and senses revealed other items. She was dressed in the commune blouse and skirt but also had her jacket on. As well, she was wearing heavy shoes and socks. This was unusual after months of just having only slippers to wear.

She stretched her arms out and touched walls, three of them all within an arm's reach with the door in front. It must be a closet or cupboard of some sort, perhaps the one in her room. But, no, it was a smaller than where her clothes hung. She realized her legs were cramped so staggered to her feet and reached up. Yes, the ceiling was also within an arm's reach.

God, she felt terrible. Blotches of purple competed with the blackness of her vision and she felt so sleepy everything was probably a dream.

Something, however, nudged Jane's mind. She remembered the nocturnal visit, the brief fight and the needle. Yes, the needle dripping liquid onto the floor, the prick in the arm... Perhaps only some of the drug entered her system and if she could stay awake now... Yes, she must stay away. It was essential to stay awake. But she couldn't!

When Jane awoke again, she felt a little better. Her throat was parched and the headache a dull throb but she immediately remembered where she was ...or had been. It smelt the same. She felt out with her hands. Yes, she was still in the closet.

This time, though, she was on full alert. She stood and spent several moments feeling the door. Hinges were on the right but there was no handle. It felt like wood, rough grain wood and not the solid texture of the fittings back in her rooms. In fact, it felt quite fragile.

Other memories came back. The women were quite agitated and Francis had mentioned something about trouble upstairs. Now, if she was unconscious and they were panicking about something, couldn't they have just heaved her in the nearest closet?

Jane grimaced, leaned against the back wall of the closet and kicked the door with all her might. There was a creak of timber but nothing happened. The sound was encouraging, though. It was a sort of echo rather than the dull thud of something solid.

Jane lashed out again, and again... a third time, a fourth until her leg ached and lungs heaved in the effort.

"Come on!" she panted and kicked once more, half way up the left side opposite where an outside latch would probably be place.

There was a twang of metal and her foot moved forward at such a speed it just kept going!. She'd succeeded! The door was open and bright light filled her prison.

*

Jane poked her head out and searched around. Expectations of instant discovery did not eventuate. Across the small room was a window with sunlight coming in. Sunlight! She had almost forgotten how wonderful it appeared.

She searched what appeared to be the interior of a storage shed but it was empty. Only a pile of dust and wood shavings were scattered across the floor. She noticed, though, that the window was clean and free of spider webs. The shed had been used recently.

With heart fluttering she slipped across to the window and peeped out. There were fir trees only a few meters away, a small grass area and the trees, nothing else. Jane turned, saw a closed door and groaned in disappointment. It was shut and probably locked; the window was minuscule so she was probably still imprisoned.

Expecting the worse she turned the old brass handle and pushed the door. It opened without even a squeak of the hinges.

She could go. She was above ground and free!

*

Jane realized if anybody saw her, they would be enemy and also the chances of overpowering or avoiding them was infinitesimal. Thought of survival over a longer term of time did not enter the equation.

She absorbed the outdoor smells like an addict and relished the aroma of the trees, moisture in the air, grass, flowers, damp earth and wood smoke. Life, itself, had returned in those few glorious seconds as she walked outside onto a small gravel path. The sun was high in a blue sky so she estimated it to be the afternoon. She walked to the edge of the building and her thrill turned to instant fear.

Shouts and voices were coming from beyond the shed. She dropped to her knees and peeped around the corner. In front, was a small beach, deep blue water and, less than a hundred meters away, an amphibian with its propellers still and hull tied to a long jetty unfamiliar to her. Men and women stood around tractors loaded with suitcases and other equipment near an opened door of the aircraft. While she watched, a man climbed aboard the tractor and backed it off the jetty, swung around and headed away out of sight.

Jane shrank back and headed in the opposite direction and saw a wire fence. This made her a little more optimistic as it was obvious she was outside on the beachfront of the lake. The shed she'd come out of was the size of a one-car garage so she was soon at the other end. Again, she took the precaution of dropping to her knees before leaning forward to look around.

"Oh hell!" Her gasp was audible. Two women in the commune uniform were walking up the path straight towards her.

Jane almost panicked. She stepped back and tried to decide where to go. In one frantic move she was on her knees and pushing through the boughs of the nearby firs that reached almost to the ground. The tang of needles hit her nostrils as she crawled forward and found a steep bank ahead. She grabbed a branch and pulled herself up to the next tree trunk. The trouble was it was too open. If the women heard her and followed through the initial low boughs, they'd see her for certain.

Jane grabbed a tree root higher up the bank, hauled herself up and just kept going.

In her mind, the tormenters were right behind. She was free and intended to stay that way. Adrenaline flowed and with a superhuman effort she pulled herself up to another fir and another. Her feet slipped, knees became grazed and the rough stones embedded in the dry needles. Every so often, a small root or branch would come away in her hands and once she slipped back on her knees for several meters but she continued on until utter exhaustion made her halt.

She stopped, heaving in exertion and took stock. Her hands, an elbow and two knees were grazed and bleeding and perspiration poured off her face. Her back was wringing wet and a sharp pain cut across her rib cage. As well, her heart was thumping rapidly and she found it difficult to catch a breath.

She grasped a bough, sat down on the uphill side of a fir and forced herself to breathe in a slow rhythm. In this way she managed to slow her racing heart, the stitch appeared less painful and rational thoughts returned.

Now her internal noises had subsided she listened for other sounds. There were no voices, no footsteps or branches being pushed aside. It appeared she had not been seen or followed. But for how long? The pair would have discovered her disappearance by now and the logical place for her to be would be in the trees. A search party could easily surround her and everything would be lost.

She decided to keep going uphill away from the living hell of the commune, if it was the commune! She stood and, at a more leisurely pace, continued climbing for almost an hour, she guessed. She never had a watch; the sun was out of sight so there was no way to tell the time. She was hot from the physical effort, her lungs began to gasp again and leg muscles ached. A gap appeared in the trees ahead and a small patch of sky came into view. She was almost at the summit or a ridge. With a little luck she would see the commune or lake and be able to take her bearings.

With this new motivation, she pulled herself up onto another protruding root and made her way forward. She walked out of the trees onto a small grass area. It wasn't the summit or even a ridge but an overgrown slip. In other ways, though, it was exactly what she wanted for far below she could see the lake stretching in both directions. The section in view, though, looked different. It was long and narrow, really not much wider than a river. Across the water, more fir forests rose above a tiny shingle beach and further back still, snow covered mountains hugged the skyline.

She just stared. "Where am I?" Nothing looked familiar.

Jane realized she was hungry, in fact so hungry her empty stomach rumbled and added its complaint to the others her body was protesting about. She sat down in that tiny clearing and gathered her thoughts.

"Think, girl," she muttered to herself.

What had happened? She remembered being attacked by Francis and Carmel, the needle being thrust aside and the room spinning but now more visions were returning. She was being dressed; no she dressed herself and was provided with the new walking shoes. They felt so heavy on her feet after all this time. Afterwards, she was led out through the cave and upstairs. They were in the administration building and it was still dark outside. They went outside and everything was fire and fluttering lights!

Jane stared at her arm and saw a long scorch mark. She felt a tender and sore area on her cheek. The building they'd left had been aflame. She remembered the searing heat and the women screaming at her to run.

She frowned for the next memory was different. There were people everywhere, waiting in front of a gigantic aircraft with four engines roaring. It was a military type machine with a glass nose and two wide hatches open along the side.

She remembered feeling violently ill but there were no more memories. The next memory was the most recent one of waking up in the closet she'd escaped from.

"Oh hell," Jane muttered.

She wasn't at Eagle's Claw Lake at all but somewhere different. Probably, Francis had given her a second needle to knock her out. She could have been asleep for hours or even days. There was no way of telling. Rumors of a new Elf Commune in Canada had even reached her in the prison. Some of the women who visited with her meals talked too much, not that she minded. The company for a few minutes helped to relieve the boredom of her existence.

So what choices were there? Basically, she could stay in the fir forest and die of starvation or return. If they were at this new camp, the reason for her imprisonment didn't matter any longer. She'd be reprimanded and possibly beaten but still be alive. Erika and Lorie could be at this new camp, too. Jane smiled for the first time. What a surprise there would be when they found she was alive.

With those thoughts in mind, she studied the lake below. The sun was now shining down the lake so she must have come southwest from the camp. If she went straight down and headed away from the sun, the camp would not be far away. She would swallow her pride, walk in and surrender to the commune members.

"Okay, girl," she muttered to herself, pulled the zip of her jacket up and headed down through the trees.

*

"I'm sorry, Lorie. I didn't mean to end up this way," Doug said in a quiet voice. "We've been good friends and I hope we can remain that way. It's just that Jessica is closer to my age and..."

"Just go!" Lorie screamed. "Take your bloody clothes and go. That's what you want to do, isn't it?"

Doug shrugged and glanced up at Erika for support.

She, though, was uncompromising. "Now you have a new girlfriend, Doug, it may be difficult if you continue to stay with us," she said in a neutral voice.

Doug pouted. "She's not a girlfriend, I mean, not a steady one. It's just a girl I met at the market and we went out to a bar and..."

"Yeah, and I'm too bloody young to go into those places," Lorie replied. "I can't help it if I'm only sixteen. Back at the commune I would have been considered a woman and you wouldn't have even got a look in, Doug but now I'm not good enough for you." She glanced at him for a second, burst into tears and ran from the kitchen.

"I'll pay you for my share of the expenses, Erika," Doug said and brought two bags, already packed, from his room.

Erika nodded. "That's okay, Doug," she said. "Remember, we still have a lot in common and you're welcome back any time."

"I know," the youth replied. He gave Erika a slight hug and kiss on the cheek. "Anyhow," he added in almost a confessional whisper. "I'm closer to your age than Lorie's, aren't I?"

Erika stared at him. "What do you mean?" she replied.

"Nothing," Doug replied but couldn't look her in the eye. "Let's just say if I'd stayed here in your home, things would have got complicated."

Erika bit on her bottom lip. "Just go," she said. "You've hurt Lorie and I am not going be contribute any more to her distress."

"Right," Doug replied.

He gathered the bags up and disappeared out the door. Erika walked to the veranda and watched as he walked out to the sidewalk and climbed into a tiny blue Volkswagen. She saw the glimpse of a woman at the wheel; Doug waved and drove away out of their lives.

"So what now?" Lorie asked from the door.

"It's as Jennifer said. Boys will come and go but we have our friends forever but we're more than just friends, Little Sister, we're family." She tucked her arms around Lorie and held her a moment. "But, come on. Kate said we had to be over in her apartment by eight. It's almost that now."

Lorie nodded. "It's hard to imagine I knew nothing except life at the commune," she said. "There's so much to learn."

"And you're doing well," Erika replied. "Oh yes, I've got you a little something. It's in the bedroom."

Lorie frowned with curiosity and went though to the other room. There was a squeal of delight and she came running back with a new pair of top brand sneakers in her hand.

"Erika!" she laughed. "These cost a fortune. How did you know I wanted them?" She sat down, threw her old shoes off, pulled the sneakers on, did the laces up and almost waltzed around the room. "You got the size right, too," she chuckled.

*

That evening back at Kate's apartment, even Cinders seemed to notice the importance of the moment and lay down on the mat with a head on her front legs but large brown eyes were taking in everyone's body language.

"It's about your mother," Kate began. "We think she is still alive and is with the other commune members up in Canada..."

"I see," Erika replied in a hushed voice while Lorie just sat with a concentrated frown across her brow. "You have more, don't you Kate?"

"Yes," Kate replied. "She was being kept a prisoner in a cave beneath the burnt out administration block. The room where she was held was found but by then she'd gone."

"So how do you know it was Mom?" Lorie snapped.

"The FBI found a letter addressed to you two."

"What does it say?" Erika gasped.

Kate glanced around the room. As well as the two sisters, Sassy and Jennifer also sat with bewildered expressions as Reid brought out the letter and handed it to Erika. "There was a covering letter to your lawyer but it really only asks the firm to try to trace you both. The main letter is sealed and hasn't been opened."

"Not even by the FBI?" Lorie asked.

"No," Kate continued. "We were asked to give it to you. Would you like us to leave you to read it in private?"

Erika took the letter and glanced at Lorie who was biting her bottom lip in nervousness. "What do you want to do, Lorie?" she asked.

"Open it," Lorie replied. "I want Kate, Reid, Sassy and Jennifer to hear everything. What affects us is important to them too." She watched as Erika slit the envelope open and took out the pages of handwritten notebook paper."

"It's Mom's writing," Erika whispered. "I recognize her style."

She began to read while Lorie watched over her shoulder.

"Oh my God," Erika exclaimed as she reached the end of the first page and passed it to Lorie who, in turn, placed it on the table for everyone to see.

"She was there all the time," Erika continued. "Apparently Peter wanted her to sign the rights of the commune over to him but she refused to do it. It was, and those were her own words, a stalemate..." She pointed to the third paragraph of the sheet on the table.

"I don't understand," Lorie gasped as she read the page through to herself. "What are these rights she's talking about?"

"Here it is," Erika said in a hushed voice. "I'll read it out..."

The truth is, old Matthew who died a few years ago before Peter became the commune's leader was your grandfather who started the original commune back on 1974. I was eleven at the time and remember how it all began. Mom had died and Dad's idea was to have a Kibbutz type commune and invite young mothers, homeless people and others to join. It wasn't even a religious based commune. That only came later but I'll tell you the full story when we meet again. Erika and Lorie, if you are reading this I'm sure we will meet again. I cannot be held forever and, fortunately Peter and his cohorts need me alive...

"The bastards," Lorie whispered. "How dare they keep Mom a prisoner and tell us she'd died."

Erika continued to read from the letter. *Dad was an astute businessman. He was very keen on community property and the ideals of everyone sharing their material processions but he was also a realist and kept many of his personal finances separate from that of the commune, hence the house in Spokane, I hope by now has been transferred to your names. If not...*" Erika read ahead silently and glanced up. "She just included the lawyer's a name here..."

"Go on," Lorie snapped impatiently. "What did our grandfather do?"

Erika turned to the third page and read it silently before glancing up. "He owned the whole farm and commune property that he had in a trust for all ELF members to use and share but there was a time limit. It was a loan rather than outright gift."

"Interesting," Reid breathed.

Erika glanced around at the attentive group before switching her eyes back to the document. "The original contract expired last year and reverted to become our family's personal property. Unless, Mom agreed to extend the loan, which she obviously didn't do, the original contract expired and the commune's use of the buildings and farm also ended."

"Okay, so what?" Lorie asked

"The whole commune belongs to Mom and us, one third each," Erika whispered. "If Mom never extended the loan the commune had until mid year to move out."

"And that's about now," Reid grunted.

"Anything else?" Kate asked.

"Not really," Erika said. "Mom did not know what was happening and could only guess about any outcome and asked us to speak to the lawyer she addressed the other letter to." Her hand shook as she read the last bit. "Poor Mom," she sniffed. "This last paragraph is quite heart rendering. I don't think she really thought she would get out."

If you get this letter too late and Peter and the others succeed in getting the title for the commune, please forgive me, Sweethearts. I've tried so hard to protect what is yours. I hope you have the house to live in and have a wonderful life. I guess Lorie is not the little girl any longer and you, Erika are a woman. If you haven't already, please leave the commune. Evil people who are using the façade of a religious cult for their own have poisoned it. I love you both dearly, and beg your forgiveness for having failed you...Your loving Mom, Always. Jane Somerville.

Erika sighed and placed the last page on the table. "It was dated only last month," she whispered.

"Where is she?" Lorie shouted. "We have this letter but where is she?"

"Probably with the rest of the commune up in Canada," Reid said.

"Or they killed her!" Lorie cried. Her eyes stared around and lower lip quivered beneath her pale face,

"No, I don't think so," Reid replied. "If they were going to do that, they'd have done it months ago. Your mother knows even more about them than she is saying here, something that protects her from them."

"Like what?" Erika also looked apprehensive.

"I don't know," Reid replied, "but whatever it is..."

He stopped when the telephone rang and everyone swung around as Kate went across and answered it. She talked for a moment before thanking the caller and turning to the others.

"That Russian plane used by the commune has been traced by satellite and landed somewhere in northeastern Alberta."

"Somewhere?" Erika queried.

"Well it seems the destination was not near Fort McMurray after all. The aircraft flew east of the reconnaissance area the satellite was covering.

They have to either wait for the satellite to do another orbit or switch to one of those long-range stationary satellites but these don't give such a high intensive image.

"But haven't they picked up other contacts?" Reid asked. "I mean radio, phone or email messages."

"That's it," Kate answered. "Since they've flown out of the satellite's range, there's been no news what-so-ever. It seems that they are purposely trying to avoid contact with the outside world. The only thing they know is that the aircraft is not now flying. It must have landed on a remote lake somewhere." She gave a slight smile. "We're reassured that as soon as it takes to the air again there will be an immediate trace. Earth bound military early warning systems as well as tracking satellites are all alerted to keep a surveillance of the area. It's only a matter of time."

"But what about Mom?" howled Lorie and tears, that had just been beneath the surface for the previous half hour, burst from her eyes and slid down her cheeks. "She mightn't have any time. We have to go and find her!"

*

CHAPTER EIGHTEEN

Though it was just after five in the morning and the sun was already climbing the sky east of Dawson Creek, a small city in British Columbia almost nine hundred kilometers north of Spokane. The three Canadair CL-215 amphibian aircraft that flew in a loose formation over the mountains and endless forests all had bright orange tails but two carried the words Canadian Armed Forces in two languages and maple leaf ringlets on their fuselages. The third, flying slightly above and behind the military craft supported the now familiar timber wolf on its tail.

"You're lucky we're north of the border otherwise you wouldn't be here," Kate said to the three teenage girls crowded behind the pilot's seat.

"Why?" asked Sassy. She flushed a little when the co-pilot, Andy Hadfield, caught her eye.

"Well, the FBI would have used their own aircraft and not chartered us to fly them to the commune," Kate explained. "These are great aircraft but cost a mint to run. We could never have afforded to fly up here ourselves."

"And it's lucky we have a charter license to fly to Canadian destinations," Andy added. "I have a funny feeling the food and other supplies we have aboard will be appreciated by the commune."

There were three other passengers aboard. Reid and Erika sat in the main cabin chatting with Ralph Yates, the FBI agent sent by Parnell Rodriguez to accompany them. In only three days this small force had been organized. Satellite records had traced back Peter Littlejohn's flight in the SH-5 flying boat to an entirely different lake from that where the commune's northern outpost had been started. Darkwater Lake, a mere dot on the map east of Dawson Creek on the Alberta side of the provincial border was one of hundreds that covered this vast remote interior. A land of snow and ice in winter, during the brief summer season the waters melted and turned to swamps, lakes and rivers festooned with swarms of insects. It was a hostile land, largely without roads, that stretched north to the arctic in the world's second largest wilderness. The large-scale map of the area showed this lake as being half the size of Eagle's Claw Lake and completely surrounded by dense fir forests. Nothing on the map indicated any cleared land or buildings. However, an enhanced satellite photograph taken only hours before showed a small clearing in the northern corner with two buildings and a jetty tucked in between the trees.

The three aircraft droned northeast for almost an hour before Kate's radio crackled into life and a male voice informed her they'd be reaching their destination in ten minutes. In their agreed plan, their CL 215 would land after the military craft and stay away from shore until an all clear was given. No radio contact had been made with the commune members and it was only the satellite photographs that proved anyone was even there. Twenty or more minute dots on the image had been enhanced to show a group of people assembled in front of a rectangular building.

It was a stressful time and Lorie, in particular, was nervous with the thought that her mother could be below and she'd see her face to face.

"Will Mom recognize me?" she whispered to Erika. "I was a mere kid when I last remember seeing her. I'd have only been about twelve but I remember her as if it was yesterday."

Erika smiled. "I'm sure she will," she replied. "You're a young woman now, Lorie but your face is the same, not as chubby maybe..."

"I was a bit of a pudgy, wasn't I?" Lorie added. She stared out the porthole at the endless forests as their aircraft lost altitude. "God, what a desolate area. It's as if the world is just trees and rivers that just go on forever. I'd hate to crash here. Imagine what it would be like in winter?"

Erika nodded and fought to contain her own nervous anticipation at what would happen in the next hour. She reached out, squeezed her sister's hand and smiled. "Everything will be fine," she whispered. "I'm sure it will be."

*

Jane stopped and stared across the narrow lake at the opposite fir trees. Something was wrong! She had been following the shoreline for hours but had found nothing. There was no commune, cleared space or any signs of another living sole. Ahead, the tiny beach she had been walking along came to a sudden halt. Firs ahead grew right down to the lake, so close, their lower limbs hung over the water. She glanced glumly around and found a small clump of grass to sit on. Even though, she'd tried to keep fit in her prison, her limbs were stiff and sore, the summer sun baked her pale skin and she could, even now, feel the backs of her legs and neck were raw from sunburn. Small gnats hovered everywhere and her stomach was so empty she felt nauseated.

"Oh hell!" she muttered and glanced back at her footprints in the sand. It was obvious she had come the wrong way, or had she? The theory she originally had was wrong, that was for sure, so she tried to think of a rational explanation. Just going back might not help. Perhaps she had come down a different hillside and this was a completely different lake.

"Choices, Jane," she muttered to herself, a habit she had formed after her years of confinement. "I can go back but it'll probably be dark before I reach the position where I came to the lake. "

She smiled just a fraction. The precaution she'd taken of tying a strip of material on a log might prove to be a lifesaver after all. She stretched her legs out and gently massaged her calf muscles and rejected the idea of climbing the hill behind her. There was no guarantee she would reach a clearing and the possibility of being lost in endless trees sent shivers up her back.

God she was hungry! Also, now she'd stopped moving it was becoming cool, almost cold. Her clothes coped at the moment but when the shadows turned to darkness in a couple of hours she could be in trouble.

She stood and walked as far as she could out to a tiny rocky point and studied the shore ahead. Beyond this steep section was another narrow beach. The thought of going back was depressing so she decided to continue on. If nothing happened she would have to find shelter, spend the night in the forest and trace her steps back. Once the decision was made she felt a little better. At least there was water to drink. She cupped a little in her hands, drank the crisp liquid and headed into the trees.

The climb wasn't difficult and, by staying on the upside of the tree trunks, she made slow progress until a beach again appeared below. She almost slid down and heaved in relief when she was back on level ground. However, there was now another obstacle. A stream was tumbling into the lake and would have to be crossed. It looked wide and shallow and her shoes were already damp so she plunged forward. Freezing water gripped her legs almost as high as her knees and the stones beneath were slippery. However, she forced herself to be calm and careful.

My God, she'd dreamed of being free and now she was. Free but utterly alone in the middle of a stream that ran into a lake that could be a million kilometers from civilization. She stepped forward, noted that there was quite a strong current, and wriggled her foot to make it secure before moving her other leg forward. In this way, she made her way methodically to the bank and another strip of coarse sand along the lake.

After about fifty meters she walked around a ninety-degree bend and gasped. The lake was wider here and looked familiar. Perhaps she had walked right around and the commune was ahead. With this renewed hope, she stepped forward and ignored her squelching shoes.

With no watch, it was impossible to tell how long she walked along the lonely shore. The lake became wider still and the beach changed direction towards the setting sun. When she moved out of the shade the sunlight made her blink but the higher temperature was welcome. Her body, though, began to protest again, with back pains and sore shoulders adding to the stiff leg muscles.

She plodded on.

Time slipped by and the shadows returned as the sun sank below the distant mountains. The mountains! Jane gasped, wiped a grubby hand across her brow and stared at their silhouette. They looked familiar, too. She sighed. No they weren't! The jagged sections were not as she remembered the mountains north of the commune at Eagle's Claw Lake.

Oh damn! The beach ran out. There was another headland to cross. Jane sighed and headed up into the trees. But this was different. There was a trail to follow, grass had been flattened and, oh my God, footprints!

The relieved woman quickened her pace and followed a steep incline. The sky, now a pale blue was ahead. After a steep climb that left her gasping for breath she found herself on a tiny ridge with views in both directions. Behind was the beach she'd walked along but it was the view ahead that excited her.

Below her, sitting on the edge of the lake was a cabin. A small wooden jetty stretched out over the water behind it several pieces of junk and litter lay scattered around. The place looked as if it was in use but no people or animals could be heard or seen.

"Hello!" Jane screamed with unhidden relief in her voice. "Is anyone there?"

She broke into a stumbling run down the wide path that led to a wooden walkway between the jetty and the front of the building.

*

When it appeared, Darkwater Lake looked similar to but smaller than Eagle's Claw Lake with a crescent shaped strip of water surrounded by fir forest stretching away in every direction.

When asked by the pilot of the leading armed forces plane, Kate brought her CL-215 down well back from the other craft and taxied along until they were close to a strip of shingle in front of the dense forest.

"We have to wait here until the military do their thing," she explained when Lorie asked why they weren't going straight to the commune. "They don't want civilians getting in the way." She smiled at the girls who were again crowded into the cockpit. "You can help Reid take a mooring line and tie it on something ashore. He's probably got the rubber dinghy launched by now."

"Okay," Sassy replied and grabbed Lorie's arm. "Come on," she said, "Mooching in here won't help."

Her voice suddenly became loud as Kate killed engines and the roar reduced to a faint throb of the propellers slowing down. Seconds later a smaller high-pitched engine kicked into life through the opened cockpit window.

"Who's coming?" a voice yelled and the girls saw a bright yellow dinghy idling beside the forward hatch. Reid sat with a cloud of white exhaust fumes from the outboard motor surrounding him.

The girls grinned at each other, all shouted, "Wait for me!" in unison and evacuated the cockpit in a burst of enthusiasm.

"Where do they get their energy from?" Andy chuckled as he switched off some of the instruments and removed his headphones. "One minute they look completely exhausted and the next they're ready to go and save the world."

Kate grinned. "Yes," she said. "I think they have years of unused energy bottled up inside them wanting to get out. I admit I have trouble trying to keep up at times."

The two pilots watched as Reid's dinghy, now loaded with four passengers, circled around to the bow of the amphibian. He tied a rope to a hook and headed to shore. The girls, and not caring that water splashed everywhere, jumped ashore and grabbed their end of the rope.

A few moments later, the CL-215 was floating so close in; one wing was over the shingle beach.

"What a bunch of nerds," Jennifer commented as Erika, followed by the other women, stepped daintily ashore without even getting her feet wet. Andy and Ralph remained aboard to monitor any incoming radio messages.

*

It was now a time to explore their small landing area. They had landed on the western shore so the morning sun bathed them in sunlight. The temperature was still cool, though, and the lake water freezing.

Ancient firs, untrimmed and matted together towered above them, looking impregnable and unfriendly.

"I see how this lake got its name," Kate muttered. "That water on the opposite shore looks almost black."

"Yes," Reid replied. "It's pretty deep, I'd say. Even here it goes straight down."

"Desolate," Kate shivered. "I can't say I like it very much. At least Eagle's Claw Lake has personality. This is like the end of the world, all dark colors and so quiet. And this is summer. Imagine the place in winter."

"Yeah," Reid replied. "It would be thirty below." He slapped at insects circling around and tucked an arm around Kate's shoulders. "I can't see a commune even surviving the winter here, let alone being able to become self sufficient. I doubt if much can grow. The growing season would only be a few weeks, if that."

"Perhaps that was the idea," Kate whispered. She stared up the beach and saw Erika and the girls were out of earshot.

"What do you mean?" Reid replied.

"Well, there was their foiled mass suicide. Now, if the commune members were just left here and never survived the winter, wouldn't Canadian authorities just put it down to an unfortunate accident of foolish outsiders trying to handle the sever conditions?"

"I see what you mean," Reid replied. "Twenty years back without the sophisticated satellite tracking they'd have never been found. Years could have gone by before anybody even found any remains."

They watched as the others returned from a brief exploration of the shore.

"There's no way out," Erika commented. "The beach just fizzles out and then there's just trees. I guess we could walk through them, if necessary, but I wouldn't like to do it."

*

At the other end of the lake, the two dozen troops in full camouflaged fatigues were finding the thick forest a real hindrance. Low boughs caught on their uniforms while backpacks and rifles had to be held close as the men and two women circled around the rear of the commune buildings. They were the advance party whose orders were to surround the commune.

The lieutenant in charge grunted as another branch swung across and struck his arm. "If they wanted a prison, they came to the right place," he retorted to the sergeant beside him. "It's taken us half an hour to go less than a hundred meters."

"But we've made it, Sir," came the reply. "There's a clearing ahead."

"Right. We'll fan out then. Remember, nobody is to move out of the trees until the signal, then we all go together."

Within ten minutes the boundaries were sealed and a brief radio message informed them the boats were waiting beside the two CL-215s for an all clear.

Their caution, though, was unnecessary as commune members were gathered on the jetty. No weapons were evident and the men in the group were conspicuous by their small numbers as they stood in a line behind the women dressed, as usual, in red tartan skirts and white blouses. Expressions on everyone's faces were of relief rather than fear and even, when the troops sprung out from the trees with rifles ready, the commune members merely waited.

"I am Lieutenant Norman Shelton of the Canadian Armed Forces," the officer snapped. "If any of you have arms they are to be placed on the ground. Who is in charge here?"

A woman in her forties glanced at her companions and stepped forward. "You're too late, Lieutenant Shelton. The leaders have gone. We have no weapons and no wish to fight you."

Shelton frowned and looked almost surprised. "If this is a trick, Madam and you are hiding your leaders..." he warned.

"I am the leader, I guess" the woman replied. "My name is Annette Bulmer," She gave almost a shy smile.

"Where are the others?" Shelton asked. "We have a list of people we wish to interview."

"You're too late," a second woman answered. "They abandoned us, Lieutenant Shelton. We have no communications equipment and only enough food for a month. Everything else has gone."

"We were left to perish here," Annette continued. "I don't know how you found us but, by the grace of God, you are the answer to our prayers."

Shelton frowned and turned to his sergeant. "Send a detail to search the buildings," he ordered. "Remain on full alert. The so-called leaders here are known criminals and highly dangerous."

"Yes, Sir," came the crisp reply. The sergeant gave a brief wave to the encircled troops and half moved cautiously towards the two buildings while the others stood on full alert covering them. Unseen, another ten troops were still hidden in the trees and ready for any unexpected counter moves.

It took thirty minutes before the sergeant reported the buildings were empty and secure. There was no evidence of explosives or booby traps.

Shelton nodded. If his sergeant said the buildings were clear they would be. These were crack anti-terrorist troops used to operating in inner city high-rise buildings and left nothing to chance.

"Give the all clear, Sergeant," he ordered and turned to Annette. "We have brought supplies for you Ma'am; food, clothing and other materials. Tell your people they are free to carry on with whatever they were doing and we apologize for any inconvenience we may have caused."

Annette merely nodded. "Your precautions were justified, Lieutenant Shelton," she said in a serious voice. "If Peter and the other were here, I'm am sure there would have been almost fanatical resistance and lives would have certainly been lost."

*

As the Timber Wolf Air amphibian was loaded with the bulk of the supplies, it was guided into the jetty while the two Canadian Armed Forces CL-215s anchored off shore.

Erika waited by the forward hatch as the gangplank was lowered and surveyed the sea of faces waiting to on the jetty. Nearly all were familiar but there was no sign of her mother. She tried to hide disappointment from her eyes, as she knew Lorie was watching. "Come on," she said and stepped off the amphibian to where Annette Bulmer waited.

"You're looking well, Erika" the new commune leader said and turned to the girls. "And Lorie, Jennifer and Sassy. My, I'm sure you've all grown. How are you all?"

"Is Mom here?" Lorie spurted out.

Annette frowned. "What do you know about her?"

"Just that her death was a lie," Erika said. "We heard she was held beneath the administration block as a prisoner. We found her cell but she had already gone."

Annette's surprise looked genuine. "She was?" she whispered. "I didn't know. "

"So she's not here," Lorie gasped.

"I'm sorry, Lorie," Annette replied, "She isn't but may have been."

"What do you mean?" Erika retorted. She tucked an arm around her sister's shaking shoulders.

"The flying boat we came here in had two cabins. We were all in the main one and never had access to the rear. Peter and the others kept going back and forth. We were sure others were at the back and thought it was the prisoners. It was only later we found out they had escaped back at Eagle's Claw Lake. Your mother could have been in the aircraft without our knowledge."

"So where is she now?" Lorie demanded. Again her eyes were wide in frustration and worry.

"If she was in the aircraft, she would have been on board when the leaders flew out."

"Couldn't she be in a cell here?" Lorie persisted.

"There aren't any cells, Lorie," Annette replied. "Only the two buildings you see and three small implement sheds that house a generator and pumps. I'm sorry, Dear, but if your Mom was here, we'd know." She grimaced and glanced around. "As you can see, we are surrounded by forest. If your mother is alive she must be either in the plane with Peter or still back at Eagle's Claw."

"She isn't there!" Lorie retorted. "We searched. Oh hell!" She turned to Erika. "We came all this way for nothing!"

"Possibly," Erika replied and squeezed Lorie's hand. "But don't give up, yet. I doubt if the flying boat will get far. You never know, she may be sitting in a warm airport terminal somewhere worrying about us."

"Yeah, and pigs might fly," Lorie retorted. She swallowed, brushed away tears before they formed and strutted off the jetty.

"We'll look after her, Erika," Jennifer said quietly and, with Sassy, ran after Lorie while Erika turned to Annette. "So how is everyone here?" she asked and turned the conversation to wider issues in an unsuccessful attempt to hide her own frustration.

*

CHAPTER NINETEEN

The door of the cabin was unlocked so Jane pushed it open and stepped inside. Though she continued to call out there was no response. Curtains were drawn and the furniture pushed back along the walls.

She turned on a light switch but when nothing happened it didn't really surprise her. By the look of the fittings the cabin was supplied with electricity from somewhere so, the chances were, a generator would be somewhere around. The kitchen, though, made her smile. The cupboards were filled with supplies; cans of food, packets of dried milk, coffee, baking materials, a box of vegetables, another box of apples and other fruit all crammed on every available shelf. Another box contained cans of dog food. It looked as the people who stayed here had recently restocked. Perhaps it was a weekend hunter who stocked up for the summer and would arrive back by floatplane.

Jane grimaced. She had no idea what day of the week it was!

Further searching found the bedrooms had been in use with a man's clothes filling one wardrobe. The beds were made but the sheets and appeared ruffled and used. There was, though, no note or indication where the owner might be or how long he had gone. She hunted around for a cell phone or radio, found none but, on the positive side, found the generator in a tiny cellar and a tank almost fill with fuel oil. The starter batteries worked and after a couple of splutters, it burst into live and all the lights came on.

Her conflicting emotions turned from jubilation to disappointment then hope as she took stock of the situation. She was safe, now had food and someone would be returning at some stage. Her immediate safety was assured and it seemed unlikely that the occupier was connected to the commune.

"Well mister," she said as she walked back into the kitchen. "I'm sure the wilderness hospitality works out here and you won't mind me making myself at home."

First she had to eat, and then get herself dry, warm and clean. She grabbed an apple to munch, sat down, took off her wet shoes and socks and sat back for a moment to relieve aching bones. Her intentions were to cook a hot meal but now the pressure was off, she succumbed to weariness and drifted asleep.

*

Jane jerked awake to find lights blazing and a chill in the air. It was dark outside the two windows where she had pulled back the curtains. The outside door was ajar and moths fluttered around the light bulbs. She must have been asleep for hours!

She stretched, stood up and called out but again there was no reply. The outside darkness, though, made her confidence wane, as she almost crept to the door and stared out. There was only the faint lapping sound of water slapping the jetty and a sigh of wind in the trees. A million stars shone overhead in, what must be a cloudless sky. Straight ahead it was black and she guessed that was a hill beyond the lake.

She was used to being alone but this expanse of wilderness made her feel afraid. This was so different from the months of being confined in a cell; her heart suddenly pounded and perspiration soaked her back. Her hands became damp and she began to feel faint. Agoraphobia, the fear of open spaces, seized her. She gasped, slammed the door and found a latch to click across. In a state of panic, she crossed the room and pulled curtains across then ran through a small corridor to a back door but this was already shut and bolted.

For a minute she stood holding the kitchen doorframe and gasped for breath like an asthmatic with eyes darting everywhere and ears attune to every sound. But the sounds were friendly and helped. She knew the swishing noise was the wind in the trees, the faint chopping sound, water outside but what was the gurgling noise? Jane stared around. It was coming from the kitchen!

She forced herself to become rational. She was safe, probably far safer than she'd been for months. If she hadn't found this cabin she'd be in the pitch-black forest now, without food. Food! God she was still hungry. She stared across the room, laughed and her fears evaporated almost as quickly as they arrived. There on the mat was the half-eaten apple she was munching when she fell asleep.

Jane swallowed and walked through to the kitchen. The gurgling sound came from a tank next to a wood stove. She reached forward and touched it. The pipe was hot. My God, she had hot water and it was water bubbling in the pipes.

Emotions changed again, fear changed to exhilaration and, seconds later settled back to a guarded confidence. She even smiled and openly laughed when she found another sign of civilization. Above a corner shelf was a wall clock, one of those battery driven ones and it was going. The time said five to eleven. It was late but somehow the knowledge that it wasn't yet midnight, made her feel even more secure.

She plucked up more courage and walked around the house, checked window latches and turned off lights in the rooms she wasn't using. Next she returned to the kitchen and found a pile of dry wood beside the stove and a box of matches waiting to be used. Moments later she had the small fire blazing away and two saucepans bubbling on top. One contained vegetables and the other the contents from a can of beef stew.

After a delicious meal and a hot shower, Jane went into one of the small loft bedrooms, found a bunk and, just dressed in underclothes, crawled in under warm blankets and dropped asleep.

*

Reid glanced up at Kate, who was helping as his nurse and sighed. "How many more patients are there?" he asked. "I reckon everyone here suffers from some sort of complaint."

"You've done wonders, Reid," she replied "There's only two more, another woman who is running a high temperature and is covered in that rash that swept through the commune and a young guy who tried to fix his own cut arm and it's turned septic."

"Okay," Reid replied and smiled. "Send the man in first. The woman can be given the usual antibiotic injection. You can do that."

"Me!" Kate gasped. "I'm a pilot, not one of your underlings."

"But you're learning fast," Reid complimented. "I'd have asked Erika to help but she looks stressed out and the girls are a little young."

In a little over two hours Reid had seen close to forty commune members whose medical problems ranged from bruises and cuts, to one young woman in an advanced stage of pregnancy. Most common illness though was a variety of virus including an itchy body rash, high temperature and throbbing headache. The stress and worry the members had gone through had not helped.

The pair had learned that Annette and three other older members who had been voted in as the new leaders after being abandoned by the elders had worked tirelessly trying to help the ill ones but medical supplies were almost non-existent and commune rules forbade artificial stimulants. It was only after much persuasion that Reid had convinced most commune members the drugs he prescribed would be helpful. As it was, several of the older women still refused any medical help except warm water and clean bandages.

"So what happened to you?" Reid asked the man in his early twenties as he unwrapped a grubby bandage on his arm to show a long wound that was purple and swollen.

"My name's Cooney," came the reply and a free hand was held out to shake Reid's. "I had a bit of a disagreement with Peter. The bastard hit me with one of those whips."

"And?" Reid asked.

"I was trying to get him to take everyone on the flying boat and, at least drop us off near a town." Cooney grimaced as Reid pulled the last piece of bandage away and began to clean the wound. "He said I could go with him but all those not of the inner circle were sinners who had to prove their worth by surviving here. It was God's orders."

"But you didn't believe him?" Kate said in a quiet voice.

"No," Cooney replied. "Most of us have seen through his deceit for months now. After the girls escaped, everything came to a head and attempts to reform the commune really split us into two camps." He glanced at Kate. "You saw how those women were treated back at Eagle's Claw Lake, didn't you?"

Kate and Reid both nodded.

"In my eyes, they were the brave ones who spoke up. Others agreed with them, and I guess I was one, but were too scared to act."

"I see and what of the commune members we have here, now."

"Most see things as Annette and I do. The few are still trying to cling to the original ideals. They are disillusioned but stubborn. Even they, though, realize we can't stay here once summer is over. Before you came, we had no alternative so their ideas still influenced many but now..." he shrugged. "I don't know."

"So that is why were having a meeting in an hour," Kate said. "The police officers will explain what it will be like here in winter and you will all be given a choice of staying or returning to Eagle's Claw Lake."

"But nothing is there," Cooney said. "The place has been razed to the ground. It was aflame as we left..."

"Only the administration block was destroyed," Reid said. "Everything else is fine. The women and children there are being protected by local police officers and FBI agents."

"Oh hell," Cooney gasped and stared at Reid. "If that's true, we've been fed more lies. We were told the women were all taken off to a remand prison and the children forcibly removed, separated and placed in foster homes throughout the state. That's why many of the mothers here are so distressed. They think they'll never see their children again."

"Well," Kate added grimly. "We'll just have to set that record straight, won't we?"

"But what about Jane Somerville?" Reid added. "Annette told us she hasn't been seen here but could be in the flying boat."

"Annette is one of the real genuine ones we have," Cooney replied. "She and the other women we voted as our new leaders were all that kept us going over the last few days. She never gave up and..."

"Jane has never been seen?" Kate interrupted.

"Not as far as I know," Cooney replied. "I'm sure if she was here, Annette would know. We all heard the rumor Jane was still alive but that is all."

Kate glanced at Reid and grimaced. Everyone else they'd spoken to had given a similar reply. Perhaps Erika and Lorie had built their hopes too high.

*

The massive HAMC PS-5 flying boat was of Chinese, not Russian manufacture and had been sold to Aeroflot, the Soviet Union's only state airline two decades earlier for service north of Viadvostok. After the collapse of the communist regime, the aircraft had sat for months in an abandoned base on the shores of the Sea of Japan before being sold to a Columbian syndicate. It, however, was too large and conspicuous for smuggling drugs north to United States so was sold to The ELF Commune, complete with Canadian registration on condition that Peter forwarded the load of drugs aboard to a Seattle syndicate after it was delivered.

After leaving Darkwater Lake, Peter and his inner team had spent several days hiding out at another remote lake in the comparative luxury of an up-market hunter's lodge owned by Canadian business people who used the retreat for just about everything except hunting. Now, though, the last stage of their plan was in action and the PS-5 was on a flight west over British Columbia

Suddenly, the pilot swore and turned to Peter beside him. "The Canadian military air control want to know our identification and flight destination," he muttered. "What do I reply?"

"Damn!" Peter retorted. "I thought that by staying low and following the mountain passes we would avoid being picked up on radar."

He thought for a moment and considered another bluff. However, this was stretching their luck just that little bit too far. "Ignore them and head west to one of the remote lakes. There must be dozens to pick from. We'll sit out the night and fly over to Vancouver Island in the morning."

His intention was to refuel on the western shores of the island at a remote lumber camp where he had connections and head south over international waters to Central America. The phase of his life as prophet and leader of the religious commune was over. The members he'd abandoned at Darkwater Lake could rot in hell as far as he was concerned. Everything of value was in this aircraft behind him right now. Turning the members' cash to gold bullion over the previous two years had been a brilliant idea.

He grunted. Perhaps it had turned out okay after all. The mass suicide would have created worldwide publicity but the movement of a small commune to Canada was not news and would be hardly mentioned in the media. Of course, his identity would need to be changed again but that was a minor inconvenience.

His thoughts were interrupted when the pilot frowned at another incoming call. "This is a last request, he said.

"Ignore it!" Peter snapped. "Drop lower between the mountains and find that lake."

"You're the boss," the pilot shrugged but looked worried.

*

Eight minutes later, four CF-18 Hornet attack jets appeared from out of nowhere and surrounded the flying boat. Peter could clearly see the blue and red maple leaf ringlets on the fuselages. The pilot paled and clicked a switch so an incoming voice filled the cockpit.

"This is the Canadian Armed Forces. You are directed to head for Prince George and land. The coordinates are..."

"Shit!" Peter snarled. "What if we continue to ignore them?"

"I wouldn't advise it," the pilot replied. "The Canadians are pretty ruthless and have had to contend with aircraft smuggling Asians in from the Pacific. We'll get one more warning and they'll shoot us down."

The warning came, all right!

The fighters peeled away but seconds later there was an enormous hiss of a rocket and the area in front of the windscreen exploded into a ball of orange flames. The flying boat shuttered as superheated air buffeted it. Seconds later, a Hornet screamed over and circled up until it was a mere vapor trail in the sky.

"Unless you respond by radio and alter course to Prince George, the next rocket will hit your starboard engines," a crisp voice came through the radio speakers. "We cannot guarantee that your aircraft will be survive this attack."

"Acknowledge and change course," Peter barked but his scheming mind was already forming another plan. After all, they were flying a Canadian registered aircraft. They could be held for failing to file a flight plan but little else.

*

When the PS-5 lumbered into a Prince George military airfield, a dozen armed personnel carriers immediately surrounded it. Troops, in full combat gear, fanned out in a circle with weapons directed at the aircraft.

Peter gulped and attempted a smile at the others of his inner circle. He stepped out with his arms extended wide and was immediately seized and forced to the ground.

A man in civilian clothes walked up and stared down at him. "I am Inspector Jack DeHaven of the Royal Canadian Mounted Police," he said in a cold voice. "Your aircraft and all the cargo aboard are hereby seized by the Canadian Federal Government. You, Peter Thomas Littlejohn, also known as Jonathan Samuel Griety, are under arrest on a multiple of charges including the illegal flying of aliens into Canada and attempting to smuggle gold bullion over international boundaries. As well, the states of Washington, California and Montana are seeking extradition rights against you to answer warrants in their territories." DeHaven turned to a police officer standing beside him. "Handcuff him, Constable," he snapped.

"Yes, Sir," the young woman replied and clapped cold steel around Peter's wrists.

Across the tarmac the others were all suffering a similar indignity as RCMP officers and the Canadian Armed Services men and women carried out their duties.

Jack DeHaven grunted and watched as a police van drove in through the outer cordon and the passengers from the HAMC PS-5 hustled aboard. The operation was a success but Jane Somerville was not aboard. He was sure, though, it would only be a matter of time before she was found. This part of the operation was over. Now he'd take an aircraft across to that lake in Alberta. He'd been kept fully informed on what was happening there but wanted to see the situation for himself

*

It was late afternoon when the floatplane glided in over the fir forests, landed on Darkwater Lake and taxied up across the jetty from where the Timber Wolf Air CL-215 was moored. The two military amphibians had returned to their base with most of the troops, except a small rear guard platoon that had set up a row of tents along the shoreline.

Jack stepped ashore and was met by Ralph and a small contingent of people including the two Somerville sisters. He walked across and reached our to shake their hands. "I'm sorry," he said quietly. "As no doubt you know, we arrested Peter Littlejohn and confiscated his aircraft. Unfortunately, your mother wasn't aboard. Are you quite certain she isn't here somewhere?"

"Look around, Inspector," Erika replied. "Except for this small cleared area, there are only fir trees. None of the locals have seen her here, on the aircraft or at Eagle's Claw Lake."

"I do have some news," DeHaven replied. "One of the arrested women, you'd know her as Sister Carmel, squealed like a pig when she thought we'd place a murder rap on her shoulders. She insisted they brought Jane out of the cave before the administration block was set alight. It seems they doped and left her in one of the sheds near the jetty, She doesn't know what happened after that as everything was in a bit of a panic when they were all ordered onto the flying boat."

"So we know no more," Erika replied, "Mom might have been put on the aircraft, but what of the time gap from between when they left here and were forced down at Prince George?"

"They stayed at a hunting lodge east of here, one of those flash outfits executives use as a retreat for conferences and so forth. Like here, the only access is by float plane."

"That could be it?" Lorie interrupted. "She could have escaped from the plane and be there all by herself."

"Could be," DeHaven replied. "We have a plane flying in right now in another surprise raid. As soon as we hear anything we'll tell you."

"Thank you, Inspector," Erika replied. "I realize you're doing all you can and it is appreciated."

"So where is everyone else?" Jack asked and gazed at the empty clearing around the buildings.

"There's a commune meeting," Reid replied. "They're having a closed session to discuss and vote on what they want to do. We told them the children and the other women were safe back at Eagle's Claw Lake but Lieutenant Shelton who's in charge of the troops here hasn't told them about the SH-5 being forced down and all those aboard arrested. He is waiting for further orders."

"A wise precaution," DeHaven grunted. He gazed around. "Desolate, isn't it?" he added and nodded to two police officers standing beside him. "Guard the jetty and don't let anybody near either aircraft," he ordered.

"There're already guards posted," Ralph assured. "Lieutenant Shelton is very thorough. I doubt if he'd trust his grandmother to do the family cooking."

"And so it should be," the inspector retorted. "Okay, while they're having their meeting you can show me around. Afterwards, I want to interview the remaining leaders. There are still many loose ends to tie up."

Flanked by his staff, he strutted off the jetty followed by Erika and her friends. Reid slipped back to tuck an arm around Lorie.

He caught her sad eyes. "It hasn't really been bad news," he said quietly. "Nothing found out so far has shown your Mom to be hurt."

"I guess but if she is safe, why hasn't she contacted us? The police here or at home would pass on any message, wouldn't they?"

Reid nodded but didn't know what to say to reassure the youngster. Perhaps it was a good moment to remain quiet.

*

CHAPTER TWENTY

Annette Bulmer sighed and gazed at the commune members. What seemed to be a logical choice was turning out to be a long drawn out argument with the final vote showing twenty-three members wanted to stay at Darkwater and continue the commune along the same lines as at Eagle's Claw Lake.

She coughed after the secret votes had been counted and waited for the mumbles to drop.

"Okay," she said. "We've discussed everything, the terrible conditions expected in winter, the lack of time to establish a farm, if indeed one will even be functional here and what we'd be going back to."

"But our ELF commune has been violated," Sister Marionette, who refused to be called anything else, argued. "The animals have been sold to the Native Americans and everything is owned by the Somerville sisters and their mother, if she is still alive." She swung her head around defiantly to glance at the congregation. "I don't believe she was even held prisoner nor that Peter has deserted us."

"Yes," added one of her supporters, an elderly woman in her sixties, "It is the devil at work. We have only the Canadians' word of what happened. Peter said he would return with implements and supplies. God will protect us. We have to overcome these adversities and pray for guidance."

"We did," Annette replied quietly, "and the Canadian forces found us. That was a miracle, Mary." Her eyes bore into the women. "We don't expect you to change but we cannot leave just a score of you here, alone. Come back to Eagle's Claw Lake and there, you can set up a separate commune if you don't like our changes."

"But it is not ours," Sister Marionette retorted. "What's to stop the Somerville sisters from selling everything? They are, after all, heretics who chose to abandoned the Real Way."

"Come off it, Marionette," an angry male voice sounded from the rear of the room. "Imagine where we'd be now if they and their friends hadn't decided to help us."

"They're sinners," Mary whispered.

Annette glowered. They were getting nowhere. "I propose the motion that, as Peter and the elders are not present, the decision of two thirds of our congregation here today is binding to us all, as set out in our original constitution," she stated in a quiet voice.

"You can't!" screamed Sister Marionette, her eyes angry and desperate.

"I second the motion," the same male voice came from the back, "and wish to add the amendment that if this motion is passed, those opposed are forcibly taken back to Eagle's Claw Lake and released there to do as they wish."

The room erupted into mutters, rumblings and even angry shouts but finally Annette restored order, the amendment was passed and attached to the original motion. In the final vote only twelve opposed and another ten abstained.

"It has been passed," Annette announced. "I shall tell the authorities here, we would all like transport back home. Will you please begin packing your possessions?"

She glared around. "Unless there are any other items, I declare this extra special meeting of the Eagle Love Family closed and suggest we have another meeting to write a new constitution one week after our return to Eagle's Claw Lake."

Her lip quivered with emotion but she avoided Mary's or Marionette's eyes, turned and walked out into the evening light.

"We're going home," she said angrily to Erika who met her outside the door, "but I am afraid it wasn't unanimous."

"Don't worry," Erika replied softly. "Some people cannot cope with change. Who was it, Mary or Marionette?"

"Both," Annette answered. "Oh, I know I shouldn't be angry but..." she sighed and glanced over to see Lisa, Jennifer and Sassy a few steps away. "I also spent my life serving the commune but it took those three and yourself to show that we had strayed from the original ideals your grandfather set up." She switched her attention back to Erika. "I am also afraid. It's as if my whole life has been a lie."

"Don't be, Annette," Erika answered. "Without those criminals running the place, the commune will survive stronger and freer than ever before. With people like yourself as leaders it will become a place of love, rather than fear, again."

Annette nodded. "Thanks, Erika," she said quietly and turned to meet the others filing out from the building.

Most smiled at her, some came up for a quiet word and several embraced her. Even the frosty looks from Mary's eyes as she swept by did not stop Annette from feeling that she had made the correct choice for everyone.

Everyone was having breakfast when a rumble of aircraft engines sounded above and the massive HAMC SH-5 landed. When it moored off the beach up from the jetty, two strangers in Canadian Armed Forces uniform appeared and paddled ashore in a rubber dinghy.

Jack DeHaven met the pilots and shook hands. "Thanks," he muttered. "So everything is arranged?"

"Yes Sir," the pilot replied. "We've been cleared to remain with this flying boat and transport the people here back to Washington State. The American authorities have given us flight clearance."

"And afterwards?" DeHaven asked.

"As you directed, Inspector. You were correct. The plane has illegal Canadian registration so remains confiscated by the Federal Government. Once legalities are sorted out, it will be sold and any profit from the sale returned to the commune."

"Good," DeHaven grunted. "We'll get loaded and get this lot back south of the boarder. They won't be our concern, after that."

*

Lorie stared out the windshield of the CL-215 as Kate flew low around the perimeter of Lake Darkwater. The shoreline, though, was no different than she expected. The water was met by dense firs and, except for a few stretches of shingle beach and a small river feeding the eastern end, desolate.

"What about that other lake a few kilometers away?" the girl asked.

"It's no different, Lorie," Kate replied. "I've got fuel for one low run over then we have to leave. Okay?"

"It doesn't matter," Lorie whispered. "Just head home."

Kate nodded and reached for the throttles. The two engines roared and the Timber Wolf Air aircraft increased height to head south. It was mid-afternoon and the other aircraft had already departed. The lake looked deserted and alone, as it became a spot on the landscape behind them.

Lorie sat in the seat behind Kate and studied the scene below in silence for almost five minutes before she swished back her blonde hair and left the cockpit.

"Poor kid," Andy commented and caught Kate's eyes. "It's so hard having your hopes built up and then swept away."

"Yes," Kate replied. "But her mother isn't at Darkwater Lake, that much I do know."

*

Cinders bounded out of the kennels where he had been boarded while her master had gone north and ran with tail lashing from Reid on to Kate, the girls, Erika and back to Reid again.

"Yeah it's been a while, Girl," Reid laughed. "Tomorrow when we head back up to Eagle's Claw Lake we'll take you with us."

Cinders gazed at him with her large brown eyes and wolfed as if to say she didn't want to be left behind again.

Because of their fuel supply Kate had decided to return to Spokane rather than have an extra landing at Eagle's Claw Lake. They had also agreed to spend the night at home and transport their load of supplies to the commune in the morning. Radio contact with the flying boat had assured them everyone was safely back at the ELF commune and the women and children there had met the returned members enthusiastically. No news of Jane Somerville, though, was forthcoming.

It was early morning, therefore, when everyone except Ralph and with the addition of Cinders left Felts Field Municipal Airport and headed north on the almost routine run to Eagle's Claw Lake. Lorie and Erika's subdued moods reflected on the others but little was said for what else was there to say? They all felt for the two sisters but a growing pessimism filled the aircraft.

The weather was clear as Kate flew in from the northeast with the intention of following the northern arm of the lake around before landing near the commune. As usual, all three girls were crowded in the cockpit taking in the scenery.

"All I wanted to do was leave the place, but it's like returning home," Jennifer commented.

"Yes," Sassy added. "It's so beautiful here compared with Darkwater. That place was awful. Even in the commune I expected a wolf or something to jump out from the trees at me..."

Lorie suddenly gasped and grabbed Kate's shoulder. "Look!" she said.

Kate frowned. Nothing seemed unusual.

"Reid's cabin!" Lorie continued.

Everyone stared out the port window to where, far below, the cabin sat bathed in summer sunlight. The jetty, boat shed and everything were crisp and sharp in the morning air.

"There!" Lorie yelled.

"Oh my God," Kate whispered. "I can see it."

From kitchen chimney at the back of the cabin, a small column of white smoke rose into the air.

"Someone's there," Lorie gasped. "Kate can we go down and look."

"Get Reid," Kate replied and glanced up a moment later when he walked in. "What do you think?" she asked.

"Nobody should be there," he replied. "I still have the leasehold until the end of summer and I know the agents aren't doing anything until I bow out." He glanced at Lorie. "It could be anyone, though. Hikers or hunters..."

"Where's their floatplane?' Lorie retorted. "It's too far to walk."

"Someone from the commune, perhaps," Andy suggested from the co-pilot's seat.

"Exactly," Lorie replied and her eyes sparked in anticipation. "It must be Mom."

Kate smiled. "Well, we'll land and have a look but don't built your hopes too high, Lorie. There could be a dozen reasons for someone to be there."

After they landed, nobody came out to meet the amphibian as it nudged the jetty and Reid scrambled ashore with a mooring rope. Cinders Lorie and Cinders immediately ran towards the cabin.

"Lorie," yelled Erika from the hatch door. "Wait!"

"Let her go," Reid advised. "If it's a stranger, Cinders will look after her and we're mere seconds behind."

"Okay, Erika replied. "I don't want her to be disappointed, that is all."

*

When she arrived at the front door, Lorie lost her nerve. It was shut and everything remained silent. She gripped Cinder's collar, bit on her bottom lip and knocked.

Nothing!

She glanced back and saw Reid wave. The others were still in the amphibian. She knocked again and was sure she heard a cough. With infinite slowness, she turned the handle and pushed the door open. Everything inside looked familiar and she could smell the aroma of burning wood. It was warm and cozy with the sun pouring through the windows.

"Hello!" she called. "Is anyone here?"

Somehow she expected no reply and jumped in fright when there was a reply.

"Coming!" A woman appeared at the kitchen door. "I'm sorry. I was asleep. Was that really an aircraft...?" She stopped and stared. "Oh my God! It can't be..."

Lorie gasped. The woman's face was covered in a red rash but she recognized it at once. "Mom!" she screamed. "Do you know me, Mom?"

"Lorie!" Jane Somerville whispered. "Oh, my God! How did you get here?"

Lorie ran across the room, met Jane in the middle and grabbed her while tears of sheer emotion burst from her eyes.

"Erika's here, too, Mom," Lorie managed to get out. "This is Cinders, our dog. We saw your smoke Mom. Kate wouldn't...oh hell..." She burst into tears again.

*

Jane held her daughter and wept. After all this time, her daughter was here in her arms, her beautiful little Lorie. But she wasn't little any longer but a mature young woman actually taller than herself. But the long blonde hair was as she remembered.

"Oh, My Darling," she sobbed and looked over her shoulder to receive another shock.

Erika stood there, her face awash with tears.

"Hello Mom," the elder Somerville daughter whispered and stepped forward to hug them both.

*

"It's the same virus half the commune members came down with," Reid said sympathetically a hectic fifteen minutes later. "I'll give you an injection and your fever will be down within an hour."

Introductions were over and Lorie still clung to her mother. "How long have you been here, Mom?" she asked.

"Several days, "Jane replied. "I just stayed put and waited. I knew it was safe and had food for weeks. Yesterday morning I woke up with this terrible headache and rash all over me. I though I must have walked through some poison ivy or something. " She smiled and squeezed Lorie's hand that was still in hers. "I had no idea I was still at Eagle's Claw Lake." She glanced up at Reid. "So you worked out I must have gone over the hill to the middle spur and followed it around here. In retrospect it seems so logical but at the time..." She smiled. "My God, I am so glad to see you all ...I heard the aircraft land but thought I was hallucinating. It happened to me a lot in the cell. It got so bad at one stage I could hardly tell the difference between reality and my dreams."

"This is real, Mom," Erika said and hugged her mother again. "It was Lorie who never gave up. She said we'd find you, and we did! We love you, Mom and are going to make everything up for all those horrible months. We got your letter and..."

"My letter," Jane responded. "What letter?"

"The one you wrote in your cell," Lorie explained. "That was when we knew for certain, you were still alive."

Jane frowned. "Oh I see," she whispered. "Peter told you I was dead, did he?"

"Yes," Erika replied. "That was before I escaped from the commune and found our lawyer. We're living in your house, Mom. It's there for you."

"Oh my God," Jane responded, yet again. "There's so much to catch up on," She turned and smiled at the faces around her, some familiar and others, until now, strangers but there was love in that cabin that morning and she realized she'd never be alone again. Even the Black Labrador with big brown eyes and thumping tail entered her heart and made her welcome.

*

The Elf commune looked little different when the CL-215 arrived fifty minutes later but the atmosphere was a complete contrast to any of the crew or passengers' previous visits. For one, the gate was wide open and people rushed down to the jetty to meet them. Jane was greeted like royalty and dozens of willing hands helped to unload the cargo. Children shouted and laughed and the vast majority of the adults were wearing jeans or even shorts.

After everything possible was told to everyone, Kate and her companions were ushered into the dining room and treated to an enormous meal while, again, children ran everywhere, and teenagers came up to chat and long lost friends spoke to Jane or the girls.

"The first thing to go was the electric fence," Annette said when she finally got them on their own. "All the stringent rules go next. If people such as Mary wish to continue wearing the commune uniform and have twice daily chapel meetings, they may along with anybody else who wishes to attend." She smiled. "Knowing human nature, I think they'll have a very tiny audience for the first while but people will drift back. We're also going to have to do some urgent thinking about the coming winter. The vegetable gardens that are usually flourishing at this time of the year have gone..."

"How?" Kate asked.

"Somebody let the cattle in and they ate or trampled everything." She screwed her face up. "Other things were destroyed too but, luckily, nothing too severe. Except for the burnt out administration block, the buildings are all in good condition, the generator works and the water supply is sound. We'll need to spend some of our capital to buy in food and other supplies but, with care, we'll be fine."

"And what of Marionette, Mary and those others made to return against their wishes?" Reid asked.

"They've been told of the changes we anticipate making, they'll be allowed to participate in the decisions but the majority decision will prevail. If they disagree we've given them a choice of leaving or using one of the buildings as their own commune, you know, a group within a group. There they can continue exactly as they did before but without the compulsion and fear where everyone had to conform."

"You sound very tolerant," Jane said in a quiet voice. "I'm afraid I would not have been so accommodating."

"After everything you went through, I cannot blame you, Jane," Annette replied, "but most of those who want to cling to the old ways are more elderly and apprehensive. The ruthless ones have gone. Even Marionette isn't too bad. I feel sorry for her in many ways." She reached across and took Jane's hands. "I guess it's a stupid question but, you know there will always be a place here for you." She chuckled. "You are our landlady, anyway, I believe."

Jane also smiled. "Don't worry about that part of it and thanks, but I want to get to know my two wonderful daughters all over again and try to make up all that lost time. They aren't children any more and don't even need me, I guess, but I certainly need them."

"It works both ways, Mom," Lorie interrupted. "We need and want you."

"Yes," supported Erika.

*

Kate watched the three and turned to Reid beside her. His eyes were on them too but he had almost a glazed expression as if his mind was a million kilometers away. She dug him in the ribs and he immediately flicked his attention to her.

"Yes, of course," he muttered. "They can certainly stay with us as long as they like."

"Reid," Kate whispered. "What are you talking about? You never heard a word of the conversation, did you?"

Reid flushed. "Sorry, Sweetheart," he replied and glanced around but everyone else was chatting to each other and nobody was listening to them. "I was thinking about things, that's all."

Kate frowned and fixed an intent gaze on her partner. "Like what?"

Reid shrugged. "Here, the cabin and what's going to happen. If I'd stayed in the cabin over summer as I was going to do, my time would be almost up. In fact, in a week from Tuesday my lease and the option to buy expire. I was just thinking about what might have been, that's all."

"Regrets?" Kate whispered with almost a pout on her lips.

"No," Reid replied and a smile crossed his tanned face. "Not one. I'm just damn glad I was referred to the Timber Wolf Air hanger. I almost gave up looking for it, you know. Now, if I'd got that other airline..." He clicked his fingers as if he was trying to think of the name. "Resolution Air..."

"They're the ones who went broke," Kate laughed and placed an arm through his. "Come on, I think Annette wants to show Jane and everyone around. I want to head back soon, too. From here, my apartment looks mighty comfortable."

"Even with a couple of stroppy teenagers?" Reid chuckled.

"Yes," Kate replied. "It wouldn't be the same without them."

*

CHAPTER TWENTY-ONE

The largest storm of the winter had dumped an unprecedented amount of snow on Spokane over night and even by midmorning the airport could barely cope. Snowplows had cleared the main runway but the snow continued to fall.

Kate sat in her warm office and felt relieved all her flights for the day were cancelled. Andy was at the coast with the CL-215 to do some contract work in the San Juan Islands so, at the moment she was alone. The amphibian operated well in the salt water but was too large, in Kate's opinion, for working the frozen lakes of the interior. The Timber Wolf Air Beaver, though, had the floats replaced by skis and they had a lucrative business flying skiers to winter resorts and ski fields in the mountains.

The telephone rang.

" Good morning. Timber Wolf Air. Kate Meltz speaking."

"You're just the person I want," said the somewhat rushed voice at the other end. "This is Annette at Eagle's Claw Lake here."

"Hi, Annette. How's the satellite phone working?"

"Expensive but fine. We have a medical emergency here and need help."

Kate frowned and stared out at the snow-covered parking lot that had only been partially cleared.

"It's Jonathan," Annette said. "Remember him?"

"Can't say I do but go on."

"He's one of the older boys, the tall thin lad. Anyhow, he's had a high fever all night and terrible pains across the stomach. I rang the Spokane emergency center but it seems they're all tied up with a major pile up on the freeway. Nobody is available to fly here until mid afternoon." Her voice sounded desperate. "Jonathan is in pretty bad way. He needs immediate help."

"What's the weather like there?" Kate asked in a serious tone.

"Cold, but clear."

"And the lake?"

"Frozen. The tractor has driven on it towing a sled. I'm sure a ski plane could land."

Kate nodded. The lakes in the high country this late in the season were frozen solid and the Beaver could get in unless there were blizzard conditions.

"Okay, Annette. It's snowing here but the runway is open. We'll try to be there as soon as possible. Please ring back if the weather closes in."

"Thanks, Kate," Annette's worried voice replied. "You have my number, I believe."

"Yes," Kate replied. "Hope to see you before lunch time. Bye."

She hung up and immediately punched in another number, spoke crisply and frowned. "Okay, thanks anyway," she said and continued with two other numbers.

However, every emergency service was stretched to its fullest. No doctors, nurses or paramedics were available.

"Damn!" she retorted and rang home.

"I need you, Sweetheart," Kate said when Reid answered and explained why.

"Right," Reid replied. "Give me fifteen minutes. That's if the road's open."

*

He was there in twelve to find the Beaver on the tarmac with the engine idling ready to go.

"Come on, Cinders," he yelled. "We're going flying. It's not as good as your bed by the boiler at home but you're getting lazy, anyway."

The Labrador, though, never hesitated. She jumped from the car and ran to the Beaver. Kate opened the cabin door and the dog was inside in one bound, followed by Reid with his medical bag.

Kate smiled and immediately contacted the tower for permission to fly out... They were soon between two commercial jets and everywhere hot exhaust fumes shimmered in the frigid air. The runway lights disappeared in a haze of white ahead and the windshield wipers scratched the frozen glass. Inside, it was cold but powerful heaters began to blow warm air in.

"You're clear for take off, Timber Wolf Air Beaver," the anonymous voice crackled but then added a personal comment. "Take it easy up there in the mountains, Kate. Heavy snow showers are coming in from Canada."

"Thanks, Tower," Kate responded. "Will do." She smiled sideways at Reid and moved the throttle forward.

Reid marveled at his companion's skill in the conditions. There was no chance of flying above the cloud bank so Kate kept low in conditions that were akin to flying through a tunnel with no lights on. Only the glow of instrument lights in their eerie blue or red added color to the almost complete white out. Snow gripped the wipers and piled up so high the view disappeared, not that there was anything to see, before being caught in the wind and flung aside.

"That's better," Kate gasped and reached forward with a gloved hand to wipe the interior of the glass that had begun to steam up. She kept her eyes on the instruments and maintained constant contact with ground control. That reassuring voice below was their one contact with normality.

Twenty minutes later they flew out of the cloud into a crisp blue sky with the sun quarter way up the eastern sky. Below, was a world of white clouds and to their left two mountain peaks stretched skywards.

"The ski resorts will be happy," Kate commented, glanced in the mirror and laughed.

"What is it?" Reid grunted.

"Look," Kate said and nodded back.

Reid turned and saw Cinders sound asleep on a blanket at the rear of the cabin.

"Complete trust," he commented.

"Or ignorance," Kate responded. "My God, that was rough going for a while."

*

Eagle's Claw Lake appeared in a crisp world of white but at least it wasn't snowing. The scene was like a Christmas card with the firs covered in new snow and the lake surface like sheep's wool as long waves of snow made 'W' shaped patterns from bank to bank. Kate's frown turned to relief when they turned into the upper arm and she saw two lines of flickering orange lights ahead. The snow had been scrapped off the surface to form a long, clear, ice runway. A tractor was at the side and several fur dressed figures waved as they approached.

"I was worried there for a moment," she whispered and again showed her skill as a pilot as she brought the Beaver down between the lights with perfection. The engine throttled back, there was a slight shudder and cutting noise filled the cabin, the tail dropped and Reid held on, more nervous than the pilot He noticed the lights were oil drums burning fuel oil. Black smoke rose straight up into the air above the flames. The Beaver wobbled slightly, slowed and slid to a halt adjacent to the tractor.

*

It was frigid outdoors; over ten degrees colder than at Spokane and the heavily clothed people waiting were surrounded in little clouds of condensation as their warm breath immediately froze.

Four children, though, were with the three adults on a massive sled connected to the tractor. They waved and laughed when Cinders jumped from the Beaver, skidded across the ice and found it difficult to stop her four legs from going in every direction. One of the men on skates rescued her and, in one almighty heave, deposited her between the waiting children's arms.

"Hi Cinders," they yelled and hugged the dog.

"It's good to see you."

"How are ya, Girl?"

Kate and Reid, meanwhile, made a more sedate exit from their aircraft and moments later the tractor and its passengers headed for the oasis of colors and chimney smoke that was the ELF commune.

*

"He has appendicitis," Reid diagnosed as he continued to examine the gasping, perspiring boy. "You were right to call for help, Annette. He is too ill to move out in the aircraft. I'll need to operate here and now."

The ELF commune leader paled a little but nodded.

"Is it possible?" she asked.

"Your medical room here is hygienic and well set up. I have operated in far less desirable spots. Do you have any nurses who can assist? "

"No really," Annette whispered. "A couple passed first-aid courses..."

"I'll help," Kate volunteered and received Reid's appreciative glance.

"And I'll do what I can, " Annette added.

"Okay," Reid replied. "We need it to be a little warmer in here and..." His directions were curt and professional before he turned to the pale youth and smiled. "Don't worry, Jonathan," he said softly. "It is a straight forward operation. You'll have an injection in the arm and when you wake up it'll be all over."

"Thank you, Doctor Tucker," the boy of about fourteen whispered and attempted to smile. "I'm sorry you had to come all this way in such lousy conditions." He grimaced in pain and switched his eyes across to Kate. "How's Lorie and the others?" he asked.

"Fine, Jonathan," Kate replied. "They're all sophomores at our local high school. Sassy's into sports and Jennifer is more the academic sort. Lorie is somewhere in the middle, I guess."

"We miss them," the boy replied. "For a while last year they were the only ones who kept us going." He shrugged. "It's much better here now but is still strange without them."

"Okay, Jonathan. I'm ready to start," Reid interrupted and brought out a hypodermic needle. He reached forward, dabbed the boy's forearm with an antiseptic swab and the operation began...

*

"Reid's excellent, isn't he?" Annette commented seemingly mere minutes later as the patient was bandaged up, minus a bloated appendix that was due to burst and Reid had departed to clean himself up.

"He is," Kate agreed with pride in her voice. "One of the best."

She never told Annette that Reid had refused to return to medicine but had become quite despondent over the last couple of months. Sure, he'd done an excellent job as secretary for Timber Wolf Air and had, in fact, been the one responsible for obtaining the San Juan Islands' contract over two Seattle firms. He'd persuaded a local fishing firm the larger aircraft was exactly what they needed to get their catch to the Seattle markets every day. It was a two-month contract that made perfect use of the CL-215 over the winter months.

"Jonathan will be fine, now," Reid told Annette a few moments later. "We won't take him back to Spokane. The aircraft journey will jolt him around too much. Just keep him warm and change the bandage tomorrow. I'll try to get back to remove the stitches in a week but, if not, it's not a hard job to remove them," He turned to Kate and kissed her affectionately. "Thanks again, Sweetheart. I'm back in your hands."

"We have to leave," Kate replied. "The weather is closing and I was told, snow will be here any moment."

Freezing air gripped them again as they moved outdoors into strange yellow light caused by inky black clouds passing in front of the sun. They clamored aboard the tractor sled and headed towards the lake.

"I placed a heat unit in the Beaver's motor. It should start okay" one of the men shouted with clouds of white condensation puffing from his mouth. "God, it's cold," he added.

They roared around by the dining room where the door opened and half the commune's children population followed Cinders out to the sled and waved as he jumped aboard and wriggled in between Reid and Kate.

"Bye, Kids," Reid shouted. "Get back inside to the warmth, do you hear?"

"Bye Reid. Bye Kate. Bye Cinders," a score of voices sounded.

"They sound happy," Kate commented to Annette who accompanied them on the sled to see them off.

"Oh they're grand kids," Annette replied. "I think everyone's happier here, now. Even old Madeline and Mary are, though they won't admit it." She smiled. "Remember. You're both welcome back anytime. It doesn't have to be an emergency, you know."

"I know," Kate replied. "We will."

They arrived at the Beaver and clamored aboard, Kate started the engine and, after a final wave good-bye, Kate turned the Beaver onto the ice runway and accelerated forward.

*

"You did well, Sweetheart," Kate said a few moments later as they headed southwest.

"Yes," Reid replied with a shrug. "I used to do two or three of those a week. They're pretty rudimentary but Jonathan's would have been in real trouble if it had burst. I reckon it would have done so if he'd been left a few more hours. At least Annette has her head screwed on. I doubt if any praying would have helped him."

"Kate gazed across at her partner. "Are you being cynical, Reid?" she asked.

"No, just realistic.

"You miss being a practicing doctor, don't you?"

"A little," Reid admitted. "Of course, for every operation where you directly help someone like Jonathan, there are probably a dozen reports one has to do for the bureaucrats. I don't miss those one bit."

"Well, go back and get a doctor's position," Kate snapped.

Reid stared out the windscreen at the darkening sky. "I can't," he whispered. "I wish I could, but I can't. It's too late for that, now."

"Why," Kate persisted. "You still have your license to practice."

"You don't understand," Reid replied.

"No I don't," Kate retorted. "I saw your performance today and numerous other times since we've met and I know you're an excellent doctor and surgeon."

"But you're biased, My Sweet," Reid replied, reached across and squeezed her arm, and changed the topic

Kate glanced at him and decided she was going to do something to get Reid re-established as a doctor, with or without his immediate help. After all, if the situation was reversed and, through some complaint or whatever, she lost her aircraft operating license, he would certainly help her. He was that sort of man!

"Snow!" Reid exclaimed and Kate's mind switched back to the present situation.

*

It was as if someone had switched off the light in a movie theater. In one minute they flew from pale winter sunlight into clouds so thick the propeller at the nose of the Beaver could barely be seen. Again, it was only the instruments and voice from ground control that guided the aircraft to Spokane. But the rugged little plane never missed a beat with the engine continuing its comforting rumble.

The snow arrived, so thick it was like flying into a tunnel of white bats. For another thirty minutes they flew onwards until they lost height and Reid could just make out foggy lights of the city below.

Kate's face was expressionless as she received landing instructions and banked to the starboard. In front were the blue approach lights and the runway itself.

"We're the last plane in," Kate muttered. "They've already diverted the commercial jets over to the international airport and all takeoffs are cancelled."

She set the Beaver down and followed the taxiway along beyond the terminals to the Timber Wolf Air hanger. There, she activated the remote control, the giant doors rolled back and they taxied inside under a blaze of floodlights. The doors closed behind and Kate shut down the engine.

"We made it," she said with a sigh of relief. "God, I feel exhausted."

"And we have company," Reid observed.

Jennifer and Sassy were waiting at the side of the hanger and stepped forward to meet them as they climbed down from the aircraft with Cinders right behind. The girls both looked relieved but, Jennifer, in particular, appeared pale.

"What are you two doing here?" Kate asked. "I thought you'd both be home in the warm."

"Why didn't you tell us?" Jennifer accused and her chin quivered. "We were worried about you and then the radio news broadcast that..."

Her face contorted with emotion and, without warning, tears flooded from the youngster's eyes.

"There's a small plane overdue," Sassy explained in a hushed voice. "We thought it was you. Jennifer refused to stay at home so we took a cab out. We've been waiting over an hour."

"You could have told us," Jennifer wept. "Why didn't you phone school and get a message to us. We came home to an empty house to find even Cinders gone."

"I wrote a note and left it on the kitchen notice board," Reid explained, reached out and wrapped his arms around the distressed girl.

She cuddled in close but continued to weep shuddering tears. Reid stroked her hair and frowned over at Kate. Jennifer was so upset she was almost incoherent. Tears just poured down her cheeks and plopped onto the concrete floor.

"Is something else wrong?" Kate whispered and stared at Sassy.

"No," Sassy replied. "We were worried about you, that's all. The radio news is full of emergency instructions and accidents. Half the city is without electricity, there's a pile up on Interstate 90 and they're advising everyone to stay at home. Then twenty minutes ago they said this airport was closed and a plane was missing. When she heard that, Jennifer just broke down. I tried to reassure her but..." She frowned and gave a tiny shrug.

"It's just that... "Jennifer stood back and wiped her eyes. "It's just that... Oh hell. I don't know..."

"We're fine, Jennifer," Kate said quietly. "Are you sure there's nothing else?"

"I don't want to lose you, that's all," Jennifer sobbed. "I love you guys. When I heard a plane was down I thought you'd crashed somewhere and..." She shook her head and wiped away still more tears. "It's just me. I'm acting like a little kid, aren't I?"

She squatted down and hugged Cinders, who perceived something was wrong, dug her long nose into the girl's cheek and licked her face.

"No," Reid replied." We feel honored, Jennifer." He shivered in the cool air. "But let's head into the office where it is warmer."

"We cooked supper for you," Jennifer sniffed.

"Where?" Kate replied.

"Here in the break room. We couldn't stand just sitting around so we went over to the terminal, bought some food and..." She smiled and linked her arms into Reid and Kate's "Come and look."

The office was warm and the aroma of hot soup filled the air. On the tiny break room stove a saucepan of vegetable soup simmered away with steam drifting into the air above it. The gas heater blazed away and the room's curtains had been drawn to give an oasis of warmth and security.

Kate smiled at Reid and went and hugged both girls. "Thank you," she said. "At the moment there is nothing in the world I could think better than a bowl of hot soup."

"Next time, tell us," Jennifer whispered and managed a tiny smile. "I've never been so happy since I've moved in with you, two. The thought of you not being here just got to me, I guess."

"We never found any message," Sassy added. "Perhaps it fell off the notice board."

"We'll we're back and safe," Kate said. " Reid did a marvelous job. He had to operate on Jonathan, you know..." She reached for some bowls on the bench and began serving up the soup as she told the girls everything that had happened.

*

It took a while but Kate and the others managed to get home that evening and everything slipped back into the usual weekday evening routine with Jennifer spending two hours doing homework and Sassy managing to get hers whipped up in forty minutes. Afterwards, it was television and everyone retreated to bed.

It was well into the night when Kate heard a tiny knock on the bedroom door. Reid was asleep beside her so, for a second she became alarmed until she realized it was Jennifer.

"Hi Kate," the girl whispered, "I think I remember something. Can I talk about it?"

Kate frowned. She was about to ask why but decided not to. This was not something Jennifer had ever done before so it must be important. "Okay," she said instead," I'll come out into the kitchen and we can put the coffee on."

"I had the strangest dream," Jennifer said after they were seated around the table. "It seemed so real but can't be."

"Why?" Kate asked. "I mean if it seemed so real why couldn't it be so?"

"Because you were in it," Jennifer whispered. "You were exactly as you are now but I was only tiny, four or five I guess."

"I see," Kate replied.

"I was running out of this building, a school or kindergarten it was..."

"See you tomorrow, Jennifer," the teacher said as the five-year old grabbed her lunch box and headed out the door with the other children.

"Bye Miss Dunne," Jennifer replied.

It was a beautiful summer's day and Mommy was going to take her to the beach for a swim. She loved swimming and could already kick her way across the swimming pool down the block.

Outside there were cars everywhere but she knew the large white Cadillac was Mommy's. She stopped and glanced around but it wasn't there. Well. Mommy was sometimes late and she knew she should go back to the small playground next to the building and play there. Normally, this didn't worry her but today with the special trip planned it was a nuisance.

She turned and was about to walk back through the gate when a lady came up to her. "Hello Jennifer, Honey," she said. "I'm Sylvia, you know, from your Mommy's bridge club. The game's gone on a little too long so she asked me to come and pick you up. We can go to the club, Mommy's game will be over then it's off to the beach."

"Yes," Jennifer replied doubtfully and stepped back.

"It's okay, Honey," the lady said and took her hand. "Mommy told you she'd be playing bridge, didn't she?"

Jennifer nodded. Wednesday was Mommy's bridge day. Of course, that was why she was late!

"I'll tell you what," Sylvia said. "We'll stop and get a soda at the mart. Mommy gave me some money to but you one."

Jennifer smiled. That was true, too. Whenever Mommy was late she bought her something, a Popsicle, candy or soda. Perhaps it was that that made her decide to trust the lady and she followed her to a large modern blue automobile.

However, mere seconds later she cried out in distress. As they drove out the driving lot, the white Cadillac drove in and her Mommy, Kate was at the wheel.

"It was you, Kate right down to the little dimple on your chin. Everything else was so real, it was as if it happened yesterday."

"Did anything else happen in the dream," Kate asked

"Just terrible visions. The woman started screaming at me, I tried to open the door but the handle didn't work. She turned and slapped me across the face, so hard I was flung back against the seat. I was crying and then I woke up."

"So couldn't the vision of me have been someone else? You were calling me Mommy so couldn't this have been your real mother?"

"Possibly," Jennifer replied. "At the commune, I was told I was an orphan and my parents were dead." She stared at Kate. "But I've had this dream before, ages ago when I was ten or eleven. I remember talking to one of the sisters in the commune just as I'm talking to you now. She, though, was annoyed with me for some reason." Jennifer bit on her lip. "I remember that after that when I had the dream I told nobody, not even Sassy or Lorie. I must have stopped the dreams for, until now, Id forgot all about them."

"And perhaps the fear that our plane crashed today, triggered them in your mind," Kate said.

"I was worried about you," Jennifer admitted, "Suddenly didn't want to be left alone. It was totally irrational, I know but..."

"I don't think so," Kate replied. "Look, why don't you tell Reid about it. He's the professional..."

"Tell me what, Kate?" a male voice interrupted and Reid walked in the room. "I saw the lights on then heard your voices," he added almost apologetically, " "

"Something more than a dream, I think," Kate replied and turned to face the teenager. "I think it fits in with how you felt this afternoon. Tell Reid about it, Jennifer."

"Now I'm wide awake, it seems so silly," Jennifer responded.

"But tell me, anyhow," Reid replied in a soft voice. He sat down on the carpet, smiled and listened without interruption as Jennifer retold her story.

*

CHAPTER TWENTY-TWO

Because of the storm, there were a hectic few days with Kate making six flights to various parts of the Washington State and one to British Columbia. Saturday arrived and by noon she found herself finally free and headed across the city to Erika's place. Only Jane was home but she was the one Kate had really come to see.

After she told her about Jennifer's nightmare, the older woman went quiet. "I see," she said in a whisper. "I had hoped she had forgotten. Poor Jennifer was such a sweet little kid and I did all I could for her." She shrugged. "She was one of the reasons Peter Littlejohn couldn't kill me. He thought I had information stashed with my lawyer. It was, though, merely a bluff that I used to save my own skin."

"Tell me, Jane. What happened to Jennifer?"

"I feared being implicated and Dad did too, I guess, when he was still alive so we all kept quiet."

"About what!" Kate began to sound exasperated. "For Jennifer's sake you have to tell me."

"I guess you noticed there are quite a large number of children at the commune?" Jane began.

Kate nodded.

"About half are children of commune women and the rest were orphans. In Matthew's day back when Lorie, Jennifer and Sassy were little, he applied officially to adoption agencies for children and commune members officially adopted them. Sassy was one but, unfortunately Peter and his henchmen were getting firmly established and children were arriving with more sinister backgrounds. Most were tiny babies who would have no memories of their background but Jennifer was older when she arrived, five I think she was."

"Sinister?" Kate queried.

Jane sighed and her hand holding a coffee mug shook. "I'm an accessory, I guess but I tried to help." She glanced up at Kate and blinked back tears of emotion or, perhaps shame.

"Go on," Kate whispered.

"Jennifer was the first but there were several others over the years, children who are still at the commune. You see," she said quietly, "Jennifer came from a businessman's family in San Francisco. She was kidnapped and held to ransom."

"Oh hell!" Kate gasped.

"That was when I realized the direction the ELF camp was going. Dad did too, but he was old and weak."

"So what happened?" Kate whispered.

"Oh, Jennifer's parents paid up; two or three times but she was never returned. The poor little kid had been kept somewhere for weeks before arriving at the commune. She was a thin as a beanstalk and covered in needle pricks. I think they kept her more or less permanently sedated. It worked, too for she had almost no recollection of where she'd come from. Only that her name was Jennifer. We added the Mears surname, as it was as close as she could remember her real name. I'm sure it was one of those East European names that she had trouble pronouncing."

"Peter and his henchmen wanted to kill her but we managed to persuade him it was safe to integrate her into the commune and she was." She shrugged. "She's grown into a wonderful girl, in spit of her experiences. Lorie and Sassy became her inseparable friends. Until they matured, I believe they had a very happy life..." She stared at Kate. "We weren't all monsters there, you know?"

"Oh Jane, I know that," Kate replied. "Look at Annette running the commune now, for example." She hesitated. "But you have to tell the authorities, Jane. Think of Jennifer's parents whom, I guess, belief she is dead. Think of the other children who were also kidnapped and are still at the commune."

Jane nodded. "I'm afraid, Kate," she said. 'I would not survive a prison sentence."

"But you didn't do anything," Kate argued.

"But I knew about it. This amounts to the same thing in the eyes of the law." She sniffed and blew her nose with a tiny handkerchief. "I'm like Reid."

"What do you mean?" Kate snapped.

"His trial, Kate. I read it all up. He knew nothing about the illegal operations going on at the Northern Lights Hospital. In fact, that consulting surgeon covered his trail so well Reid was completely ignorant about what was going on."

Kate's face was now pale. "I don't know a lot about it," she whispered. "I guess I've been too afraid to research the details. All I know is that Reid is an excellent doctor and I love him. I don't really care what happened."

"He was innocent, Kate," Jane added. "However, because he was in charge he was still brought to trial. He got off all except a minor charge of failing to account, I think it was and was allowed to go free. In my case, kidnapping is a more serious offence. I knew about it, Kate, but didn't report the crime. I'm an accessory!"

"Then we won't involve you but I have to go to the police and report this for Jennifer's sake, her parents and the other children. Do you understand?"

"Yes," Jane whispered.

" I promise not to mention your name."

"But the police know I'm from the commune. They've already spent hours interviewing me so they build a case against Peter Littlejohn and the others. Their trials are still to come up."

" That's The Royal Canadian Mounted Police," Kate said. "The local police or FBI will be handling this."

"But they all work together." Jane added. "Oh hell. I know I should have done something, years ago..."

"But you were a victim, too, Jane. Look at all your time they kept you in that cave. Nobody could blame you..."

"They blamed, Reid," Jane said bitterly.

"I still have to do something," Kate responded. "I'm sorry, Jane, but for Jennifer's sake, I have to report this."

"Of course you do," Jane whispered. "In fact it will be an enormous weight off my own mind." She smiled faintly and stood up. "Another coffee?"

"Yes please," Kate replied. She sat, deep in thought, as Jane walked across to the coffee percolator and refilled both their mugs.

*

It was five weeks later when a white Pontiac pulled up to some wrought iron gates; the driver stared at the remote camera lens and ignored the view of San Francisco Bay behind him.

"Officer John Livingston of the FBI," the man said and flashed an identification badge at the blinking eye. " Captain Parnell Rodriguez needs to speak to Mrs. Melhuish-Toland on an important personal and confidential matter."

"She cannot be disturbed Sir," replied a somewhat abrupt male voice. " She is hosting a charity dinner for Congressman Parsons at this very moment. Could you please return at a more suitable time? If you wish I shall..."

Parnell leaned across his driver and glowered at the lens. "Son," he said with his voice like ice. "If you don't open this Goddamn gate pronto, I shall be on your front lawn in a police helicopter within fifteen minutes. Get it!"

He grinned at the woman in the back seat. "I'm sure your approach wouldn't be so direct, Bree but, frankly I am not impressed by these society types."

Bree Nolan, a local police psychologist, laughed. "No, I'm impressed Parnell," she said.

There was silence on the speaker for a moment before the voice came back while, at the same time, the gates swung open on well oiled hinges.

"Please take the left hand driveway to the rear entrance, Captain Rodriguez. I shall meet you by the service entrance." There was a click and the instrument went silent.

"Go to the right, John," Parnell snapped. "Right up to the Goddamn front door!"

"Yes, Sir," the officer replied with a grin.

*

The butler must have been forewarned for not a word was said about the vehicle sitting mere meters from the ornate glass doors.

"Please come in, Captain Rodriguez," he said. "I shall show you to the visitors' reception lounge. I am afraid will be a fifty minute wait."

"Will there?" said Parnell and held a business card out to the man. "You show this to Mrs. Melhuish-Toland and inform her I wish to speak to her, immediately." He stuck his chin out at the man. "And I mean, now!"

"Yes, Sir," The butler hardly blinked. "And what I shall tell is the reason for your visit?"

"A confidential, personal matter," Parnell snapped.

"Very well, Sir. If you will take the door to the left and I shall inform Mrs. Melhuish-Toland the matter is urgent. Help yourself to refreshments."

"Pompous twit," the FBI agent snorted after the man had left. He stalked into the room that was as large as an average household's living room and glared around. On the far side was a bar filled with every drink imaginable and a coffee percolator bubbled away on a small hot plate at the side. Coffee mugs, milk, cream, sugar and artificial sweetener were arranged neatly beside it.

"The other half," John added softly.

"Yeah," Rodriguez replied and reached for a coffee mug. "Damned pity we're on duty."

*

The woman that walked in moments later was a stunner; tall, slim and brunette, she wore a clinging white gown with bare tanned shoulders exposed and expensive but not ostentatious jewelry, earrings and elbow length gloves. Parnell estimated she was in her mid-forties. In contrast to her staff, she seemed perfectly composed.

"I am Danielle Melhuish-Toland. How can I help you Captain Rodriguez?" she asked in a natural voice.

"This is Officer John Livingston and Police Psychologist Bree Nolan," he introduced after shaking the woman's extended hand.

The woman frowned. "Psychologist?" she said. "This sounds serious."

"It's about your daughter, Ma'am," Parnell began.

"What's happened to Kirstine?" Danielle gasped. "Has there been an accident?"

Bree glanced at Parnell and switched her attention to their host. "Can I call you Danielle?" she asked in a soft voice.

"Please do but what's happened?"

"Your daughter Kirstine is not the reason for our visit, Danielle."

"I have no other daughter," the woman's slightly relieved voice replied. "Only two younger sons."

"We have traced Jennifer, your elder daughter," Bree continued. "She is sixteen now and…"

Danielle Melhuish-Toland stopped and just stared. Her eyes grew wide and color drained from the attractive face. For a second her mouth hung open before she swallowed, staggered and reached out for a chair to steady herself.

"Jennifer!" she finally managed to stutter.

"Sit down, Danielle," Bree continued and reached out to guide the stunned woman to one of the comfortable armchairs a few steps away. "She is in perfect health. I have a photo of her taken only yesterday."

The psychologist opened a small handbag and took out a colored portrait showing Jennifer dressed in casual school clothes and smiling at the camera. "I'm sure you will see the likeness between her and yourself. We have taken DNA samples that prove this is your daughter who was kidnapped eleven years ago."

The well-manicured fingers trembled as they reached for the photograph and the woman studied the photograph. "Oh shit," she gasped in a very unladylike manner "It's her! My darling little Jennifer. I'd recognize her anywhere." Her repose collapsed and she burst into long shuddering tears.

Bree waited and nodded at John. "Perhaps a small drink for Danielle," she said.

"Sure," replied the officer and walked over to the bar.

"How is she?" the woman replied after she'd taken the gin and gulped it down in almost one mouthful. She wiped away her tears and faced Parnell. "Is she here?"

"No. We have not told her about you yet, Mrs. Melhuish-Toland," he replied. "As far as she knows she is an orphan. We decided to approach you first. There are many details to explain."

"Of course," Danielle replied and studied the photograph again. "She's a young woman, now..."

"Yes, a high school sophomore and, I believe one of their top academic students. I know her personally and I assure you she is a remarkable young lady," Parnell said.

"Personally, Captain?" An eyebrow shot up.

"As I said," replied. "It is a long story."

Danielle walked across to an inconspicuous intercom on the wall and pressed a button. "I shall be a while, Patrick," she said with her voice now under firm control, "Could you please extend my apologies to Congressman Parsons and the guests... No, I do not wish to be disturbed." Her lips twitched slightly in annoyance as she switched the instrument off and turned to the FBI agent. "Tell me everything Captain Rodriguez," she said. "I want every detail about Jennifer."

*

Kate was nervous and, for once, it showed. The suggestion by Bree that Danielle Melhuish-Toland make a casual visit to Kate's place and be introduced to Jennifer, as an acquaintance was about to take place. As Bree said Jennifer would eventually have to be informed about her mother because, as a sixteen year old, state laws allowed her to make a decision about her own future.

"At the moment she is a state ward under your foster care," she pointed out to Kate in a long telephone conversation the evening before. "We have no desire to force her to move in with her mother or, for that matter, stop her if she wishes to go."

"I understand," Kate replied in an enforced neutral voice.

"However, as a psychologist, I know springing the information about her mother will be extremely traumatic for Jennifer, especially with her recent experiences escaping from the commune. Her mother has been told everything but wants to see her daughter incognito, before deciding what she wishes to do." Bree coughed. "Parnell gave a glowing report about yourselves and how you're caring for Jennifer but I'm sure she will be studying you both, too. Danielle is a very sophisticated and astute woman."

"What about Jennifer's father?" Kate asked.

"That's interesting, too," Bree replied. "Danielle divorced Conrad Melhuish a year after Jennifer's disappearance. Apparently, the kidnapping wrecked their marriage. She remarried soon afterwards but kept her first husband's name hyphened onto her new surname. She told me it was in case Jennifer ever came back and tried to trace her."

It was seven in the evening and Kate had arranged for Lorie to also stay the night. The woman was due in fifteen minutes and the girls were all in the living room spread out across the floor doing homework. It was a perfect middle class domestic scene but Parnell had warned Kate that Danielle Melhuish-Toland was anything but middle class.

"I'm nervous, Sweetheart," Kate confessed to Reid. "What happens if she up and demands to take Jennifer? What can we do about it?"

"She won't," Reid replied. "That psychologist from San Francisco assured us that." He glanced up as the buzzer from the basement car lot sounded. "Anyhow, it's too late now. This must be her." He clicked the receiver and listened as a female voice identified herself as Jennifer's mother. "Yes, come on up," Reid replied.

When Kate answered the door a few moments later she almost gasped out loud. My God, the woman looked like an older version of Jennifer with the same hair coloring, slim frame and narrow chin. The next thing Kate noticed was that the woman appeared quite nervous as she waited across the entrance foyer.

"Kate and Reid, I believe," she said in a quiet voice. "I'm Danielle."

"Good evening Danielle," Reid replied who stood just behind Kate. "We spoke to Bree on the phone who explained everything and Parnell dropped in and had a chat, too."

"And Jennifer still doesn't know about me?"

"No," said Kate. "She's doing homework in the other room with Sassy and Lorie right now."

Jennifer's mother smiled, walked in and was shown through to the kitchen. She glanced around and waited quietly while Reid shut the door.

Kate was tongue-tied. Her planned speech was forgotten so she just smiled and stuttered, "Teenage girls can make quite a mess but come on through."

Danielle nodded and followed the pair into the other room. Sassy was watching television, Lorie sat at Reid's computer doing something on-line but the object of the adult's attention lay on the floor with one leg kicked up in the air as she wrote furiously on a lecture pad.

"Girls," Kate said in a shaky voice. "An old friend has just dropped in and just wants to say hello."

Two girls turned around, said a polite greeting and returned to their activity but Jennifer looked and sort of blinked twice at the visitor. Her leg went down and she sat up. With her head slightly tilted she stared at Danielle who had paled slightly.

"Oh my God," Jennifer said. "I know you, don't I?"

Kate's eyes caught Danielle's. This was completely unexpected. How could Jennifer remember her mother?

"I'm not sure." Danielle stuttered her first words to her daughter in eleven years.

"Mommy," Jennifer whispered. She used the name from her childhood memory but instantly corrected herself. "You're my Mom aren't you? I recognize you and know your voice."

Danielle looked stunned and only managed a tiny gasp and it was Reid who stepped in.

"Yes, Jennifer," he said. "Danielle is your mother. She wanted to see you without letting on. None of us guessed you'd know her after all these years."

"Oh hell!" Jennifer replied and just sat there biting on her lip. "I don't know what to say... It's so sudden."

Danielle studied her daughter before she spoke. "Well, you could start by showing me the homework you're doing, Jennifer," she said. "I heard you are doing very well at high school." She stepped across the room, smiled at the gaping Lorie and Sassy, squatted down and picked up the lecture pad Jennifer had been writing on.

Kate looked at Reid. She was impressed by Danielle; no tears, no gushy outburst but a realistic approach in a dramatic situation.

"It's an essay on genetic foods," Jennifer said in a quiet voice as if she was talking to her teacher. "There must be a balance between the ban the greenies want and the commercial needs of society."

"It's well above my head," Sassy interrupted. "Jennifer's the brain box here."

"No I'm not," Jennifer replied with a pout. "We're just good at different things, that's all."

Danielle smiled and asked Jennifer more questions about the subject and the fact that they were mother and daughter wasn't mentioned.

It was only half an hour later when she was about to leave when Jennifer said, "I love it here with Kate and Reid, Danielle. I hope you like them, too."

Her mother nodded. "You know, Jennifer. I feel very humble and proud this evening. I met hundreds of people every year and I can see Kate and Reid are wonderful people. Sassy and Lorie are real friends, aren't they? " Only then did her voice quiver and tears spring to her eyes. "My God, I'm so glad to see you again. You turned out even better than I ever dreamed. Can I just hold you a moment."

"I'd like that Mom," Jennifer replied. "I think I'd like that."

*

The next surprise came two days later. Lorie had just left Jennifer and Sassy after school and was walking home. The weather was quite mild and she pulled off her cape to let her long blonde hair flow free so, unwittingly became easy to recognize from behind.

Unnoticed, a massive cream Rolls Royce limo pulled to the curb, the rear door opened and a little boy of about six jumped out. He had a massive grin on his face and ran as fast as his legs could carry him towards the teenager.

"Lorie!" the little boy yelled. "Wait for me."

Lorie turned, frowned for a second and realized she knew the child. It was one of the commune children.

"Trevor!" she laughed and stooped to grab the little boy who ran straight into her arms.

"We were coming to visit you and I saw you walking along the pavement," Trevor said. "I'm with my mommy and daddy."

Lorie glanced over her young friend's shoulder; saw the vehicle and two adults standing a few meters away. Both the man and woman wore crisp business suits and were smiling.

"We're the Hannah and Dennis Wilcox," the woman said. "You must be Lorie."

"Yes," the girl replied.

"I believe you were the one that set everything in motion," Dennis Wilcox said and held a massive hand out for Lorie to shake.

"Me," gasped Lorie. "I don't understand."

"Like your friend, Jennifer, Trevor was a victim of kidnapping," the man explained. "He was only five weeks old when he disappeared and now we have him back because of the efforts of yourself, your mother, sister and brave friends. We were coming to thank you all when Trevor saw you."

Lorie flushed. "Well, come in," she said and nodded at a house up the block. "Erika will be at work but Mom's home."

*

Jane appeared shy but welcomed her guests. "I'm afraid all I can offer you is a cup of coffee," she said. "I'm just back from another lengthy interview with the FBI."

"And how did it go, Mom?" Lorie asked.

"Fine," Jane replied. "No charges are filed against myself or present commune members. When the kidnapping trial comes up against Peter Littlejohn and those others arrested at Prince George we will have to be witnesses, though. Addition charges here in Washington have been filed against them."

"Can you get your friends, Jennifer and Sassy?" Dennis asked after the conversation about Peter Littlejohn continued for a few moments. "We have a tiny token of appreciation for you all."

"Sure," Lorie responded. "I just left them. They should be home by now." She took out her mobile phone, punched in a memorized number, spoke a moment and clicked off. "They're coming over," she said.

When Jennifer and Sassy arrived, Hannah took five tiny velvet cases from her purse and handed them out. "I'm sorry we missed Erika," she said, "There is one for her, too."

The, so-called, tiny tokens were five almost identical bracelets made to look like interlocking golden maple tree leaves. On the back, the girls had their names inscribed and the words. *Thank you for looking after me -Love Tony* while the two for Erika and Jane were inscribed. *For everything you did for Tony. An appreciation. Love, Hannah and Dennis Wilcox.*

The girls' eyes shone and Jane seemed overwhelmed, "But I did nothing," she said in a whisper.

"You did everything, Jane," Dennis replied. "If it wasn't for yourself, your daughters, Jennifer and Sassy, the commune could still be under control of those gangsters and we would think Trevor was dead. Three years ago the police told us the chance of ever finding him again was infinitesimal, yet here he is with us."

"But," Jane protested, "These bracelets are solid gold."

Dennis shrugged. "We're also going to make a donation to the commune," he said quietly. "There are five families, like Hannah and myself, who found their children. We have set up a trust fund to restock the commune's farm and provide help for the children who were genuine orphans."

"But there's been nothing on television," Jane said.

"We wanted it that way," Hannah replied. "All the parents agreed to keep everything secret and the FBI have supported us. No doubt there'll be publicity when the trials start but all we want to do now, is thank you for this miracle and continue our lives."

"Oh my God," Sassy replied as she turned the bracelet over, reread the inscription and slipped it on her wrist. "Thank you Mr. and Mrs. Wilcox."

Jennifer and Lorie also thanked the visitors, Tony was given a big hug, everyone promised to keep in touch, his appreciative parents chatted for a while and left.

"And you thought you'd be in trouble, Mom," Lorie retorted after the visitors departed." It's turning out well, isn't it?"

"It is, Sweetheart," Jane replied. "Like the Wilcoxs said, far better than I could even imagine."

"And these bracelets. They'd be worth a fortune," Jennifer added. "When could I wear mine?"

"On every important occasion," Jane laughed. "Like this year's prize giving at school. I heard you are in for a stack of certificates."

"I guess," Jennifer answered.

She flushed while her friends laughed and gazed affectionately at each other. The wonderful gifts made them all feel somehow valued and appreciated.

*

CHAPTER TWENTY-THREE

From Kate's point of view, one of the unexpected outcomes of the meetings with Jennifer's mother and Tony's parents was the reaction of Sassy. Jennifer became quiet and thoughtful but Sassy looked depressed, so much so, that Kate took her aside three evenings later and asked her what was wrong.

Sassy sighed. "Is it that obvious, Kate?" she asked.

"Yes," Kate replied. "You are usually our bright, happy one who tells everyone to buck up. To tell you the truth, I expected Jennifer to be the one that was downcast once the knowledge she has a mother, sister and two brothers was known. She though, seems completely unaffected by the events yet you are looking so miserable, I just wondered what was wrong."

"It's just, I'm the one left," Sassy whispered.

"How?" Kate asked.

"Lorie's got Erika and Jane; Jennifer has a mom who is stinking rich and look at Tony's parents? I have no parents. Oh, I know I found out about them and I was a genuine orphan but it seems unfair, somehow. I think about my parents, too Kate. I wonder what they were like and I'll never know, will I?"

"We can search old records and find out," Kate suggested.

"But it's not the same," Sassy said. "Lorie's living with her family, the chances are Jennifer will move out and that leaves me." She looked at Kate with serious eyes. "Hell, I'm just feeling sorry for myself, aren't I? I'm as moody as old Reid."

Kate nodded. "You noticed, did you?"

"Reid? Yeah. Oh he's still great with us; I don't mean it that way. He just looks sort of sad when he is by himself or with Cinders."

"And Jennifer?" Kate said.

"She's said nothing. If my mother turned up I'd be so excited I'd be running up and down the stairs whooping with delight. All she said was, 'It looks like I've got half a family, Sassy,' and that's it."

"So it seems to me that Reid and Jennifer both need your company and happy face to cheer them up." Kate stopped and turned serious. "I cannot replace your parents, Sassy; nobody can but I can be your friend to talk to. We've already told you this can be your home as long as you wish; Jennifer's too if she wants to stay." She stopped and walked across and stared out the patio windows that led to the balcony. "You know, I once had this apartment all to myself then I met Reid and later, you girls." She swung around. "We've helped you but it's gone the other way, too you know." She hesitated. "I'm just trying to say we want to be your family, Sassy, if you want us."

Sassy also looked out across the balcony. Below was a small park and beyond it another tall condominium block. "You're all I've got, now," she whispered. "I don't want Jennifer to leave but don't think it is fair to tell her."

"Possibly," Kate replied. "I've been a bit of a coward, too and haven't said anything to her. She says nothing but thinks a lot."

"Yes, that's Jennifer," Sassy replied and broke into a smile. "Thanks, Kate. I feel better now so there's only Reid to cheer up, isn't there?"

"Yes but I'm working on that, too."

"The true diplomat," Sassy replied. "Anyhow, I'll go and drag Jennifer out of the bathroom. God, she hogs that place!"

"And you don't?" Kate chuckled. She turned and spied Jennifer standing at the door staring at her with a towel wrapped around her hair. 'Hi Jennifer,' she said.

'You just said you haven't talked to me about my mother but never told Sassy what you thought either. What do you think, Kate and none of that nonsense about what I want, what's best for me and so forth?"

Kate gulped and decided on the truth. "Remember when you first came here you asked almost exactly the same thing. Nothing has changed. We would like you to stay with us, Jennifer," she said.

Jennifer nodded and turned to her friend. "I wish your parents were still alive Sassy. I overheard most of your conversation. Tragic as it is, your decision has really been made for you. In some ways, my mother turning up has just complicated things for me. I've been so happy here but there is now one more person I have to consider. Nothing's easy is it?"

"No," Kate said. "There is always one more decision to make. That's what life is. One last point though. Whatever you decide to do, Jennifer, we'll support you all the way."

"I know," Jennifer rubbed her hair for a moment before gazing intently at Kate. "Somehow, that makes it more difficult for me."

*

The following Friday evening, the three girls flew out to San Francisco for the weekend; business class with all tickets paid by Danielle.

"It was kind of her to invite all three of them for the weekend," Kate commented to Reid as they picked up Cinders from the Timber Wolf Air hanger and headed to the apartment.

"Yeah," muttered Reid, "She can afford it, though."

"Reid," Kate responded. "What's wrong? You've been moping around for days now. Even Sassy mentioned it."

Reid smiled slightly. "Oh, Sweetheart," he said. "I'm sorry. I should be the happiest man in the world with a beautiful woman beside me, my dog, and two over active boarders who certainly stop me becoming bored."

"But you miss being a doctor, don't you?"

Reid heaved. "Yes but we've been through all that."

"Except there is absolutely no reason why you can't apply for a position here in Spokane." She sucked on her lip. "Unless you want to go back east."

Reid turned and broke into the grin he usually wore. "No," he said and stretched across to squeeze Kate's leg. "If you'll have this moody old fellow, I think I'll stick around for a while,"

"A while?" Kate whispered.

"A long while," the man replied.

"And you'll think about being a doctor again."

"Yes, Dear," Reid responded. "I'll think about it. "

*

After an unusually quiet weekend, Sunday afternoon arrived and Kate and Reid were back at the airport. The girls arrived back with tales of their up-market life in San Francisco. Sassy and Lorie hardly stopped talking about everything they did, what Jennifer's new family was like and the sheer opulence of the mansion where they'd stayed. Again, though, Jennifer said very little until late in the evening.

"It was different than I expected," she said when Kate tried to draw her out. "Oh, Mom tried so hard and Frank, her husband, couldn't put himself out more."

"Kirstine is a spoilt little brat though and the two boys are little better," Sassy added

"She's eleven but thinks she's my age," Jennifer continued. "She goes to this private girl's school and wears make up.

"Yeah," Sassy butted in. "Jennifer gave her the evil eye a few times and that shut her up."

"Mom wants me move back with her. She said I could go to the high school part of Kirstine's school or the local state high school, whatever I preferred. I can have my own apartment in the south wing of the house and really anything I need, including a new car."

"But?" Reid noted Jennifer's lack of enthusiasm.

Jennifer glanced up at him. "Mom argued that I've really only known you two a short time." She sighed. "I told her I needed to think about everything."

"And what did she reply," Kate asked.

"She told me to take all the time I wanted. I was welcome to live with her but if I found the change too great, she'd understand."

"That's fair enough," Reid replied.

Jennifer glanced up. "How do I tell her I'd rather stay with you and not hurt her feelings?" She gulped. "Because that's what I want.'

"Your mom wasn't going to tell you who she was when she called in that day you recognized her," Kate replied, "I'm sure wants what's best for you."

"Can you tell her?" Jennifer pleaded.

"Okay," Kate replied softly and glanced at Reid. She didn't relish the idea but could understand Jennifer's reluctance to talk herself. "I'll give her a call."

The phone call went through to Danielle almost immediately and it appeared she'd given instructions to have any call diverted directly to her. Against the background mumble of a crowded restaurant or meeting place, the woman greeted Kate with warmth and listened as Kate repeated Jennifer's wishes.

"What is your opinion?" Danielle said in a bluntly. "I know you took the two girls into your home and all three said nothing but praise about Reid and yourself. You are, however, both young and have your own lives. Don't two teenage girls place heavy demands on your own lives?"

"No," Kate replied in a frank reply. "They really look after themselves and actually help us by cooking dinner and doing much of the housework."

"Fair enough," Danielle replied. "How do you cope, financially?"

Kate explained about the welfare grant they received for the pair. "They don't have big demands," she added. "At the commune they led a frugal life so don't expect everything normal sixteen-year-olds want."

"Well, Jennifer can come off the welfare," Danielle almost snapped before her voice softened. "Oh, Kate, she's so mature and graceful but somehow remote. I look at her and think of my little darling who went missing as a five-year-old and my heart goes out to her. But she's not a child, is she?"

"She isn't," Kate replied softly and smiled at Jennifer who was standing beside the phone listening to her end of the conversation. "Do you want to talk to her?"

"Please," Danielle replied.

Kate handed the receiver to Jennifer. "Hi Mom," the teenager said. "I loved it at your place over the weekend. Sassy Lorie and myself have never, ever, had such a grand time but, Mom..." Jennifer hesitated before blurting. "I can't come and live with you. There's no real reason. You and Frank made us so welcome and..."

"Jennifer," interrupted her mother. "I understand."

"You do?"

"So how about regular visits? Bring Sassy and Lorie, too." Danielle laughed. "Perhaps Kirstine might be knocked off her pedestal. She is a bit overbearing at times, isn't she?"

"Yes," Jennifer replied. "I don't think she liked me very much but, as for your first question, we'd love to visit."

"Good," Danielle replied. "Can you put Kate back on, please?" When Kate came back on the line she continued. "I want to deposit a regular amount with you for Jennifer's keep," she said. "As well, I want her to have a regular allowance without it spoiling her. Do you have any suggestions?"

"Ask her," Kate replied and flicked the speaker button so Danielle's voice filled the room. "I've switched on the extension speaker. Sassy and Reid are here too, if you don't mind them joining the conversation."

"Not at all," Danielle replied. "Hello Sassy. Hello Reid..."

They spoke for almost quarter an hour before Danielle concluded with a promise to keep in touch and an agreement to set up a bank account with Kate and Reid as trustees. "It is for both girls and also Lorie," Danielle insisted. She quoted an amount that made Reid raise his eyebrows before continuing. "My only request is you withdraw both girls from the welfare program," she added with a chuckle. "It might hurt my image if it became known I had a daughter on welfare..."

"There you are," Kate said after they were disconnected. "That wasn't too hard, was it?'

Jennifer nodded and stepped across between her and Reid. "Thank you," she said with gratitude in her voice and tucked her arms around them both. "I'm glad Mom included Sassy and Lorie in everything. We're more like sisters than Kirstine will ever be."

Reid's thoughts of returning to his profession again received a sharp jolt only a week later when a letter arrived for him. It was Monday evening and the family were all home when Kate noticed the unopened mail sitting on the bench. She thumbed through the usual envelopes that contained nothing of real importance until she came to one addressed to Doctor Reid Tucker with the words *White Knight Medical Center* across a stylized knight and sword on the envelope.

She wrinkled her forehead up in curiosity. "Letter for you, Sweetheart," she called and handed it to her partner after he walked in. "What is it?"

"I have absolutely no idea," Reid responded. He frowned, slit the envelope open and read the one page letter. His frown became deeper as his mind absorbed the information before he looked up. "What have you done, Kate?" he breathed.

"Me?" Kate replied in all sincerity "Nothing. Why!"

"Read this," Reid replied in a monotone. He handed Kate the page.

Dear Doctor Tucker, the very formal letter began. *Your application as Head Surgeon and Medical Officer at the White Knight Medical Center has been received. We are please to advise that you have been short listed and we wish to interview you on...*"

"Reid! You never told me," she said with a smile.

"You know nothing about it?" a stern Reid whispered.

"No?" Kate replied.

"I never sent in any application," Reid continued. "If you didn't, who did?" He scowled and suddenly strutted to the living room door. "Sassy, Jennifer. Get in here!" he yelled as if he was calling up Cinders.

The two girls looked sheepish as they slid into the kitchen and stood staring at Reid. "What do you know about this? " he growled and tossed the letter across the table.

Jennifer picked it up and flushed a deep red. "Oh hell!" she gasped and handed it onto Sassy who blew out through her cheeks and also looked embarrassed.

"Well?" Reid retorted.

Sassy turned to Jennifer. "You sent it?" she gasped.

"Of course," the taller girl replied. "You told me to."

"I think an explanation is necessary, young ladies," Reid replied in a whisper while Kate tried to suppress a smile.

"We only wanted to help," Jennifer replied.

"It was advertised on the web," Sassy continued.

"Go on," Reid hissed.

"It was one of those electronic application forms. You know, where you fill in the gaps then send it off."

"And you did?" Kate gasped.

"Yeah, well," Sassy stuttered. "We got the details from that brief case Reid keeps in the top cupboard and just answered the questions or copied appropriate bits in."

"Then I clicked "send"," Jennifer admitted. Her red face turned pale and she blinked as if she was on a verge of tears. "There's a copy saved.

"I see," Reid answered but still looked grim. "We'd better go and have a look, hadn't we?"

The copy of the application form was surprisingly accurate with everything of Reid's medical history included except the court case conviction. There was even a testimonial under Sassy's name that told of everything Reid had done as a doctor at the ELF commune including the emergency appendicitis operation.

"Jennifer wrote that and I stuck my name on it," Sassy admitted. "Oh Reid, we're sorry. It just started as a bit of fun. We heard Kate trying to persuade you to apply for positions, you've done so much for us and..." She stopped and bit on her lip.

Reid stood tall and stroked his chin. "Okay, girls," he said. "I know you were trying to help but we now have to go and withdraw my application, don't we?"

"Why?" Kate cut in.

"Because it isn't honest," Reid replied. "Nothing was mentioned of my trial and conviction."

There was silence in the room. The two teenagers made faces of each other but didn't answer while Kate scanned though and reread the application form.

"There is nothing dishonest here," she said.

"No, but a glaring omission," Reid answered. "It amounts to the same thing."

"Then we'll explain it to the White Knight Medical Center," Kate replied. "You want honesty. What say we all go down there tomorrow and tell them everything? At that stage, you can withdraw your application if you think it is ethical to do so." She turned to the girls. "You'll come, won't you Jennifer, Sassy?" she almost ordered.

"Yes, sure," Jennifer gulped and Sassy nodded.

*

Fifteen hours later, Reid walked out of the modern medical center building with three women filling the sidewalk on each side of him.

"So your application stays in?" Kate said.

"I guess," he replied with a shrug.

"They had the full transcript of your trial there on the table," Sassy whispered. "It didn't seem to worry them at all."

"But how did they get it?" Kate replied.

Again Jennifer flushed. "I did it," she admitted. "Last night after everyone went to bed I felt so bad, I sent in an amendment to the application. I told them about the trial verdict and gave them the Minneapolis Courthouse email address. They must have downloaded all the information before we arrived this morning."

Reid stopped and, without warning, swept Jennifer in his arms and plunked a kiss on her cheek. "You are the limit, you know," he laughed for the first time since the letter arrived. He turned and hugged the other girl, too. "You, as well, Sassy. What am I going to do to the pair of you?"

"Keep us," Jennifer whispered in solemn reply.

*

Five days later Reid was appointed Head Surgeon and Medical Officer at the White Knight Medical Center and asked to begin in six weeks.

*

CHAPTER TWENTY-FOUR

The Cessna 208 Caravan lowered its ski undercarriage and circled over Eagle's Claw Lake while the twenty or more children skating on the ice all moved to the shore. It glided down and landed with a swish before turning to taxi to the jetty. After the engine stopped the rear door opened and a woman dressed in a white fur coat, gloves and up-market jeans stepped out. She smiled at a group of curious children gathered nearby and made her way across the icy surface of the jetty.

"Hello," she said to a young woman in her late teens who came to greet her. "My name is Danielle Melhuish-Toland. I'm Jennifer Mears' mother."

"Hi," replied the commune girl, "I'm Geraldine. Welcome to Eagle's Claw Lake and the Elf commune." She smiled, "How are Jennifer and the others?"

"Fine," Danielle replied. "She's still with Kate and Reid but I guess you know that."

"Yes," Geraldine replied. "Kate flies in quite regularly and often the girls come with her. We rarely have other aircraft visit, though." She screwed her nose up. "Well, there was plenty of activity with the police and FBI for a while. Is there anything I can help you with?"

"I'd really just come to see the place where Jennifer lived for most of her life and to meet Ms Bulmer, your leader."

"Well, you're in luck. Annette is just coming."

They glanced up to where a snowmobile howled in from the commune and pulled to a halt at the end of the jetty. A woman climbed off and walked forward with a curious expression on her face.

"I thought it was the police again," she said after Geraldine introduced the visitor. "It's a clear day so all the kids are getting a bit of exercise," She blew a cloud of condensation into the air. "It's still about ten below freezing so I wouldn't leave your aircraft engine off too long. You might have trouble starting it again."

"Oh it's fine," the visitor replied with a wave of her gloved hand. "It's got an in-built heater coil..." She chatted away, followed Annette and Geraldine towards the commune and ignored the two crewmembers still on the aircraft.

"There's been changes since Jennifer left," Annette remarked and pointed along the shoreline where piles of snow had been scooped up to make a row of snowmen. "There was an enormous fence around the commune that we had pulled down. Come spring and we will restock the farm."

"I see the burnt out administration block hasn't been replaced," Danielle said a few moments later as the small group made their way towards the dining room that now served as the commune headquarters.

"I guess Jennifer told you a lot about us," Annette replied.

"Not really," Danielle replied. "I learnt more from the other parents who found their children here. Jennifer hasn't said a lot." She smiled at Annette. "Is it inconvenient or would it be possible for me to look around? I'd love to see where Jennifer lived, of course, but am also interested in everything else."

"No problem. We'll show you our home," Annette replied. "We're a bit disorganized at the moment. Fifteen children have left not counting, Jennifer, Lorie and Sassy and we're short of adults with all the old leaders arrested."

"So what happens, now?" Danielle asked.

"We voted to keep going," Annette replied. "There have been changes and, no doubt, more will follow. It will be hard but I'm sure we will become self sufficient in time."

"And until then?" Danielle became blunt.

Annette sighed. "Like yourself, Mrs. Melhuish-Toland, most of the parents who found their children with us are supportive and we have been given some quite large donations. Two families, though, have filed court cases against the commune. They blame us for the loss of their children and want the commune disbanded. They don't realize we have many other children who are genuine orphans and we are their only home."

"Sounds typical," the visitor shrugged. "Anyhow, there's another reason for my visit to Eagle's Claw Lake. I believe there is a cabin here for sale."

Annette frowned. "No, I don't believe so," she replied.

"Yes, there is, Annette," interrupted Geraldine. "The cabin where Reid was staying. He was going to buy it but after meeting Kate, gave the idea away."

"Of course," the camp leader replied. "That's at the other end of the lake, over four kilometers away."

Danielle looked disappointed. "Oh I see," she replied.

"Why? Is there a reason you asked?" Geraldine replied.

"Just interested." came the uncommitted reply. "I suppose you are short of space."

"We have less mouths to feed now," Annette said, "but yes, the admin block had several recreation and storage rooms attached that we miss.

"Oh well, " Danielle replied with a shrug and changed the topic.

An hour later, after politely turning down an offer to stay for lunch, she shook hands with her two guides and departed...

"Another woman rolling in money who wanted to see how her daughter survived all those years in poverty," Geraldine retorted as the Cessna aircraft flew away.

"No, I don't think so," Annette replied. "I was quite impressed with her. She reminded me of Jennifer, you know."

"She looked like her," Geraldine admitted, "but it was hard to tell what she was thinking."

"And wasn't Jennifer like that?"

Geraldine smiled. "I guess you're right. It was Sassy and Lorie who made all the noise."

"Anyway," Annette replied. "Ring that bell. The kids have been outside for the whole time Danielle was here. They must be frozen and starved. Lunch is late."

"They don't mind," Geraldine laughed. "I reckon we've had more snowmen built, more sled rides and skating than I ever remember."

"Yes," Annette replied. "Going on the ice was banned, remember."

"Everything involving fun was banned," the younger woman replied philosophically as they headed into the warm indoors and were greeted by the smell of hot soup and toast waiting for hungry little tummies.

*

Kate had just returned from a two hour round flight in the Beaver and welcomed the mug of coffee Reid had waiting for her. It was still a cold day but, at least, the snow had stopped falling and all the airports were open. She welcomed the break while the ground staff refueled the aircraft and did the routine checks.

She was about to return to the hanger when a knock sounded on the door. It was Erika.

"Oh hi, Erika," she said. "What are you doing out here at this time of the day? Shouldn't you be at work?"

"I've got the day off," Erika replied. "Whenever we see each other at your place or mine Mom or one of the girls are around. I wanted to speak to you alone."

"Do you want me to leave?" Reid asked.

"No," Erika replied. "I came to see both of you. It's Mom. I'm worried about her."

Kate frowned. "Well come in. It's freezing out here. Coffee?"

Erika walked into the warm room, took off her coat and gloves and sat at the tiny table. She smiled but failed to hide an apprehensive look.

"What's wrong?" Reid asked. "I thought Jane had settled down well and was enjoying being with Lorie and yourself."

"She puts on a good face but is sort of withdrawing into herself. She hardly leaves the house and I even have to get the groceries from the market, now. Oh, she does everything for us, the house has never been so spic-and-span, I reckon she even irons the towels, the meals she cooks are fabulous and she helps Lorie do her homework."

"Is she happy?" Reid asked.

"That's it," Erika replied. "I don't think she is. I came home from work early yesterday before Lorie arrived home from school. She was just sitting in a kitchen chair crying. She didn't see me so I sneaked out, pretended to come in again but made the door bang to warn her. By the time I walked in the second time, she was at the sink preparing supper and pretended to be okay."

"Sounds like post-traumatic stress," Reid said. "She was locked away for all those months and things may have happened to her that her subconscious has suppressed. Now she is free and with her loved ones she relaxes. However, little things might trigger her memory or she might be scared of something without really knowing why."

"I know she doesn't like crowds," Erika said. "We were at the mall last Saturday morning and you know how crowded it gets?"

"I do," Kate replied.

"Well, she went as white as a sheet and just stopped walking. I thought she was going to faint. As soon as we went outside away from the crowd she was okay again." Erika looked up and was close to tears. "She's thinking of going back to the commune."

"Did she tell you?" Kate asked.

"No, she told Lorie we were getting on so well together she wasn't needed around the place. That's when it came out."

"And what would you think if she went back?" Reid asked.

"Hell, I don't know," Erika whispered. "But why would she want to? We've done everything for her. We love her, Reid. I think Lorie would be devastated if Mom left."

"Then tell Jane that," advised Reid. "I think she looks at you as a sophisticated adult and even Lorie is not a child any more. She thinks you both managed without her for years and are staying with her out of duty rather than because you want to."

"But that's not true."

"Then tell her that, too," Reid said. "Tell her everything you just told us."

"Maybe I can help," Kate said. "You know Reid's starting at the Medical Center soon."

"Sure and we're all thrilled," Erika replied.

"Well, I need a new secretary here in the office. I reckon it'll suit Jane down to the ground. Half the time there's only Merve and a couple of other ground crew around. The pilots come and go depending on the flights. Three quarters of our business is freight and orders come on the phone, by fax or through email links..."

"You mean she won't be overwhelmed by people..."

"Exactly. Look around. This office is tucked away from everything. Half the time I don't even realize we're in the middle of a large airport."

"But she knows nothing about modern methods, operating a computer and..."

"Erika," Reid said. "Perhaps that's the trouble."

"What?"

"You're over protective. Your Mom needs to do things for herself and feel useful."

"She just try to make things easy for her. We love her, Reid."

"Of course you do but is your Mom stopping your own social life?"

"What do you mean?"

"You also went through a traumatic time at the commune. You escaped, went back and were attacked. Are you using your mother as an excuse not to get on with your own life?"

"What are you, a psychiatrist?" Erika snapped.

"A little," Reid admitted. "I think Jane is as concerned about you as you are about her. You're all trying so hard to make up for those lost years you're afraid to let go."

Erika nodded and sipped her coffee silently for a moment. "I guess we're all screwed up a little. Lorie still mopes around and talks about Doug and I admit the thought of going on a date scares me. A guy at work kept asking me out but I make excuses not to go. Poor Michael's given up asking now" She sighed. "Perhaps you're right."

"I've another idea," Reid added.

Erika glanced up but said nothing.

"If we take Jane back to the commune on a visit, she might decide it's not what she wants, after all," Reid continued.

"... And if she doesn't?" Erika whispered.

"Let her go back without feeling guilty about letting you or Lorie down. Even if you disapprove, don't let it show."

"If she went back, you could still visit," Kate added. "I call there at least once every two weeks and they have the satellite phone now. They aren't cut off from society like they used to be, remember."

"I suppose," Erika said.

"So I'll offer her the job and invite her to Eagle's Claw Lake?"

"Okay," Erika replied and smiled.

"Danielle Melhuish-Toland has hired me to take a load of Christmas stuff out the day after tomorrow. I think she's bought a present for every child at the commune, there's a ton of decorations and four massive hampers of food coming. She seems to have taken quite an interest in them all. I guess she's grateful for how Jennifer has turned out."

*

There were so many supplies from Danielle for the ELF commune that Kate decided to fly the CL-215 in. The larger aircraft was back from the coast and, for the first time, skis had been added to the undercarriage. After a trouble-free journey from Spokane, Kate, with Andy and Jane aboard, stared nervously at the frozen lake below.

"I've never landed anything this big on the ice before," she remarked to Andy in the co-pilot's seat. "I'm glad there's plenty of room."

Andy grinned at Jane sitting nervously behind the pilot. "You'll do well, Kate," he chuckled.

And she did. The yellow amphibian landed gracefully, stopped several meters away from the jetty and was immediately met by a tractor pulling a massive sled crowded with waving children. Something else of intense interest to both Kate and Jane sat mere meters away.

Sitting on giant skids and behind two massive Caterpillar bulldozers, Reid's cabin towered above them on the icy shore.

"Oh my God!" Jane gasped. "How did that get here?"

Geraldine and Annette, who were both at the hatchway to meet them, laughed.

"It's another donation. Danielle and the Wilcox, Tony's parents, bought the building. It was jacked up on those skids and pulled around the frozen lake by those two bulldozers,' Geraldine explained. "They're going to place it where the old administration block was."

"It will be our new school," Annette continued. "We have enough pupils for a elementary school. The state authorities told us if we could provide a building, they'd equip it and pay for a registered teacher. We're hoping to have one here in January." She smiled. "The only condition was that we send the high school aged children off to a boarding school in the city. We agreed to that so it's all go."

"Oh my God!" Jane replied. "And look, no fence, kids everywhere and a Christmas tree!"

Above them in front of the dining room, a massive fir tree had been raised. At the moment, there were two giant stepladders around it and several people were stringing up a set of decorative lights. Children's voices were shouting everywhere and the number of snowmen had increased to almost a score. White smoke spiraled into the air from the main furnace in front of a pale blue sky. Closer, the trees and fields were covered in snow. It was perfect scenery for Christmas only three days away.

"It's so different," Jane remarked an hour later after a scrumptious meal in the dining room. "The place is like a little town, not a prison. Everyone looks so happy."

"We like to think so," Annette replied. "That is our aim anyway. We will all work together but encourage our followers to be individuals as well. We already have three new children, here."

"You have?" said Kate.

"Yes, all orphans, poor little dears. Again, the state authorities visited us and imposed a few conditions but we're now registered as a charity institute. We're hoping to encourage a few adults to join us, too, " Annette replied. She glanced at Jane. "You're welcome back anytime, Jane," she added.

Jane glanced at Kate and gave a tiny grin. "No," she said in a whisper. "I'm thrilled to be here but I can't come back. I've my two daughters and home are in Spokane." She laughed. "Also I'm employed now; secretary for a run down little airline that needs a bit of a push along."

Kate smiled. Up until now, Jane would only say she'd consider the offer proposed to her. It seemed that everything was fitting into place after all.

"Oh there's one more thing," Jane said. "I had a big discussion with my lawyer but haven't mentioned this to anyone else. It's not finalized yet and I want my daughters' opinions." She raised her eyes at Kate and Reid. "As you know, my father owned this property..."

Annette nodded and a worried expression crossed her brow. "We can't afford to buy you out or pay a high rental," she muttered.

Jane laughed. "Oh, Annette," she replied. "If Erika and Lorie agree, I propose to renew the lease on the commune and farm for another ten years with the right of renewal if both parties agree at that time." She grimaced. "My lawyer suggested I put the last clause in just in case another Peter turns up."

"It sounds fair," Annette replied but still looked serious.

It was Reid who asked the question Annette was probably worried about. "How much do you propose to ask for the lease, Jane?" he asked.

"I rejected my lawyer's suggestion," Jane said with a tiny grin on her face. "You must realize I have two daughters as well as myself..."

"Go on..." Annette whispered.

"It will be a contract based on the farm," Jane replied. "You will have full rights to use and run the commune and farm. You'll be responsible for all maintenance and operating expenses. Capital expenditure will be by mutual agreement."

Annette nodded but still looked expectant.

"In exchange, we expect five percent of any profit the farm makes."

"What?" Annette gasped.

Reid grinned. "And if there is no farm profit?" he asked.

"No profit, no fee," Jane replied with a chuckle "I was going to make it free but I do have daughters, you know."

"Oh Jane," Annette gasped when she realized the significance of the offer. "Thank you. After the way you were treated, I thought..."

"We held out against Peter and his cronies and we won, didn't we?" Jane said. "I have had everything ready to sign but needed to sort myself out. Now I come here and see wonderful things happening. I'm sure this is the type of commune Dad visualized and ran when I was a little girl. If he could be here now, I'm sure it is what he'd want."

"I think he would," Annette replied. She stepped forward and wrapped her arms around Jane. "Thank you." Tears swelled in her eyes as she just held on.

*

On the way home Kate found out something else about Jane. Andy had apparently asked her to go to a Christmas Charity Concert with him and she'd accepted. Kate knew Andy had been alone for many years now and, though older than Jane; he was a great character and perhaps just what she needed.

Her mind switched to Reid and his enthusiasm about his new position. He was due to start after Christmas but had already visited the medical center several times to get to know the staff and look around.

The only thing that had annoyed her was that, only two days earlier he'd shaved off his beard and come out grinning at her with a clean-shaven white face.

"Beards can be a nuisance when you're trying to scrub up," he chuckled at Kate's retort. "Cinders likes it."

"Oh Reid," Kate replied as she grabbed him in a massive hug and kissed his bare skinned cheek. "I loved that beard but I love the man behind it even more."

Their eyes met and lips touched. It was as everything was meant to be.

*

It was snowing again when the amphibian touched down at Felts Field Municipal Airport and followed the Boeing jets before it went past the main apron and onto the Timber Wolf Air hanger. As they turned in the apron and switched off the engines, Kate noticed four girls standing by the building with a Black Labrador dog.

"Oh hell, what's wrong?" Reid muttered. "Why aren't they at school."

"It's Christmas Vacation time," Kate laughed. "Who's number four?"

"Beats me," Reid replied.

They opened the hatch and were instantly surrounded by three girls and a dog while the stranger hung back.

"Mom's in town," Jennifer chuckled. "I said I'd ask you if Kristine could stay with us for a couple of days." She flushed slightly. "I promised her a ride in the amphibian too. I hope that's okay."

"Kristine?" Kate said. The name had escaped her for a moment.

"Oh Kate," Sassy laughed. "It's Jennifer's sister."

Lorie dug Kate in the ribs and whispered "She's really a nice kid, you know; another Jennifer."

"Oh my God," Reid retorted. "Two of them!"

Jennifer glanced into his eyes and saw the twinkle. She turned. "Come over here, Kristine," she yelled. "Meet Reid and Kate. Reid used to look real savage but he shaved his beard off. He's a doctor, you know." There was pride in her voice as she grabbed couple's hands and almost dragged them across to the younger girl.

"I love Cinders, Doctor Tucker," Kristine said in a soft voice and reached out to pat the dog that trotted in beside her. "Mom won't let me have a dog at home. Jennifer said it would be okay if I stayed..."

Behind them, Jane smiled and accepted Andy's hand as he helped her down off the amphibian. They walked forward to where all four girls appeared to be talking at once and the dog ran back and forth between them with her tail wagging.

She stood beside Kate and pulled her collar up against the snowflakes. "It's good to be home," she said.

"It is," Kate replied.

Their eyes linked and they both smiled. Indeed, it was good to be home.

The End